T0304895

I Will Live

I Will Live

LALE GÜL

TRANSLATED BY KRISTEN GEHRMAN

virago

VIRAGO

First published in Great Britain in 2024 by Virago Press
Translated from *Ik ga leven* published by Prometheus Uitgeverij, 2021

1 3 5 7 9 10 8 6 4 2

The publisher gratefully acknowledges the support
of the Dutch Foundation for Literature.

A CIP catalogue record for this book
is available from the British Library.

Hardback ISBN 978-1-4087-1680-9
Trade paperback ISBN 978-1-4087-1681-6

Typeset in Sabon by M Rules
Printed and bound in Great Britain by
Clays Ltd, Elcograf S.p.A.

Papers used by Virago Press are from well-managed forests
and other responsible sources.

Virago Press
An imprint of
Little, Brown Book Group
Carmelite House
50 Victoria Embankment
London EC4Y 0DZ

An Hachette UK Company
www.hachette.co.uk

www.virago.co.uk

For my late grandmother and Defne

If I'd just gone with the flow, I never would've been condemned to life as an outcast. Sometimes in life you get these ideas that seem really great at first, but you have no way of knowing how serious the consequences will be.

I'm going to tell you my story. My only hope is that it has some kind of ripple effect.

Oma

It's after eleven when I wedge my key into the lock in Oma's front door and turn it. I'm immediately struck by the familiar, nauseating smell of her house, but after a few seconds I don't notice it any more, or at least it doesn't bother me, which is a good thing I guess. That's how bad smells work. The moment you go from a neutral-smelling environment to a foul-smelling one – high-school toilets, the locker room at Fitness4Me Ladies Only in Bos en Lommer, Lucas's room when he's been smoking cigarettes or weed, my parents' apartment when Mother's been deep-frying (there's no ventilation in those old chicken coop flats in Amsterdam-West) or when the dead sheep is delivered for Eid al-Adha, after which the whole place smells like fresh sheep's blood for at least three days (which is basically how Oma's house smells all the time) – you're overwhelmed by the stench, but after a while you get used to it. There are a lot of things in life you can get used to.

I saunter into my room, yank back the curtains and throw open the windows. I've placed scent diffusers around the house to mask Oma's unpleasant odour, but all this does is create a mélange of disgusting smells with hints of green apple and baby lotion. I've resigned myself to the fact that there's nothing more I can do – the source of the smell remains: Oma.

Every time my eighteen-year-old brother Halil walks in he feels the need to make the same stupid comment: 'Jesus, the *smell* in here. Ever try opening a window?' I just ignore it. I mean, what would be a reasonable response? He knows it's because Oma is sick in bed, growing fatter by the day, wrapped in layers and layers of clothing even though it's sweltering outside. It's as if her body has been consumed by the rolls of fat, as if she's literally drowning in them. The worst is when she tries to stand up. She suffers from 'erosion of the knees' (something to do with her ligaments – Father can't quite explain it to me, his Dutch isn't very good and he's the one who talks to her doctor, so I don't really know the details). She also suffers from calcification, asthma, diabetes, Parkinson's and God knows what else. The bottom line is that she can't really move. The doctor said she has to lose at least sixty-five pounds before they can operate on her legs. Well, that's never going to happen. Those white coats have been telling us that she needs to lose weight for years, but there's just no way. Oma doesn't give a shit about her health. If it were up to her, she'd just die. 'Then I'll be redeemed,' she says.

She's been gloomy and cynical for a long time now. The only thing that seems to cheer her up a little is sugar, which she greedily consumes in all its forms, and I'm not about to rob her of that last remnant of pleasure. Almond-filled cookies, apple pie, fizzy drinks, ice cream, crisps – we buy her whatever she asks for. She's completely illiterate, so she can't occupy herself with the kinds of things that other, literate grandmas enjoy, like reading, sudoku or watching the news – she can't follow TV programmes or documentaries. Her Turkish is farmer's level at best. She never went to school, so she has a very limited vocabulary and narrow perspective. Even modern Turkish television is way over her head. Her general knowledge is so poor that she thinks there are only three countries in the world: America, Turkey and the Netherlands. She only knows America because people talk about it all the time – it's that wicked place, the geographical embodiment of evil. When she left home, the modern world was so new to her that a lot of things didn't even have a name; all she could do was point. So, you understand why I can't have much of a conversation with her – it's small talk at best. Still, when I'm not there, all the quietness makes her anxious, or just bored.

It's not that different with my parents (I prefer to call them my 'begetters'). They were equally illiterate when they came to the Netherlands at the age of twenty-five (approximately, their exact dates of birth were never registered). Though this particular problem was partially addressed back then, there are still plenty of other things they desperately need to catch up on, as will become clear as you read on. They might have heard of a few more countries and have basic knowledge of current events, but their entire worldview is based on what they've seen on Turkish media outlets tailored to a reactionary, collectivist, ultra-religious audience, and dripping with nonsense and melodramatic rumours; in other words, media that is totally devoid of fact, deafeningly kitsch and riddled with inflated propaganda. Its goal is to spread a one-sided message – not just about domestic matters but about international affairs as well. Recently, I was exposed, against my will, to one of their Turkish broadcasts, and I learned that Prime Minister Mark Rutte had told all the Turks to get the hell out of the Netherlands and that right-wing politician Geert Wilders was promising to return Holland to its pre-Islamic state. To be fair, I have to give the producers some credit for

3

not being entirely wrong about these things – given the whole 'Holland for the Dutch' thing (whatever that means) and the prime minister's use of mildly offensive language in statements towards easily agitated bicultural youth – but anyway, slightly more accurate quoting and translation would have made a significantly different impression on the audience, I suspect. The Turkish broadcast also made sure to include bombastic sound effects and images of a furious, roaring Geert, as we know him in his natural habitat, and played it all on repeat, like an infomercial, as if their viewers were troglodytes.

Oma is exempt from all household chores. I do them for her, though I should note that Mother has been doing them more often lately since I'm hardly ever home. I'm currently working two side jobs, studying at university and trying to maintain a secret, fairly long-distance relationship. (More on that to come.)

The smell of all the pills that Oma consumes on a daily basis seeps from her pores. It doesn't help that she never opens the balcony door or a window herself, so after I've been gone for a whole day, you really smell it. I have requested, demanded, even begged, that she air the place out a little while I'm away. She refuses. The woman doesn't give two hoots. She's a heap of misery, wrecked on all sides by her past, worn out by life and utterly depressed. And on top of all that, she's no longer able to function normally, so I can't really blame her. Oma has endured a lot of misery in her life, so much that it's a miracle she hasn't gone insane. She grew up incredibly poor, with no mother and an ailing, dependent father, was married off at the age of twelve to her cousin, raped and abused in her marriage, subjected to atrocious domestic violence and became a mother at thirteen. Her husband gambled away everything he had and turned out to be a brutal, unpredictable villain with a hot temper, who killed and abused several of their children (including Father) and beat Uncle Bahattin so hard that he was disabled for the rest of his life. Eventually, he divorced Oma after they arrived in the Netherlands and married a woman forty years younger than he was, from some Turkish village. He managed to lure her away with his Dutch passport – which meant money – and convince her to marry him. Now he's got five children with her, one of whom, word has it, was born just a few days ago. Grandpa is over seventy by now, but apparently his reproductive system is still going strong.

I have never seen Grandpa. He lives in Amsterdam too, so maybe I've seen him without knowing it. Father occasionally has contact with him, but the rest of us only know him from all the blood-chilling stories. Every now and again, Oma will mention Ayse and Atikè, her two daughters who were choked to death by her husband. They squawked too much and it drove him mad, especially after he'd lost all his money playing dice. One day, Oma was furious about it and had the nerve to lash out at him. Before she knew it, he had taken the pan of boiling milk from the stove and tossed it over her legs. And that's just one of countless stories about him, but I'll leave it at that. We need to keep things a little upbeat.

In her youth, Oma was aesthetically endowed. She had all kinds of suitors, men who wanted her hand, but it didn't matter. Her father had already promised her to her cousin at birth. They called it a cradle vow. Parents got together and decided that two infants – who were usually related because you could trust family – would be married when they were ready. Physically speaking, that is. So yes, Oma has seen her share of misery, and all pigs are sent to the slaughter. The long road has made a tired woman. And consistent apathy is more radical than suicide. Life has at least graced us with

5

the capacity for indifference. She has managed to keep an appropriate distance from every latent spark of enthusiasm. Indifference is self-protection at other people's expense.

The most unfortunate part of all this is that she's also incontinent: she can still make it to the toilet to poop, but she pees in a nappy. And that you can smell. Everywhere. All day. The house reeks of urine, and in the summer it's especially unbearable. The outdated flats we live in are mostly made of wood, and they're incredibly small, so small that you're basically living on top of each other and can barely turn around, which doesn't make sharing a household with Oma any more comfortable. But all of these disadvantages are trumped by one single advantage that I have with Oma: she is unfailingly kind to me. She is my companion for life.

The flats have two bedrooms; everything creaks and squeaks and the walls are so paper-thin that you might as well shit with the door open. They're forty-eight square metres and incredibly cheap, which is why we live here. We pay just 450 euros a month in rent, which is what you'd pay for a cot in Amsterdam these days. My fellow students pay 700 euros a month for their studios, all on their own. This favourable price is not because the housing corporation is particularly philanthropic or likes having us around, it's because we've been living there for more than twenty years. If we were to leave, the rent would most certainly be jacked up for the new residents – those house-milkers would have no shame in demanding 750 euros a month for a worn-out shoebox flat in a poor neighbourhood. Or an 'up-and-coming neighbourhood', 'an investment neighbourhood', whatever they want to call it. And that's the price for subsidised housing. Don't even get me started on the private sector.

Not too long ago, our neighbourhood, Kolenkit, made the

news: we had received the honourable distinction of the worst place to live in the Netherlands. This award was based on the considerable economic dependence of residents, the significant language barriers, the rate of juvenile delinquency, the amount of vandalism and, above all, the downright pitiful school performance. In the photo that accompanied the article, you could just make out Oma – she could still walk outside then. The whole neighbourhood went on and on about Oma being in the (free local) newspaper. The article's content was all but completely ignored; most of them probably couldn't read it anyway. Or they didn't care. Or both.

Mothering

As a gatekeeper of the unwritten laws of the Code of the Turkish Conservatives, Mother experiences any violation of these laws as a nefarious personal attack. Oma has broken all conventions, and I've broken a few myself, which has been known to cause a flare-up every now and then, but it has also strengthened the bond between Oma and me; she always stands up for me in arguments and tries to ease the tensions as much as possible. The moment the begetters start going after me, she and I close ranks. I do the same for her. Oma curses or calls for death, even in the presence of others, which is a terrible sin in our religion. You're supposed to bear your suffering with 'dignity' and 'patience and restraint' and all that, because that's the 'noble' thing to do, or at least that's what Mother says. In other words, we all have our cross to bear – only without the cross. It's not up to you to call upon death; only Allah can decide when your time has come. The suffering is your test and part of God's plan. By now I know that the best plans are the ones that are fundamentally impossible to carry out.

'He wants to see if you can handle it without moaning and groaning or questioning your faith in Him,' Mother said.

Even as a child, I had trouble grasping this concept. Back then, whenever my questions became too difficult to answer, Mother would just say that I was too young to fathom it, but that hasn't improved much over the years. On the contrary, in fact. Once she tried to explain it with an analogy: 'At school, the teachers make you take tests even though they could just tell you all the answers, but they would never do that, no matter how difficult it is, because they want to see if you can do it yourself. This life is a test from Allah, He's the one administering the test.'

A test it was, in an experimental sense at least. Even as a child, I had already realised that the sample I was working with was fairly problematic, but deep in my bones I knew that I just had to live with it. It's a feeling that hasn't gone away.

Oma has a deep aversion to all things divine, although she doesn't dare say so out loud. Mother is constantly having to remind her that it's time for prayer, which happens five times a day, so it's pretty damn hard to get out of it. Oma doesn't participate in Ramadan either. Now that she's ill she has an excuse, but even before that I spotted her sneaking little snacks. And to make sure that her illegal behaviour remained secret in the occult caverns of our zealot household, she used to pay me off; it's not like she had anything else to spend her government subsidy on anyway. Back then, Mother kept her fed and clothed (Mother happens to be an excellent seamstress, as well as, in my opinion, the incarnation of the devil), so there was always money left over for bribes.

Whenever Oma starts bemoaning her physical pain and her very existence, which in Islam is equivalent to expressing grievance against the Creator, Mother admonishes her and tells her to turn to prayer or recite chapters from the Quran, that this will help. At this, Oma's mood turns even more sour.

9

She doesn't say a word, but you can see her boiling like a volcano about to erupt. The other day, a valve burst: 'Oh come on,' she said irritably when Mother advised her to pray about something. At that, the despot of the house asked God to pardon Oma's slanderous words, which had been whispered into her ear by Beelzebub, and rebuked the sinner. She told Oma she better watch out and quickly fill her rebellious heart with godliness, for she would have to account for her sins in the afterlife and accept the wrath that she had brought upon herself. And since her day of judgement was dangerously close given her current condition, she'd better be careful. It seems that, as you get older, the temporary loses more and more of its original, theoretical nature.

As I take off my bag and toss my keys on my desk, I spot Oma in the living room. She's got the heat turned up to 27 degrees, it's burning up in there. But as usual, she's wearing a long, floral dress, a knit cardigan and a white headscarf. I can't remember the last time I saw her without it; it's almost as if it's grown into her head. That's a habit among elderly women – they just stop taking it off, except to take a shower, even though they technically don't have to wear it at home. That's what I learned in Quranic school, where I spent every weekend as a child and teenager.

In practice, many of the rules are based more on culture than the Holy Scriptures; the doctrine I was taught doesn't actually reflect the lifestyle of many of the Muslims around me, which was something I struggled to understand as a teenager. Now I know that hypocrisy and discrepancy are integral parts of the pious life. I'm willing to bet that there are more Muslims out there than people who sincerely believe in Allah. Way more. A pious pagan is less unlikely than a devout Muslim.

Case in point: in Islam, any kind of transaction involving interest is an unforgivable sin, yet plenty of people still take out mortgages or loans, including my own family members, who then, in turn, like to berate me for violating the rules. My begetters would never approve of me coming home with a Muslim convert. People who play with tar eventually get covered in it, that's the argument. Also, things like over-the-top, fairy-tale weddings have no place in the Islamic doctrine, which calls for simplicity in earthly life and forbids extravagant spending on worldly things. And praying five times a day is non-negotiable, but many people, especially men, don't do it.

More than anything, people get competitive and coquettish when it comes to luxury, money or a high standard of living; all of these things are denounced or extremely marginalised in the doctrine. They love going all out for celebrations; the women are addicted to all the soap operas about forbidden romances on Turkish and Arabic satellite channels; and young people are willing to shell out for expensive, brand-name clothing, even when their parents earn next to nothing and they live in the poorest part of town. Then there's the music they listen to – drill rap by people of their own ethnicity, such as the famous Boef and Lijpe, whose lyrics promote an aggressive, promiscuous, criminal, nihilistic existence. Their words toss out shards of Islamic doctrine, producing a toxic mix that's beyond my comprehension, seeing as music is forbidden in the first place. Just as rain and wind are perfectly tolerable when experienced separately but a massive pain when combined, so it is with religious doctrine and the glorification of street culture. Together they create a sort of Islamic gangster culture. Our religion, which most of these people could go on about endlessly, is entirely incompatible with such a profane, materialistic, superficial hip-hop culture, but this is somehow completely lost on them. They're like Catholics preaching the tenets of Calvinism.

Now, of course, the question remains as to what the Islamic doctrine actually is. I've had countless lectures on it, but I won't bore you or myself with that. What I'm talking about is my doctrine, *our* doctrine, the one I learned at the Quranic school run by the Millî Görüş Foundation, which I was forced to attend from the age of six to seventeen by Mother, the embodiment of evil, the tyrant of the nest, a virus against which no antidote can be found, a woman bursting with hatred and resentment towards me, the instigator of all molestation and the source of my tragedy.

Halil had to go to Quranic school too. He came home with stories about teachers who administered corporal punishment if you didn't do your homework or failed to fluently recite verses from memory. My begetters, who believed that physical violence was an indispensable tool in any respectable upbringing, were happy to hear it. 'Otherwise, you'll never learn what discipline is. A man is not at his best when he's totally free; freedom makes you lax. Adam's son [this means "man" in zealot jargon] needs guidelines and direction. Discipline and fear are necessary devices for civilisation. Those who experience fear are strengthened for battle. Those who do not, become lazy. One must submit to authority, pay no attention to the drivel of Westerners who unconditionally embrace latitude, autonomy and boldness. Unbridled casualness threatens a man's happiness and with it the peace and harmony of society and the home. Fear is the mother of morality, one must learn to face it,' Mother claimed. I can say a lot of things about Mother, but I can't say she possesses any cognitive ability. Still, there's no lack of vision. It's vision that holds her together, it's just that her ideas are incredibly rigid and utterly simplistic. It's ludicrous how she sprinkles her wisdom on all sorts of topics, always with a tone of certainty and a nod to the facts.

Fortunately, I myself hadn't been subjected to any disciplinary measures of this calibre; that only happened in the boys' classroom. Defne, my eight-year-old sister, is currently being cultivated at the same Quranic school I went to. Sometimes she tells stories from class that make me wonder whether these children will ever recover from the constant intellectual mutilation they're being subjected to. It's downright disastrous. And her indoctrination has been even more extensive and devastating since she also attends an Islamic primary school, whereas I didn't. But still, I think about how I turned out and try to hold out hope.

The Quranic school is an institution designed to stifle any form of truth-seeking, with no regard for science and reason. I hated it there. I never wanted to go, and begged Mother to let me stay home, but every weekend I still found myself in a tiny room crammed with way too many girls around a rickety little table reading the Quran, ready to pound sacred texts into our tightly wrapped heads. But if I, being the simple soul I am, have managed to untangle myself from the shortcomings of our religious doctrine despite being dispossessed of all instruments of scepticism and open-mindedness, my little sister might be able to do so too. But I also know that a person's path in life is largely determined by a series of circumstances and thousands of other variables, and that most people don't stray from it. Or at least I didn't know anyone else who had, so I can't say if my hope for Defne is reasonable or misplaced. Most of the time, hope is just a way of outsourcing one's responsibility. Nietzsche said that no victor believes in chance, so neither did I. The trick is to be able to decide which responsibilities are best outsourced to fate. The future is not beholden to us. I spent half my time trying to turn the tide, but I could never shake the feeling that I was trying to use the eraser at the end of my pencil to rub away letters written in permanent marker. For the most part, though, I consider humans to be system managers of an infinite network of possibilities that they create themselves, not pawns of fate, regardless of the situation.

Recently, Defne and I were out shopping for Oma when she spotted two men kissing. 'Eeew!' she squealed. 'That's disgusting!' The couple probably thought she was my daughter given the significant age difference between us, which unleashed a deep feeling of shame. I scolded her and told her to apologise, which she politely did, and informed her that, as an upstanding citizen, one shouldn't make fun of people's affection for each other or the way they manifest it, no matter their gender. She was quickly forgiven; she was just a kid, after all, and she was clearly ashamed. Shame is another sign of affection. We are only ever ashamed of those who are dear to us. Shame for one's own stupidity combined with the recognition of it is the definition of true wisdom.

Children can get away with a lot, and as someone who always had to pass for an adult, I sometimes envied that. In the end, naivety is a luxury that not everyone can afford. Comfort is always the privilege of the weak.

Defne was a quick learner; she recognised her mistake and repented. In that sense, children are empty vessels; you can fill them with whatever you want. An intolerant person never starts out that way. We humans are so fond of pointing our arrows at those who are the least like us or whom we struggle to understand. Being civilised means being able to curb that tendency. Being able to behave better than you are.

Sometimes, after a weekend of indoctrination, she'll come home with flyers listing all the Israeli companies she's supposed to boycott. Nestlé, Coca-Cola, Danone, Evian, Colgate and Maggi, for example. And a list of items, such as dates and figs, that we're not supposed to buy at big chain supermarkets like Albert Heijn. Recently, after Erdoğan accused Macron of Islamophobia in his response to the murder of Samuel Paty, she brought home a list of French products we couldn't purchase any more either.

From time to time, she'll ask a question on a topic I prefer to avoid, such as why Christians and Jews hate Muslims, why Muslims in Iraq have been bombed by Christians, why Bosnian Muslims were betrayed in Srebrenica, why Muslims are in concentration camps in China, why the world allowed the Palestinians' land to be taken away from them, and why as many as ten thousand people assembled on the Dam Square in Amsterdam to protest police violence against people of colour, yet no one says a word about the Uighurs or the war in Yemen. Why it's illegal to deny the Holocaust in some countries, but you can deny the Bosnian genocide all you want. The reason for all this is, of course, that the non-Muslim world has a grudge against us, which was something God had warned us about.

I reject her inferences and say that it's all more complicated than that, that reality isn't always what it seems. I have no intention of telling her that it's all a bunch of baloney, because I know she'll run off and tell our begetters. She's a first-rate telltale, I know that from experience. Nevertheless, there is one secret that she has kept for me, a secret on which my life depends: she saw a picture on my phone of me kissing Lucas, my boyfriend. I told her that if she ever wanted to see me again, she'd better not tell a soul. It's cruel to burden a child with secrets. They're so young and unsuspecting, they wear their heart on their sleeve, so asking her to keep a secret like that went against her nature, but there was no other way. If you want to make a child independent, all you have to do is steal their innocence.

Defne is doomed to grow up quickly. Not only because she has to keep secrets for her sister, who would otherwise be disowned from the family or avenged for her unforgiveable sins, but also because she already has to wear a headscarf and long abaya to school, and has girls-only gym class because her eight-year-old body has already been sexualised, because she is preoccupied with thorny geopolitical issues, because all these things make it impossible to be a child like the other children.

But, for now, both she and I can be happy; she only has to go to an Islamic weekend school, same as I did – there are also Islamic boarding schools where children spend the entire week, day and night. They're basically convents for children, where pupils are kept on a tight schedule so not a minute is wasted and they might one day become a *hafiz* – that is, someone who can recite the entire Quran, cover to cover, by heart. In Arabic. There are kids there as young as six or seven, most a little older. After graduation, many will degenerate into teachers themselves, ready to train a new generation of children in similar boarding schools, and that's how the wheels on the Islamic bus – with separate sections for men and women, of course – go round and round. After all, a lie derives its status from the number of proclaimers it manages to recruit. By comparison, our weekend school really wasn't so bad. Mother wanted us to go to a boarding school, where we would be undisturbed in our service of the Creator, but Father hesitantly objected. Children should be allowed to enjoy their childhood, he thought. And those boarding schools were expensive. Now that Mother has seen the result of eleven years of weekend school in me and Halil, how we've become too free-thinking and nowhere near as devout as she is, she has been toying with the idea of sending Defne to a boarding school. She didn't want to sacrifice a third child to the many-headed monster of individualism.

The other day, after a major earthquake in Turkey, Defne's teacher proclaimed that natural disasters are Allah's punishment on mankind, which continues to sin despite the Message. Every time Defne catches me in a sin, such as tweezing my eyebrows (women who do that kind of thing will bear the curse of Allah), wearing make-up or anything that's too short or too tight, neglecting to pray, lying half-naked on the beach without a headscarf (as proved by pictures on my phone), talking back to my begetters or chatting on the phone with my boyfriend (with whom I'm in an extramarital relationship), she says that I am partly to blame for the miserable fates of people on the other side of the world who face droughts, earthquakes and volcanic eruptions. Somehow, even in Scripture, our dear Lord has a tendency to punish not only the sinner for their sin but also complete strangers. It's a guilt sacrifice in its most repulsive, most barbaric form: the sacrifice of the innocent for the sins of the guilty – cold-blooded paganism, at least according to Nietzsche. The individual is non-existent in the eyes of God. In some ways, it's a memorable message. Environmental concerns, which only weigh on the conscience of certain people, also burden the collective. The same goes for people who demonstrate inexplicable behaviour during a pandemic. Apparently, God is steadfast in His methods of admonishment; thus, His ways really aren't that inscrutable. There's a pattern to them. But people don't learn, they don't realise that what's bad for the hive is bad for the bees.

And unfortunately, stupidity finds its strength in numbers. I belonged, according to Defne, to the category of hopeless fools. Believing in collective guilt robs a person of more than just the possibility to believe in individual innocence. Why are individuals always duped in their pursuit of collective goals?

I often feel as if I were Defne's mother. She was born shortly before I started high school, and I've been with her every day since. The years have gone by so fast. I still remember the day they brought her home, wrapped up in the Maxi-Cosi like an overwhelmed little worm. I sang her lullabies in the bassinet and watched her while Mother was off attending classes at the mosque, which she did regularly and with great passion, even when I had my own tests or exams to study for – she always considered her own education more important.

I fed Defne and played with her, I mashed her bananas every evening, I knew how to calm her down when she was crying, how to make her feel better when she was sick. Now I cared about her more than I cared about anyone else in the world. I wanted to shield her, to arm her for everything that was coming, to devote myself entirely to her protection. She shouldn't suffer like I did, she should never feel lonely, stifled, inferior, insecure, unsafe or misunderstood. I would always be there for her, I would be the one she needed as a child and teenager, her companion, her comrade, her guide, a listening ear, the person I never had. She would not be destined to wander alone in a spiritual wasteland, contemplating how to deal with her emotions and desires, which she wouldn't be able to talk about with her begetters. She wouldn't have to murder every feeling in her heart. She could come to me with all her questions, doubts, obstacles and insecurities; I would stand by her unconditionally, even if she got pregnant by a junkie at the age of fourteen, no matter if she was drugged in a dark alley or had fallen madly in love with him – I don't know which is worse, but it wouldn't matter to me. I would be there for her with my wings, I would give her the right tools, I would guide her and encourage her when she didn't know what to do, but under no circumstances would I threaten her with rejection due to 'loss of face', 'dishonour' or 'a lack of self-respect'.

In our world, people believed that you made your own bed and had to lie in it, but not me; I didn't believe in taboos, she could always come to me with her troubles; with me, she would never have to feel trapped in her emotions or obligations. If I had had an older brother or sister like me growing up, I would have been spared a lot of anxiety, distress, disappointment and suffering.

Defne would never have to hide cigarettes and lighters under her headscarf, she wouldn't have to take off her headscarf on the way to school only to put it on again on her way home, she wouldn't have to sneak out of the house from her second-floor balcony to meet up with a guy, and later, if she were caught, be subjected to slaps and blows. She wouldn't suffer from agonising guilt for kissing her boyfriend or the fear that once she did, she would be seen as some kind of half-chewed sandwich, perhaps even by him too, or that photos of her would be leaked in an 'expose group', making her the object of a scandal. By no means would she have to go through all the things I went through. I wouldn't allow it. I would take her fate into my own hands. Or at least as much as I could – I couldn't pull her out of that ecstatic, science-defying primary school she went to, or the Quranic school. Sadly, I didn't push her out of my vagina, so I had no real say.

As Nietzsche put it, 'The surest way to corrupt a youth is

19

to instruct him to hold in higher esteem those who think alike than those who think differently.' In other words, conviction feeds on one-sidedness. I found these words quite hopeful, especially given the kind of intellectual barrenness I was up against. I would do what I could.

Moreover, I would teach her that there was nothing tough about being a bully, or being obnoxious, cynical and provocative – all things that upped your status in the Moroccan hip-hop culture that was so popular in the 'black' schools. I would make sure she knew that this behaviour wasn't bravado, it was a manifestation of deep sadness. I would tell her that she was not underprivileged, that she shouldn't let anyone tell her that. If she needed tutoring or counselling, or a quiet place to study, I would make sure she had it. If she wanted books, I would get them for her, and if she didn't want them I would encourage rather than confiscate, as Mother did with my books. She thought they distracted me from memorising the Quran, the only book that was read in our house. I would teach Defne that, in this country, all paths are wide open, that achieving success is a matter of dedication, that she is not a victim, that the Netherlands is a meritocracy, unlike Turkey and many other places. And although she would still be a little behind in our pluralistic society as a young adult because of the way she was raised, at least she would be a little better off than I was at that age. There was no one who could help me with my homework, we didn't have money for tutors, I didn't have educated parents or any other educated adults around me. I had no room of my own, no bed of my own, no desk of my own, no place to study. As I got older, I started going to the library to check out some real reading material, only to have it taken away because the Quranic school took precedence. People were constantly coming over to the house. I wasn't allowed to watch Dutch TV. I wasn't exposed to sophisticated language or intriguing conversations so that I might one day be able to hold my own in an educated society. Mother sent me to the supermarket every day with one euro; back then you could buy an entire loaf of white bread and a tub of cream cheese for fifty cents each, and that was my breakfast and lunch almost every day. We didn't eat nuts, fish, special fruits or more expensive vegetables like asparagus and peppers. We didn't play sports or go on family outings, we didn't go out for haircuts. In primary school, whenever there was a field trip planned, I had to listen to my parents complain about how expensive it was. They'd ask me over and over again if I really wanted to go, if I was sure, or if they should just say I was sick. Yes, I fell significantly behind, my development was less than optimal, my weekends were consumed by illegal indoctrination, but I caught up eventually and fixed what I could. After all, ludicrous is the person who, in a country like this one, attributes their failures to a couple of minor misfortunes and serves them up as some kind of injustice against them, either by others or by fate. I would tell Defne that she, like everyone, will experience discrimination. Perhaps because of her ethnicity or religion, or because of her weight or gender or appearance, I don't know. Anything could happen – mankind is cruel and incomprehensible – but she should know that everyone everywhere experiences discrimination at some point, and most of the time it turns out fine and you didn't have to start wishing you lived somewhere else in the world (climatic drawbacks aside).

Cleanliness

Oma recently gave up deep-frying and now just eats whatever Mother makes for her, which is lucky for me as I was the one who got to scrub the splattered grease off the floor every day before class. If I skipped it just one time, I had to face the wrath of my chronically spiteful and hot-tempered Mother. She would go around checking the extent to which I was maintaining my duties as caretaker; everything had to be virginally clean at all times. Turkish housewives are obsessed with cleanliness; they scrub the floor until it's clean enough to eat off, for fear that someone might drop by unannounced. I used to moan and groan about her excessive fear of dirt, but in the end – as with the many other things that we, to put it mildly, disagree about – I resigned myself to her regime: an immaculate house. This meant vacuuming every single day, dusting, scraping bird shit off the balcony (a loathsome chore; for some reason Oma's balcony functions as a toilet for all the pigeons in Amsterdam), not leaving the dishes in the sink for a minute (and when washing them never letting the water run; we were taught to scrub and lather, otherwise it was expensive), hanging the washing on the clothes lines on the balcony, and ironing it the second it was dry, scrubbing the tiles in the toilet with bleach, and changing the bed sheets every other day. Mother has a conniption and bends my ear if she sees that I haven't made my bed, put my dirty socks in the laundry basket or jumped up to bring in the laundry the second it starts to rain. If the bin is three-quarters full or there's a single strand of hair in the shower drain or food still sitting on the stove from the last meal, there's hell to pay.

When it comes to cleanliness, both in the literal and spiritual sense, you could call Mother fairly neurotic. 'What if someone shows up at our door?! What will they think of us? Are you going to do this in your own house when you're married? Your husband will divorce you immediately!' she said when I asked why she was so uptight. Her expression was serious, as if she had just made an incredibly sound argument. Mother lives for other people; it's something I've made many futile attempts to change, but I've never been able to cure her. *Collectivum* is her middle name: all of her actions are motivated by what she thinks others will think – or worse, say. In this case, others are people of the same calibre who adhere to equally frivolous rules of decency and virtue. The fact that she has chosen to live this way is one thing, but she expects me to internalise these values as well, and I refuse to go along with it. But what I want doesn't matter; she just forces her ways upon me.

Mother had a perfect spot for every single item in our house: everything had a cupboard, a shelf, a drawer, a vase, a location. The only thing she didn't have a place for was me. She had no idea what to do with me. I wanted to be everything except what she wanted me to be: citizen, child of God, a virginal servant, a virtuous and conforming member of the community, and a chaste wife of Quranic conscience. My neck got blotchy just thinking about it.

23

Last summer, when we were getting ready to go on 'holiday' (a.k.a. torture) in Turkey, Mother was frantically cleaning the house as if her life depended on it. She required my help, but I'd had enough. I demanded to know why we were doing this. I was floored by her answer.

'What if we die on the road or on vacation? What will people say about me when they see this filthy house? That I'm a dirty slob. I won't have anyone saying that about me.'

At that moment, I knew she was crazy. All our conflicts with Mother were centred around this fact. She's a sheep that follows the flock, and I'm the thorn in her side because I don't care what other people think. I only answer to myself. Okay, yeah, sometimes our arguments are about me not complying with the rules of Islam, but even that is intrinsic to her fear of moral judgement from the Other, people within in her own community whose opinions apparently set the norm. She has an existential fear of being stigmatised and ostracised, which can happen to people with a daughter like me, a daughter who is uncompromisingly rough around the edges and so unlike other people's perfect daughters. I am too Dutch, and that worries her Turkish heart.

The Rules

I live at Oma's because there's no room for me in my parents' flat. They have the exact same flat she does, only they have to squeeze an entire family into it.

I used to share a room with Halil, and Defne slept in the begetters' room, but she got too old for that and took over my bed. At least, that's what the begetters said, without any explanation as to what exactly she was too old for, but I figured it out. It's pretty hard to have sexual relations with an eight-year-old in your bedroom, though I'm willing to bet that 'sexual relations' in their case is about as sexy as it sounds.

Halil and Defne now sleep in bunk beds in the same bedroom, which means that Halil is unable to study or relax at home. Defne is always having friends over, watching cartoons in her bed and existing in the way an eight-year-old exists. Consequently, Halil is almost never home, but at least he has the option of getting his own place if it gets too oppressive, an option I don't have, so I can't say I feel sorry for him. But he's in no hurry to move out since we are going to get a bigger apartment in a year anyway because our building is slated for demolition. Then he'll have his own room. Moreover, he doesn't want to take out student loans. His university is close by, he doesn't have to do any household chores, and he has all the freedom to manoeuvre he wants, because Halil has a penis. A woman, which is unfortunately the category I belong to, is not allowed to live on her own before her marriage because she might be tempted to sin and her parents would have no way of watching over her. Somehow this doesn't matter so much if you have a penis.

When you're living on top of each other like that, it feels like the walls are closing in on you and you don't want to come home. I know all about that. But if you think things couldn't be any worse, you're mistaken; our Moroccan neighbours live with six kids in an equally tiny apartment. They've got two sets of bunk beds in one bedroom and the two youngest children sleep on the couch, which they fold out into a bed when 'Allah spreads His blanket across the heavens'. This is not unusual, by the way. In our neighbourhood, most of the families of North African descent have at least four children and live the same way. Turkish families usually have two or three children, which gets pretty tight too. It's all relative, of course, but just because some people build their families in sixes and think enough room to breathe is the same as enough room to live doesn't mean that we don't have a right to complain.

Due to the lack of space at home, children and young people often hang out in the streets, usually in large numbers and for prolonged periods of time. It's either that or sit at home and bicker – after all, idle hands are the devil's workshop – or have your parents barging into your room at any given moment (there's no such thing as knocking at our house, or privacy for that matter) and use you as a dumping ground for all their woes, or start ranting and raving about whatever's bothering them that day, usually family matters, financial emergencies or marital troubles, or otherwise the mess in your room. They'll come in and ask you to translate the mail for them and fill out all kinds of forms, and then get angry and spiteful if you say you can't, even though you're just a kid. They'll demand that you go to mosque on Fridays, ask why you don't pray, ask what you're watching on your phone, why you're smiling at the screen, who you're calling and why it sounds like the voice of the opposite sex, or they'll just make a lot of noise while video calling family members, both those in the Netherlands and those abroad, while you're trying to concentrate on your homework or simply don't want to listen to their endless drivel. Worst of all is when they have people over, and they stay so long that you wonder if they're going to spend the night. And that happens a lot; at any given moment during the week people will shamelessly drop by and stay over until you manage to fend them off with a lot of exaggerated yawning. They say that visitors and fish keep their freshness for three days, and it seems that Turks take the three days literally, when it comes to visitors at least.

In a way, all the spontaneous visits make sense: the women don't work, so they get bored and start searching for fellow housewives to commiserate with, but sometimes they have to bring the whole family over with them, including the husband and children. They do it just because they can, because they have no better use for their time. They have to look for ways to keep busy, a mission in life, they cannot enjoy themselves without companionship, and they're obsessed with maintaining family ties. In our circles, not needing other people all the time, enjoying time alone or simply being introverted are all seen as forms of self-inflation, and signs of a cold, frigid character. Hospitality is the essence of our existence. Or of theirs, I should say.

Personally, I find solitude a severely underrated pleasure.

For me, the details of life can be so overwhelming that I often take refuge in my own space, and this makes me an apostate and the target of slander, especially from Mother. I never feel like a participant; at best, I'm a spectator or someone filling a temporary role. I'm missing a social gene. I have a fundamentally different way of looking at the world, and find people difficult. I derive no joy or satisfaction from the trivial, incessant waffling of my thirteen-a-dozen relatives. The women are more than happy to argue about whatever the affair of the day is, usually gossip, food, drink, wives-to-be, marital disputes that need to be settled (after all, marriage is often nothing more than a penitentiary microcosm in which the warden and prisoner are constantly switching roles), and other trifles. And if they find themselves in the company of penises, then the conversation shifts to the news from Turkey and intense displays of self-righteousness despite having no real knowledge of anything due to a pitiful lack of intellectual and cultural awareness, in other words civilisation. They have virtually no critical thinking skills and no ability to entertain any opinion other than their own, and if someone does voice a different opinion, they raise their voice and act all flabbergasted, because in our circles you always have to pull together, to conform, otherwise you belong to the opposition, and therefore the enemy. Anyone who ventures into unknown territory is not to be trusted, though if you ask me, their ability to conform is as dangerous a virtue as any. I have better things to do than waste my time with these overly sensitive simpletons.

In my world, other people are always so different from me that I often wonder whether I am an unfathomable mystery to them too.

Since I've been living at Oma's, and at least have my own room with a door so people aren't barging in on me all the time, I feel unchained. Not entirely, because according to Mother, moving in with Oma doesn't mean that I'm relieved of the responsibility of sitting with visitors for hours. Sometimes they knock on Oma's door too, but luckily for me Oma is as much of a hermit as I am; she doesn't like visitors, and she's not afraid to shoo them off either. This always leaves Mother red with shame. She holds herself responsible for the behaviour of her mother-in-law and daughter, because in her eyes we are all an extension of one another and together form a single entity that must observe social norms in order to uphold the family's image and honour. This means that after the guests are gone, Oma also gets a mouthful from Mother, who, like a woman stung by a wasp, rattles off all the rules we didn't comply with. But all in all, Oma's apartment has become my little safe haven from ideological short-sightedness and a place where I'd much rather lay my head. It's the one mitigating circumstance that allows me to endure life with my begetters.

Initially, Halil was supposed to move in with Oma, as Mother preferred the thought of overseeing my life to that of her penis-bearing offspring, who is allowed to do whatever he wants anyway and is almost never home. On top of that, she naturally liked the idea of outsourcing her hostess duties to her daughter, who could act as her slave. But I managed to convince my begetters that Halil would get bad grades if they didn't keep an eye on him, saving myself from a life of eternal servitude. He was sixteen at the time, I was eighteen, and his grades were plummeting due to a gaming addiction and total lack of discipline for all things school related. I knew how to scare Mother and Father by prophesising doomsday scenarios, such as their son dropping out of his top-tier high school and settling for trade school instead, where he would be led astray by junkies who carry knives. He would end up a binman or a drug dealer. Small missteps lead to huge failures. (And I wasn't even lying about those trade schools.)

All my fearmongering succeeded; I was the one who got to go and live with Oma. If they could, they'd take back that decision in a heartbeat. Over the years, they've suggested on multiple occasions that it's Halil's turn to live with Oma, but nothing ever comes of it. I will guard my territory, and the tiny bit of freedom that's come with it, with all my might. No one is going to kick me out, I hotly proclaimed. So much of my communication with my begetters was this way. In our culture, you have to speak with your entire body, not just with your words – words alone are never enough. This means that I have no choice but to respond caustically – and with zeal – whenever this recurring topic comes up. I've got Oma on my side too. It's important that I keep living with her; my company has done a lot to counteract her decreasing desire to live. Halil would be useless to her – he only comes home once in a blue moon. And for Eid al-Adha, which everybody looks forward to, except of course the calf.

So now my begetters have less knowledge of when I go out, how I dress, whether I wear make-up and who I talk to on the phone at night. There are still all kinds of restrictions imposed on me, and there's still a long road ahead if I ever hope to achieve the freedom I long for, but at least it's much more comfortable than living at home under the watchful gaze of my begetters, or more specifically, of my tyrannical mother. Father works until the early hours of the morning, so he doesn't give me much trouble. I've only ever known him this way: my entire life he's done nothing but work and was fairly absent in my childhood.

I've learned how to leave Oma's apartment without making

a sound – my begetters' apartment is right across the hall, and whenever Mother hears Oma's door close she runs out to measure my outfit with a ruler, and then proceeds to tell me everything that's wrong with what I'm wearing. When I get back, I'm equally quiet. I silently climb the stairs, silently unlock the door, grip my keys so they don't make a sound, and then I race to my room to remove all my make-up and arousing attire (arousing according to God, that is) before Mother or Father catches me. They have the key to Oma's flat and stop by regularly. This has been going on for years, and occasionally they catch me red-handed, but I'm getting increasingly fed up with the whole charade. So, we fight. They attack me with their moral blackmail and threaten to marry me off. Then comes a slap from my hot-tempered Mother, who would like nothing more than to see me boiled in my own broth. I'd like nothing better than to push her out of a helicopter over the Sinai desert. Eventually, she unleashes the bloodhound inside of her, scolding, spitting, pinching me, leaving all kinds of greenish-yellow marks that make Lucas's stomach turn when he sees me naked and make Oma livid – she's seen her fair share of the whip in her life, and to be fair I never had it as bad as she did. Still I keep inciting Mother's wrath. Because I don't want to be good, I don't want to listen, I don't want to obey. I used to cry in bed afterwards, waiting for someone to comfort me, refusing to eat or leave my room, trying to get their attention, to show them that I was really sad, but comfort never came because I didn't deserve it. That doesn't happen any more. I'm my own comfort. The playbook for these situations isn't going to change, but I'm fucking twenty now. At some point, she's going to have to give up the fight, right?

In the winter I wear a long coat, which covers my outfit,

but now that it's summer, all my sinful, promiscuous outfits are on full display. Mother makes me wear a dress that hangs to my knees at least and is loose enough to conceal all my curves. I'm not allowed to wear short sleeves or anything that shows the least bit of skin, let alone bare legs like every other girl does in the summer. I'm not allowed to wear jeans, only pantaloons, and only under the shapeless sack I just described. This is why I mostly stick to maxi dresses, the most attractive option available.

Under no circumstances am I allowed to have a strand of hair sticking out of my headscarf or tie the scarf into a turban, exposing my neck. When I was fourteen, Mother came to the conclusion that bare feet were forbidden as well. She had talked it over with the local morality preacher at the mosque, a skilled yet pernicious orator from whom she derived most of her authority over me – in other words, this person was the source of the molestation and harassment that I endured on a daily basis. Thus, Mother started complaining about my flip-flops as well, but I had managed to get other members of the family and a couple of neighbours on my side. They thought that Mother was going overboard – everybody wears sandals nowadays. 'What do I care what other people do? They've lost their fear of God, these are His rules, not mine!' Mother retorted, pointing out the flaw in my aunt's reasoning. 'She's young. You're too strict with her, be careful, that can be counterproductive you know,' my aunt warned prophetically. 'I'm just following the rules,' Mother replied, which was true. 'And she has to follow them too, otherwise she'll be sorry. God is going to ask me on Judgement Day why I didn't raise my daughter properly, why I allowed her to chase after the devil before my very eyes, and what will I say then? The imam believes that we are responsible for the deeds of our children, that we will be held accountable for them.' Apparently, our God levies a 100 per cent inheritance tax on sin. Not from parent to child, but vice versa. But if the child was going to hell anyway, you lost either way; meanwhile God's lining His pockets. Unless we all behave.

How could I make it clear to Mother that the words of Imam Blahdiblah, as someone with a clear philosophical bias, are not absolute truth and do not make him a legitimate authority? How could I explain to her the difference between facts and moral judgements? How could I make her see that objectionable behaviour – even in the name of the rights she bestowed on herself as an enforcer of morality – remains objectionable?

Our dear Lord had thought of everything to make the free individual anything but free, and certainly not an individual. Once again, I found myself still attached to the eternal umbilical cord. You can say what you want about the Islamic doctrine, but it's been systematically thought through. The ideal always goes before the individual right. There was a time when I accepted everything my begetters and the morality preachers put forth as truth and I took it all to heart, but this changed as I grew up. The adults didn't know any better, they were all too busy playing house, even the ones who didn't have children. Nobody knew what they were doing. And although that realisation was frightening at times, losing all faith in people still came as a sorrowful release. 'Come on, Fatma, you're making a big deal out of nothing, they're just feet,' Father said. In those moments, I wonder how zealots decide what's over the top and what's not, and how they reason it through in their minds. If you're able to disregard the rules in this case, then surely you can do so in other cases as well. It turns out that reality isn't willing to conform to conclusive theories. Human behaviour is so complicated and random that I'll never understand it. The priest Antoine Bodar put it beautifully: 'There is doctrine and there is life, and there is tension between the two.' Perhaps the most significant constants in history are man's contradictory nature and unpredictable behaviour.

Integration

As a kid, I always turned beetroot-red when the teacher announced that they would be making home visits to meet our parents, as if they couldn't meet our parents at the school. I don't know if all schools have this policy, but it was probably the policy at ours because it was a 'black' school – in other words, all the pupils were from a migrant background (or a bicultural background, you can call it that too). Don't be misled by the word black, there were almost no black students at our school. Based on my own, no less reliable, observation, the school's population was roughly 70 per cent Moroccan and 30 per cent Turkish (or 'Turkish Dutch', whatever), with a few Surinamese, a couple of half-diluted Germanic Dutch types, and all of two full-blooded Dutch kids thrown into the mix. The teachers tried everything they could to get the parents and guardians involved in their children's education, but most were indifferent or didn't show up at parent nights, especially those from the older generation who spoke little to no Dutch. So it was decided – just as I started attending the school – that home visits would help solve the problem. That plus I'm pretty sure the teachers just wanted to snoop around in our home lives. To see what an exotic Muslim household really looked like. How it was furnished, whether it is all so different, whether the mother wore her headscarf in the house too, whether the father slapped her around from time to time, if he had several wives, if there were bomb belts and explosives for committing holy jihad lying on the kitchen worktop, that kind of thing. However, there really wasn't that much to see: at most a dead sheep hanging in the shower if they happened to drop by during Eid, but that was about as adventurous as it got.

To my surprise, all the teachers who came over (both mine and Halil's) were enthralled by our carpets. I never knew that handmade carpets were so special until I heard Mr Albers (and the rest of the teachers who came over every year after that) go on about them. Mother had done a lot of weaving in her youth and had the dusty old things sent to the Netherlands after she got married. 'What sublime works of art!' Mr Albers exalted, 'You know, I have a Persian carpet at home myself, but this colour combination and these decorations are absolutely extraordinary! And so unique! Very different from the ones I've seen.' I translated it as 'He likes your carpets, Ma', which made Mother beam with pride. 'Tell him that I have a few more in the cellar, he can pick one out if he likes them so much!'

Typical Mother, she *was* generous. If people praised her clothes, she would jump behind her sewing machine and run up something for them; if people complimented her cooking, she would bring them a pan of food the next day; if we were barbecuing in Uncle's garden, she would take a plate of meat over to the Dutch neighbours (to their astonishment), because surely they had smelled the meat cooking on the grill and it's a sin not to share your food. So when someone praised her carpets, she was more than happy to let one go. She definitely wasn't greedy, you might even say she was altruistic, and she firmly believed that a generous hand pleases the Lord; she got that from her own mother, who was the same way. Grandpa sometimes complained that his wife gave away everything but the forks and knives in their village in Turkey. Though, in their case, that was understandable: they were the wealthiest people in town. All six of their children had emigrated to the Netherlands and become successful contractors (except for Mother, of course; she had a vagina). And Oma, being so pious, wanted to share her wealth with others, for when one hand washes the other both get clean. It was simply too much money for their frugal lifestyle. Chances are they didn't know what else to do with it. But altruism is really just the selfishness of the collective. Make no mistake. Goodness that demands admiration disavows itself.

Anyway, since I was embarrassed by the thought of giving a fucking carpet to a teacher, and at that age all I wanted was to be normal be like everyone else, I translated her offer as: 'My mother says the coffee is ready.' Knowing what I know now, I should've just given him that carpet, but as an adolescent I had an incredible urge not to be different or weird, whatever that means. It's a condition that a lot of teenagers suffer from. Before I knew it, the nutcase would tell the whole class that he scored a carpet at our house, and people would laugh at me. I couldn't have that. I wanted to be normal, and normal people don't give the teacher a carpet during a home visit.

I didn't have any objections to the teachers wanting to drop by, except that I found it extremely embarrassing. Especially when the teacher first walked in (after obediently removing their shoes at Mother's command) and saw how small our apartment was for an entire family. It was something that every single one of them made sure to comment on: 'Wow, this place is pretty small for all of you, don't you think?' Wow, what an astute observation, Mrs Kusters. You know, if you hadn't said anything we would never have noticed how small this place is. My reply was always the same: 'Yes, but luckily we're moving soon.' I figured that in these kinds of situations, it was okay to lie, Allah would understand. Fortunately, my begetters played along. Or at least, Mother didn't understand a word (and still doesn't) and Father kept his mouth shut.

The teachers were always delighted by Mother's elaborately set table and enthusiastic reception – also known as hospitality, something we foreigners are known for. My parents' limited Dutch made communication somewhat difficult, but we worked our way through it. I was the interpreter. Things were different in primary school: both Halil and I would sweat like crazy as we tried to translate everything the teacher said as quickly as possible during our report card interviews. Our Turkish wasn't nearly developed enough to translate phrases like global awareness, artistic aptitude, social skills or vocabulary. And even if I could have translated them, they wouldn't have meant anything to my begetters. The same problem arose when we had to translate letters from the Dutch tax service or the municipality. I had no idea what a 'waiver' or a 'tax-free threshold' was. All I knew was that Father liked to complain about how we were always getting the short end of the stick.

Halil had a harder time translating; his reports always contained extensive comments on his language skills. I myself got excellent grades thanks to my consumption of significantly more books. I had no trouble securing a recommendation to attend a top high school. Halil, on the other hand, was initially placed on the lowest vocational track, despite the fact his test results were technically pre-university level, because his teacher considered even the mid-level programmes too advanced for him. Halil was not verbally gifted. He sighed and huffed out his words and had yet to write a complete sentence in Dutch with correct punctuation. And yet his test scores were quite high, which nobody understood. By that time, my begetters knew more or less how the scores worked and what they meant for your future prospects because of their experience with me. They had heard from the other kids' parents that I had achieved an exceptionally high score and that they should be really proud (my score was actually the highest one ever obtained at my primary school, but it was only exceptional because everyone else did so poorly).

In Halil's case, our begetters had long since resigned themselves to the fact that he would end up a construction worker or something like that; after all, he wasn't much of a reader. 'Not everyone is good at studying, some are good at working with their hands, like my brothers, that's just how Halil is, it's the nature of the beast,' said Mother after a parent–teacher conference in which she was told, once again, that her son was way behind in terms of language skills, and that he needed to read more books and watch more Dutch television. Mother thought that was a bunch of nonsense. She claimed that it couldn't be fixed, that you shouldn't force it, it was something to be accepted, everybody was different and had different talents. I, who also served as interpreter at Halil's conferences, didn't translate that for the teacher. Instead, I said that she promised to do everything in her power to help her son catch up. I hoped that Mother would eventually be proven wrong.

When Mother heard that I got such a high score, her first concern was for the evil eye. The idea of an evil eye comes from religious doctrine and basically means that anyone who achieves success should beware of sinister looks from jealous people who are out to destroy their achievements. And this applies to everything. If you are attractive and praised for your looks without anyone saying *mashallah*, your beauty will fade. So Muslims can get pretty upset if a fellow Muslim gives them a compliment without uttering that key word; it's taken as an attempt to rob them of their God-given blessing. When a woman gives birth and everybody comes over to meet the baby, and the baby gets sick around that time or at any point after that, they blame it on the evil eye of one of the guests. If your hair starts to fall out, it's because someone has been looking enviously at it. If a recipe fails, it's because someone nearby didn't want it to succeed. If your car breaks down, it's because someone was jealous of your car, etc., etc. In other words, all of life's setbacks can be traced back to the jealous people around you, and the only weapon in your defence is the Quran and your concerted effort to keep your achievements and blessings as quiet as possible, away from the evil eye. You can also hang a *nazar boncuk*, a blue pendant with a dot in the middle, which is supposed to represent an eye. In Turkey, you see it everywhere – in shops, town halls, hospitals, bakeries, banks, homes, cars and airports. The Moroccans have a similar symbol, but theirs is a hand. In Quranic school I learned that these cursed pagan amulets are actually forbidden, that they're idols of later innovation, which basically means that they were not present during the life of the Prophet (peace be upon him) and cannot be found in scripture. Their symbolism is therefore cultural, not religious. Amulets aside, the concept of the evil eye *is* mentioned in scripture, but you can only protect yourself against it by reciting the Quran – that's what I was taught.

The evil eye is the reason why devout Muslims don't post pictures of themselves, their children or their food on social media. Imam Blahdiblah claimed that there was once a guy who posted a picture of his food on Instagram, after which he suffered an extreme heart attack. 'That's because people looked enviously at his meal without praising Allah for it. It could happen to you too!' But what if, while listening to his sermon, I gave him the evil eye? Could I give him a heart attack too?

Halil had achieved his high score by doing a couple of practice exams on the library computer right before the test. We didn't have a computer at home. This was after he suddenly realised that his results could have a major impact on his future career and thus his life. When he got to the Reformed Lyceum West, however, he was still placed in a mid-level bridge programme in light of the lower recommendation he'd previously received. If he did well, he could move up the next year. Today, he gets top marks at Leiden University, and plans to graduate cum laude and pursue a career as a lawyer in Amsterdam South. The other day, Oma asked him what he wanted to be when he grew up, but she didn't know what a lawyer was, and even after he explained it to her she didn't have the faintest idea what he was talking about.

When Halil graduated at the top of his class, he raised a middle finger to Mr Mischa (the teacher who made him do the bridge programme) and expressed frustration about how hard it had been for him to move up in the programme. Even though he had had the test scores for it from the beginning, that 'racist asshole teacher didn't think I deserved it'. I wouldn't say it was a matter of ill intent; after all, Yassine, one of Halil's friends since primary school, did get a higher recommendation from the same teacher thanks to his verbal talents, extroversion, large vocabulary, assertiveness and participation, even though he scored lower on the test. Yassine is in trade school now, by the way. So, it seems to me that this is not so much a case of 'foreigner discrimination' but rather of 'teachers reward extroversion over introversion and think they know how to detect intelligence'. I'm sure this happens among less informed white Dutch people as well. I would assume. They say still waters run deep, but unfortunately it's the fast talkers who get all the appreciation.

I felt incredibly awkward when the teacher who visited our house asked to use the toilet; we kept a watering can next to the loo to wash our behinds with. This had to be done before praying otherwise the prayer wouldn't be valid. Maybe they knew why it was there or maybe they didn't even notice it at all, I can't say, but to me it wasn't normal, which is what made it so embarrassing. Nowadays, I couldn't care less. You have to assume that teachers at a school like ours have some general knowledge of customs among the subcultures they encounter on a daily basis, surely? You know what they say about integration: it takes both sides.

Likewise, I found it extremely inconvenient when the call to prayer (the *ezan*) suddenly went off while the teacher was talking. We had a digital clock from Mecca that wailed five times a day. Teachers were always shocked by that. Chances are they associated *Allahu akbar*, the first two words of the call, with something other than prayer. Whether the teacher was done talking or not, Mother would immediately grab her prayer rug and head off to the other room to perform the necessary motions: stand, bow, stand, bow, forehead on the floor, sit, repeat. She only bothered to leave the room because the teacher was there. She never did that for me. As a kid, I'd be watching cartoons or some show on TV and had to switch it off immediately so Mother could pray. That was fucking irritating. She had to pray towards Mecca, which also happened to be towards our television, so it couldn't be on because that would make it idolatry according to Imam Blahdiblah, so it had to be switched off.

Most of the teachers also commented on the foreign-language programming that was constantly playing in the background. 'Do you ever watch Dutch TV? It's really helpful for improving language skills.' Father said we did, but that was a lie. Even if Halil and I did want to watch something in the evening, the begetters dominated the remote control and simply ignored our requests. Most of the kids at our school didn't even have Dutch channels at home; they cost money and there was no need for them. Not to mention the fact that after a certain hour of the night these naked women would appear on the screen and try to get you to call them. At one point, Father wanted to cancel his cable subscription because he had heard that it was a good way to save money, but Halil and I begged him not to because we liked the Dutch cartoons better than the Turkish ones. Father conceded, albeit reluctantly. Eventually my brother and I started speaking more and more Dutch; we only spoke Turkish to our begetters and relatives who didn't speak any other language. Alternating between the two languages took practice, but at the same time it was a blessing – by gaining a language we had gained a culture and could easily switch to another social reality. Language gives you access to the way people think, it says a lot about how they're put together, how they express themselves in different situations, how humour and ideas are formed. Words direct our thoughts. Anyone who thinks that language is merely a means of transmitting information is incredibly ignorant. I realised that, through language and translation, you can explore the limits of your own thoughts. In that sense, language is also a deceptive tool for achieving the impossible: understanding each other.

Mother didn't like us speaking Dutch, but Father encouraged it. He aspired to join the conversation but never could. He couldn't form a correct Dutch sentence if he tried. Mother refused to speak it altogether. She found it difficult, tiresome and unnecessary, and she always hoped to return to Turkey in the near future. My entire life, I've heard my chronically wistful Mother declare that one day we would 'go back', that we shouldn't put down roots, but she never knew exactly when or how. Mentally, she had never left her home country, but physically she had. Moreover, she believed that Dutch was for school and Turkish was for home; we were Turks, after all, and had to maintain our mother tongue. Ultimately, she was flogging a dead horse. She eventually threw in the towel, as I would do later too, but let's not get ahead of ourselves.

Once I got to high school, I watched Dutch shows on my phone, though that was only possible after I got an iPhone in my third year; it was also my very first phone. Teachers recommended that we watch talk shows and read newspapers, that it was important for our overall development and would help expand our vocabulary. I didn't have any newspapers – Father thought they were a waste of money – but the news was free on TV, and I could download the reruns on my phone, or at least the ones that weren't behind a paywall. That's how I first encountered the Dutch world of opinion.

Burdens

I'm exhausted, totally beat. Two hours back and forth in one day, that's the time I spend travelling between Bos en Lommer, where we live in Amsterdam, and Loosduinen, Lucas's neighbourhood in The Hague, and it's really taking it out of me. As soon as I plop down on the bed, Oma says, 'Your mother called, you're home late again. I'd call her back if I were you.'

It sucks supremely not being able to spend the weekend with Lucas and always having to return to Amsterdam in the evening because I'm not allowed to sleep anywhere but here. Having him come here is not an option. If I were to be spotted in Amsterdam with such a suspiciously Germanic-looking boy, all hell would break loose at home and I'd be facing excommunication. Or even worse: an arranged marriage and a one-way ticket to Turkey. It's something I've heard plenty of anecdotes about and even seen happen in my own neighbourhood – I'll come back to that later. I'd rather avoid that for myself, so for the time being, we have to settle for clandestine meetings outside Amsterdam.

When I'm not at the university, I'm either working at the supermarket chain Albert Heijn or at Oresti's, a 'Greek' restaurant owned by Turks, not unlike every other Greek and

Italian restaurant in the metropolitan area. Depending on the weekend, I'm either at Lucas's or at work. I want to earn enough to pay my tuition, books and other expenses, and also save a bit to help my begetters with their impending move. Father delivers the post and cleans trains for a living, so he doesn't make enough to cover all the family costs. And we want to buy new furniture. Or have to buy really; all of ours is falling apart. I've been seeing Lucas for three years by this point, and every time I go out I tell them I'm going to work, so Father assumes I've saved up a small fortune. One day, he informs me that he will need an advance and keeps bugging me about it after that. My savings are non-existent, and I'm worried that I'll eventually get caught, so now I'm scrambling to set at least a little money aside.

Mother is a housewife and Father is the sole breadwinner. She has never worked outside the home, even though Father has encouraged her on numerous occasions to learn some Dutch and get a job. This is unusual: most men of Father's generation forbid their wives to work – after all, it would bring them into an environment where they'd be around other men, and that's not proper. Moreover, they are utterly convinced that a woman's place is in the home doing womanly things. But Father is newfangled in that way, I guess. Or he just wants more income – that's possible too. Principles often give way to money, the god secretly worshipped by so many, most of whom would never admit it, even to themselves. Money, violence and power win out over law, order and art. Choices are almost never made on principle alone; most of the time they're pragmatic, driven by emotions and money.

Despite Father's exhortations, Mother prefers to uphold traditional gender roles; she believes that a woman is responsible for raising the children, cooking, cleaning, baking, sewing and maintaining strong family ties. If the woman were to work outside the home, the family would lose its balance. This is something she learned at the mosque. Eventually, Father gave up. Now that she doesn't have small children any more and we're leading our own lives, she has more free time on her hands than ever. She's like a grocer with so little to do he weighs his own balls, as the Turkish saying goes. So she's recently started a new Millî Görüş course at the local mosque. She is learning to read Arabic and, if all goes well, she should become proficient enough to read all kinds of Quranic texts, giving her a complete knowledge of scripture. She considers this a much more meaningful use of her time than pursuing worldly knowledge or work. Just as the sluggard considers himself lucky that people find him useless, so it suits Mother that scripture forbids her to work. I'm not trying to say that she's lazy; she just likes to keep things convenient for herself. That's different.

Because Father is an unskilled labourer and we're living on his income, we always have it tight; meanwhile, we have neighbours and relatives who don't work at all or who earn cash under the table and still get welfare benefits, and they have it just as good or even better than we do. Mother has heard from other women in the neighbourhood that their children get free internet, money for clothes and even a laptop from the government. Their older children got student loans that they didn't have to pay back when they graduated because their father's income was so low. They also receive allowances for rent and healthcare. Some of them even get divorced on paper so the wife can claim extra benefits as a single mother, or something like that. In the end, they have enough to cover all their expenses and still go on holiday with the money they've earned under the table. Some even buy property in

Turkey. Mother liked to remind Father that he was crazy to even bother doing unskilled labour in this country, especially since it's so poorly paid. But since the local imam said that claiming benefits when you are perfectly capable of working an honest job would be deceiving the government and thus a grave sin, Father keeps going to work.

I can never understand how this woman gave birth to me. If I didn't look exactly like Father, I would have the sneaking suspicion that I was switched at birth, that perhaps the hospital mixed me up with some immigrant child who looked just liked me, with a name they couldn't remember or pronounce that happened to look a lot like mine, Bouchra or something (my name is Büsra, by the way, nice to meet you), and so they switched the name tags on the incubators by mistake. I don't even know if there are name tags on those things, I'm just thinking out loud here. The only other possibility is that Father got some other woman pregnant and I got saddled with Mother shortly after I was born, but that seems unlikely, and I don't want to fall down some conspiracy rabbit hole here.

When I see the books, notebooks and loose papers piled up on my desk, I suddenly remember tomorrow's deadlines. I'm overwhelmed with the feeling that life is becoming too much for me. I collapse on my bed and close my eyes. Then I down three cups of coffee as dark as molten rubber so I can finish my assignments.

This morning I found myself on the train with a group of elderly women on their way to a museum. They seemed to be really looking forward to it. They were having trouble downloading their tickets to the exhibition, which was apparently necessary, and were worried they might be barred at the door. I found it incredibly endearing. They were all made up, had even painted their nails, their hair was coloured and styled.

They all looked kind of like Lucas's grandmother, actually. They were full of zest for life, which was fascinating to me. I wasn't used to seeing that. The older people in my world didn't do that kind of thing. Many of them couldn't even read, let alone show interest in art. Even the not-so-elderly people I knew, my begetters for example, talked of nothing but Allah, death and the afterlife, and particularly the prospect of hell. They weren't interested in this earthly life and its art exhibitions or other aesthetic expressions. Or earthly sciences for that matter. Mother prays, even at night, on her prayer beads, which she has in every colour. It works pretty much the same way as a Catholic rosary.

I always like it when I discover that the stories in our scriptures are the same as those in the Christian Bible. I used to have a different image of Christianity, which was mostly limited to Christmas dinner and the Bible stories we had to sit through every Monday morning at my high school. But there weren't any principles in them that could dominate my entire life. Or completely disrupt it. I read on Wikipedia that, back in the seventeenth century, Christians in the Netherlands had their own kind of burka, called the *huik*. I found it hard to believe that Dutch women would ever walk around under a black shroud, but the thought of it gave me hope: apparently, even in a deeply religious society, things can change drastically as the average level of education improves (and, of course, a little social reform, democratisation and secularisation doesn't hurt either). Change is possible. But my family had already missed the boat.

One morning last week I found myself in a train carriage that was completely empty except for an older gentleman who, for some reason, had chosen to sit right across from me rather than in one of all the other empty seats. On trains, there are certain unwritten rules: don't sit near someone if there's space elsewhere, and definitely don't sit that close.

He asked with theatrical articulation what my name was and then, pointing to his own head as if I were some kind of imbecile, whether I ever get teased about my headscarf. When I said that I do, I was told that I shouldn't let it bother me, that his own mother and grandmother wore headscarves and that this used to be commonplace. I found his unsolicited commentary oddly endearing, but I didn't quite know what to make of it. Did I look like someone who needed reassurance from random passers-by that I'm good enough and that I don't deserve to be ridiculed? Did I look fresh off the boat, like a displaced refugee from Afghanistan or something, like someone who needed him to explain to me how things are in the Netherlands? I was born here, for Christ's sake. What did he expect, for me to thank him? Surely, he didn't think for one second that I let myself be bothered by the comments of single-celled organisms who had nothing better to do than taunt strangers for their cultural attire? I did not appreciate the victim role I'd just been placed in. I was a good person, and I acted even better than I was. What I wasn't good at was being vulnerable. This gentleman was talking to the wrong person.

I had, in fact, been ridiculed, most recently at the beach in Scheveningen. 'We're not in fucking Saudi Arabia, take that rag off your head!' shouted some half-naked, overly bronzed man who was on his high horse and looking for a fight. The guy was full of rage, all the way down to his toes. I could see it in his light-blue eyes, brimming with agitation. I didn't really know what to say. What I wanted to say was 'You know, I'd like to take it off myself, it's fucking suffocating. If it were up to me I'd be lying here in my bikini with my bare ass basking in the sun, but I can't take it off, dick breath.' But I kept my mouth shut. I didn't want to make a scene. At the beach, I got more comments on my headscarf when I wasn't accompanied by a man. It seems that the people in and around Zandvoort and Scheveningen are not fond of Middle Eastern attire, but this was nothing compared to what I'd experienced in Lucas's neighbourhood: spitting, people glaring down at my head from the balcony, spewing curses at me in a thick Hague accent – sometimes, when I was walking with Lucas, they even tried to pick a fight (thank God this never happened when I was alone; that would've been below their honour I guess), so yeah, I was used to it. The man on the train didn't have to worry about that.

Out of the corner of my eye, I see the countless bottles of nutritional supplements that I've forgotten to take for several days now. Recently, I've been suffering from all kinds of bodily ailments – chronic fatigue, gloominess, irritability and shaky hands. There are moments, today included, when I stare out in front of me and burst into tears. The days and weeks fly by, I'm constantly racing back and forth between university and work, and every once in a while I catch the train to see Lucas, who's starting to complain – and rightly so – about how little we see each other. I feel like I'm living outside of time, like I'm just ticking off my responsibilities. I work without any real motivation, like a dutiful robot, wandering blindly through reality. It's a withered existence, with no lust for life. When I googled 'why am I so tired?' most of the hits had something to do with vitamin deficiencies. So I went to the pharmacy and bought everything labelled 'good for the immune system', 'anti-stress' and 'for a healthy energy level'. I still feel listless and sluggish, but I can't really blame the vitamins; it's not like they can improve your circumstances, socio-economic situation, freedom, independence or family.

My schoolwork has been piling up for weeks. Both at home and from friends – or at least from the few I still have left – I keep hearing the same thing: that I'm somewhere else. On top of school and work, I'm in a romantic relationship that comes with a lot of stress and fear of getting caught. Loose lips sink ships, as they say, and I have to play the perfect daughter, granddaughter, girlfriend and sister. The friendships I have managed to hold on to have somewhat evaporated over time. I'm chronically exhausted from trying to keep all the balls in the air, but by far the greatest source of misery is the constant battles at home. We fight about everything – about me coming home late, me not being home when relatives stop by, me working in the evening (they still believed that the night was for drunks and criminals) and me being out too much. But Mother's main grievance is my overly sexy clothes, which – even though I never wear them in front of her – she still manages to find when she goes through Oma's laundry basket and raids my closet. Then she demands to know why I own so many tight dresses if I'm not wearing them, and why they end up in the laundry basket. And of course, my cosmetics are a bone of contention as well. And that I never answer my phone when they video call to verify my location and check that I'm still alive, that I never send my live location on WhatsApp, that I have a profile picture of my face on WhatsApp, Instagram and Facebook (it's haram for women to post photos of themselves online).

I'm overheated from my frenzied life and the arguments at home, and pretty soon I'm going to explode. I don't know what to do any more, but my protests are always silenced.

I have to report to work in the bakery section at Albert Heijn at the crack of dawn. I work the 7 a.m. to 12 p.m. shift, so I have to get up at 6. Then I head to the university to listen to lectures on Dutch literature. I generally have class two afternoons a week, and on the other days I work at the restaurant, which my parents don't know about. They would never allow me to serve alcohol, or be a waitress at all for that matter – Muslim women are supposed to be modest and remain in the background, they shouldn't seek attention by serving tables in a tight uniform. The men would most certainly check you out, and then your sin record would sky-rocket. Not to mention the damage to your family's honour.

It isn't completely untrue – in our world, people often go to restaurants to hunt and scavenge since they can't go out or date, like the *tattas* do. Or, well, let me put it more precisely – the girls can't, at least not openly, they're not allowed; the boys can, of course. If they want to score a girl of their own ethnicity, the restaurant industry is pretty much their only option, apart from virtual encounters on Instagram. And if they prefer a Germanic girl, they just swipe left.

How restaurant flirting works is actually kind of hilarious. The guys sit in groups eating or smoking a water pipe while they explore their surroundings, checking the tables one by one to see if there's any good meat. If nothing catches their eye, they hop on over to the next joint and do it all over again until they hit their target. If the interest is mutual, the girl eyes him and smiles suggestively, giving him the green light. Then the guy has to have the balls to give her a wink and motion towards the toilets. The girl follows, which means she's interested.

Numbers are exchanged in the hope of one day exchanging bodily fluids. Sometimes the guy will spot a girl he likes, but she doesn't look back or busies herself with her friends, forcing him to resort to other means if he ever wants to see her again or find out whether the affection is mutual. He hopes that at some point she will go to the loo so he can strike, but if that doesn't happen, he's got one final option: Facebook. There are groups for situations like this, where you can post anonymously that you were at such-and-such restaurant at a certain time on a certain day and saw this girl with long hair and a green sweater sitting at table x, who you would like to meet. Only guys can post things like this. If a woman were to write such a post, she'd be considered 'thirsty', in other words a slut, a whore, a jezebel, a wet slice of bread. You'd be 'desperate for dick', or otherwise written off, because no girl with an ounce of self-respect would ever go after a boy, and certainly not in a public group on the World Wide Web. Most of the people in these groups are from the same background, so there's a pretty good chance that the girl will see it or hear about it from a friend. You can also secretly snap a photo and post it in the group. But in general, these relationships usually don't work out, seeing as both parties usually have staunchly religious parents who wouldn't dream of letting their child bring home a boyfriend or girlfriend before marriage.

When the weather's nice, couples can mess around in corners of parks where nobody goes; the Amsterdamse Bos is large enough, so is Spaarnwoude. Or in the car, if that's available. In the winter, however, their only option is to book a hotel. Since, in our world, the man always foots the bill, even among teenagers, a relationship like that can get pretty expensive. For instance, my chronically horny cousin Mustafa regularly complains about all the hotel and restaurant expenses he incurs. The hotels in the suburbs are more than happy with all their Muslim patrons.

But the most absurd thing of all is how the sex actually happens. Vaginal sex is out of the question; the girl's not going to give up her virginity until there's a ring on her finger. So, they have to get creative. What they do is not considered sex since she's still technically a virgin, which means it's okay. If, however, things go wrong and the girl unwittingly surrenders to the heat of the moment, allowing the hunter to strike, the consequences are disastrous. We're talking celestial, corrosive, voracious regret. A period of repentance, remorse and self-reproach, or in some cases self-flagellation. The burden of such a colossal sin is often too much to bear and can lead to depression or erratic behaviour. There is fear: what if he tells people? At worst, he will post it online and tell the girl's family; at best, he'll only tell his friends, who will then tell the other guys, who will then tell even more guys, and after that hopefully everyone just forgets about it.

If the family gets wind of the girl's disgrace, their whole life is turned upside down; their daughter is now worthless: no upstanding gentleman would ever take her as his wife and the future mother of his offspring. The family's good name is thus definitively and irretrievably ruined. Whenever her father or brother goes out in public, there will be pointing, muttering, gossiping, people staring out of the corner of their eye, whispering out of the side of their mouth – there he is, that chump, that pushover, that spineless piece of shit, couldn't raise his daughter right, couldn't protect her, guard her, keep her safe from the big bad world and now look what she's become, a whore. Gossip is the immoral revenge of a frustrated and powerless morality.

Mother told me that there are mothers out there who have become paralysed or suffered heart attacks after their daughter was *exposed* in sexy photos. We Muslims approach everything holistically: the individual does not exist, you are an extension of your family, so your life as a relative of the exposed girl will never be the same, not to mention the girl's life.

The girl's anguish after such a scandalous deed stems primarily from uncertainty about the relationship's future, that it will ultimately fail and they won't get married. After all, what man would even want her in her tarnished, degenerated state? Our men select and value their women in the same way they do their cars: zero mileage is much more desirable. Or as a cousin of mine recently put it: 'Women and cars, you drive them both.' An illuminating explanation.

If the relationship survives and the couple do make it to the altar, you're pretty much home free. There's still a chance that Allah will never forgive you, but you can negotiate that later and spend the rest of your life repenting for your sin. Much worse is when the two part ways: not only is there a guy running around with your secret, and he could ruin your life and the lives of your loved ones for ever, especially if there are pictures to prove it, you're also still stuck with your 'unwrapped cunt' that you can no longer sell as new – it's 'as good as new' at best – but nobody wants that. If you're lucky, you'll end up with a man who is divorced, has children or couldn't do any better because of his inferior looks. And most Muslim women aren't interested in that, and their father, whose opinion is even more important than their own, definitely isn't interested in it either.

There's only one way out: hymen surgery. But this only works in cases where the boy you fucked has no evidence of the act or, if he does, would never reveal it. This usually requires a little extra motivation on his part, otherwise he could ruin everything, and you'll still be known as the neighbourhood *kech*. So, you slip him a few grand et voila: you've got a pristine pussy that will bleed like an ox on your wedding night. And bleed it must because people are already suspicious. If you are unlucky and there's no blood, you could be promptly returned to your begetters with the receipt. Then again, he might turn a blind eye, as the costs of a divorce and a new marriage aren't in his interests either. However, with that kind of distrust, the relationship will be off to a very bad start and will only become more unpleasant over time, thus the best way to avoid all of this is to make sure it never happens. There are a lot of ways to go about this – feel free to google it if you like. The most common method involves a bit of fake blood in a bag. I don't have any more details for you; I haven't had to do it yet.

All of this is to say that we Muslims live and die by a cult of virginity. Or at least the women do, because, again, the sexes are not subject to the same terms and conditions. Men see 'women to have fun with' and 'women to marry', otherwise known as 'wifey material'. Until they're ready to be fully domesticated, they can play the field, which mostly consists of monocultural Dutch girls, but they're also free to dabble in their own kind. These girls can be, in their words, 'used and thrown away'. They're seen as sluts and nothing more. The woman they ultimately marry must be pristine, a diamond in the rough. If she's not, then she's inferior and promiscuous.

God makes no distinction between the sexes when it comes to virginity requirements, but in reality all hell doesn't break loose when the family finds out their son is no longer a virgin. Sometimes they even secretly encourage him to bust a nut every once in a while. 'A boy needs to experiment, it's perfectly normal, but a girl's honour is more important than her life,' my aunt said the other day when I asked her why she gives my cousin Mustafa free rein to hang out with girls, but Sema can't hang out with boys. Most of the time, parents couldn't care less what their son does with his knob, seeing as it never leads to any kind of suffering or intense scrutiny from the community. On top of that, guys who fuck pretty girls are higher in the public pecking order, a benefit that those without penises do not enjoy. Mother doesn't mind that Halil has a girlfriend, but if she knew that I had a boyfriend, she'd have a fit. I'd be slapped, disowned, thrown out on the street, shipped off to Turkey and God knows what else. And if you ever call them out on their hypocrisy, they'd come up with some kind of moral excuse to absolve themselves from adhering to their own moral requirements.

I'm in a dangerous position, not only because I have a boyfriend but also because he is as white as they come. As a woman, you can't even be in contact with a man unless your family knows him and has approved of the relationship, after which an engagement and a wedding will follow. The begetters' approval is purely based on their own preferences. Some things are set in stone and not open to discussion: the man must be of Turkish origin, he must be Sunni Muslim and of the same movement (in our case the Millî Görüş). He must have a family that supports him and endorses his choice of partner, otherwise he's no good; a righteous person knows the value of his begetters and shows them unconditional respect. A rebellious (in our world, critical also counts as rebellious) and non-conformist nature is considered the embodiment of evil. In addition, he should have a steady job and a house.

As a kid, Mother always warned me not to ride a bicycle, as I could break my hymen if I went too fast or bounced too hard on the seat. After a lot of bickering with Father about it, she decided to turn a blind eye. He thought she was being unreasonable; everybody let their daughters ride bikes. The women in the neighbourhood offered Mother their reassurance as well; they told her that it would take a lot more than a bicycle ride to break a hymen.

When she discovered that I had started menstruating, she told me never to use tampons, not even if someone offered me one in an emergency situation at school. Most kids were warned about drugs; I was warned about tampons, because apparently they could steal my virginity too. Contrary to the story about the bicycle seat, this one was confirmed by the women in the neighbourhood.

Mother didn't find out that I was menstruating until I was thirteen. I'd managed to hide it from her for two years. I knew that if I told her, I'd have to start wearing a headscarf outside the house and every day to school, instead of just at the Quranic school. According to the Islamic doctrine, a woman should start covering herself as soon as she starts her period, and at that point she also becomes accountable for her sins. Before then, your sins are automatically forgiven. For men, this responsibility begins with the first ejaculation, but they don't have to start wearing any special clothes or a headscarf.

I didn't want to wear a headscarf yet. I thought they were ugly and impractical, especially when it was hot. The kids at school would think I was weird, though there were plenty of other girls who wore headscarves. But it just didn't suit me. And I wouldn't be able to wear short sleeves any more and that would be super annoying in gym class. But mostly they were ugly, that was the main thing.

The first time I discovered blood in my underwear, I panicked; now my sins counted. I would have to fast during Ramadan, no more sneaking gummy bears with pork gelatine in them, no more swimming (at least not with men) and no more hanging out with boys. I had to pray five times a day and cover my womanly curves and hair. But I had absolutely no appetite for all that praying, no need for spiritual fulfilment; it all seemed incredibly inefficient to me, a total waste of time. So, I decided to keep the news about my period to myself. I stuffed a giant wad of toilet paper in my underwear and waddled to the chemist to buy some pads. I would have to hide them as if my life depended on it. Mother was always nosing through my stuff, so it was hard to find a suitable spot. It had to be somewhere she wouldn't look, but no such place existed in our apartment. Finally, it came to me – the lockbox a girlfriend of mine had bought at Intertoys. Granted, it was just a toy, but it still had a lock on it. The stupid thing was that all the lockboxes in the store had the same lock and key, so all Mother or anyone else would have to do was buy a second one and they'd be able to open mine. It was the same with the diaries with little locks on them. Those idiots.

Anyway, Mother probably wouldn't buy a second lockbox (incidentally, when I figured out that every diary had the same lock, I broke into my friend's, but there was nothing very interesting in it, just long, vindictive rants about her begetters, which is essentially what this book is too). When Mother asked why I had used my savings to buy a lockbox, I told her it was to keep my money in. As if I had any money left. The box and the pads had cost me an arm and a leg; I'd spent all the money I'd earned from kissing the hands of relatives at the end of Ramadan – it was the only day of the year when I got a little money. We never got any kind of allowance.

After the big investment in the lockbox, I didn't have any money left over to buy chocolate milk from the vending machine at the library or a croissant at the supermarket. I thought about stealing one once but quickly suppressed the impulse; that was beneath me.

After a while, I started thinking about switching over to tampons – they seemed much more practical – but Mother's warnings echoed through my head. I searched the government healthcare website to find out whether you could really break a hymen with a tampon. You couldn't, but the opening could be stretched. I was shocked. Apparently Mother was right, so I stuck to pads.

But, one day, it must have been all over my face, because, as the Turks say, a liar's candle burns until sunrise. Mother probably already suspected it. I was thirteen by then and the other girls my age already had their periods. She began to worry that I might be infertile or have some kind of disease. She wanted me to go to the doctor, but I told her it was perfectly normal and that there were plenty of other girls at school who hadn't started yet. I knew I would have to tell her soon, especially since I wasn't allowed to lie until the Israel–Palestine conflict was resolved. The main goal of any liar is to not get caught, but when this eventually becomes unsustainable it's better to stop lying altogether. However, the thought of having to wear a headscarf kept me from telling the truth every time. That's not to say that my conscience wasn't getting to me, when I saw the other girls wearing headscarves it was a slap in the face, a reminder of my sinful, hypocritical existence, but then I thought of all the Muslim women who didn't wear headscarves, so I wasn't the only one, I wasn't alone. But I was also smart enough to know that that was no excuse; we all dug our own grave, as they constantly reminded us at the mosque. Thus, the discomfort was permanent. I didn't know what to do. I was taught that you would burn in hell for every strand of hair you didn't cover in the company of strange men. So, every night before bed, I begged God for forgiveness and understanding; I wasn't ready, the headscarf made me feel insecure and it didn't look good on me. Surely God could understand that? Or was that a bad excuse? I didn't know, and worrying about it all the time was exhausting. I didn't want to lose my popularity at school and was afraid that people would think I was ugly, especially Harun, the cutest boy in my class. Sometimes he talked to me, which turned my face bright red and made my stomach churn. If I tried to reply, I'd find myself struck with a sudden speech impediment.

Then there was the fact that headscarf pins weren't allowed in gym class. I'd heard from the other girls that this was extremely annoying because without the pins, the scarf would slide down with every movement, especially if you had a lot of hair, and I really liked playing football. The headscarved girls never ran and never did any of the exercises. The gym teacher just assumed that they were lazy and lacked motivation. Once I started wearing a headscarf, I became 'lazy' too.

Anyway, one summer day in my thirteenth year of life, I let my guard down just once and Mother stumbled upon a pair of bloodstained knickers in my room. She assumed it was my first time, and I just let her think that.

The next day, I came home to find a red headscarf lying on my bed. 'It's time you started observing the rules. Your classmates have been wearing them for a while now, some since primary school. Ilay is younger than you are, and she already wears one. You're thirteen now. You know you have to; you've learned that at the mosque. And you should be happy, Allah will be so proud of you! Think of the blessings you'll receive. Tomorrow you'll wear a headscarf to school, I bought one for you in your favourite colour,' she said, as if she were ordering a halal ham sandwich, and then she calmly went back to making dinner, completely uninterested in my reaction or the fact that this was a really big deal to me. To her, my protests were just whining. You could say that whining is a sign of sensitivity, but to the narrow-minded, whining is just whining.

After spending hours in front of the mirror fiddling with pins and watching YouTube videos on how to style the thing – which, as with any tutorial, made it seem a lot easier than it actually was – I took a deep breath the next morning and headed off to school. I expected everyone to stare at me on the metro, but no one did.

'What a shame, Büsra! You have such beautiful hair!' said almost every teacher. 'Oh, I see you've got a new look,' said Mr Krosse. 'I didn't recognise you,' said another. 'Why the sudden change?' asked Mr Demaret. 'I just wanted to,' I replied. Their comments, along with their sullen, regretful looks, made me feel even worse than I already felt. But I smiled it off, only to weep at the sight of myself in the mirror later that day.

Once Mother had discovered my secret, the lockbox was no longer necessary. But I still needed a place to hide my monthly supplies. If she caught sight of the bright purple packaging in my room, because, say, I tossed it on my desk after buying it, she would have a fit. I should be ashamed to leave such intimate items lying around, what if Father or Halil saw them? Under no circumstances was I to ask my father to pick up pads or razors for me at the store; that would be extremely inappropriate. There were many times in my life when I felt like I should be ashamed of being a woman at all. Meanwhile the boys were encouraged to indulge in their masculinity. As a little girl, I remember family members playfully urging Halil to show them his circumcised pecker so they could judge whether he was big enough to be called a man. At first, he found those kinds of jokes embarrassing, but there came a point when he would pull down his trousers and proudly display his goods, sometimes without even being asked, and all the aunts and uncles would applaud in theatrical amazement. He was a man

63

all right, he had balls of steel and an iron cock, and one day he would devour women. What about me? I thought. What am I going to do later? Just be devoured?

I decided to see what they would do if I did the same thing. I was small, I don't remember how old exactly, but young enough not to understand why I couldn't flash my private parts in public.

Mother immediately yanked down my skirt and Father slapped me, as he would often do for the rest of my life, always with the palm of his hand. The guests were shocked by my audacity. I felt like a criminal. Mother practically sank through the floor with shame since she was naturally to blame for my poor upbringing and lack of manners. This was a low point that would remain chiselled in my memory for ever.

I cried the whole day. I didn't understand what I'd done wrong and prayed for Allah's mercy. Mother thought that it was because I had been watching *Shin-chan*, a manga series where the main character occasionally pulls down his pants and does a naked tushy dance. 'Those infidels, even their bloody cartoons encourage this kind of nonsense!' From that day forward, I was no longer allowed to watch *Shin-chan*, and that made me mad. It was my favourite show. And *Shin-chan* wasn't even to blame.

I felt the same way at Halil's circumcision party. He got to wear a beautiful gold, blue and white kaftan and carry a golden staff in his hand, like Sinterklaas. The whole family went to a photo studio to pose proudly with him in his circumcision outfit. To this day, the photos still hang in our living room, and in our grandparents' living room in Turkey, alongside the circumcision photos of all their other male grandchildren.

Then we drove to a small party hall where his circumcision

was celebrated with all the members of our extended family. Halil received money and gold coins as gifts; everyone wanted a photo with him. He got to sit on the stage in a big golden chair covered in decorations, as if he were an emperor. Everyone came by to offer him their personal compliments and to tell him that he was a real man now. Mother was glowing with pride; the whole thing brought her to tears. She kept calling Halil 'my lion' and 'my ram', and she still does. She's never called me by anything but my name. Or just 'my daughter'. In hindsight, I'm glad I've never been called a lion. They're a bunch of moral crusaders who'd rather kill their partners than be cheated on.

Everybody laughed, danced and ate. I secretly wished that somebody would throw a party for me too, so I could get some attention. And compliments for becoming a *real* woman. To celebrate my menstruation, if need be.

As we got older, I often heard remarks of this calibre directed at Halil. Even when he talked to family in Turkey on the phone, they always asked how the pretty girls were doing, whether he had one or thirty, how he'd ever be able to choose. They gave him tips on what to look for in a woman: if she had wide hips, she'd bear healthy tigers; if she had big tits, she'd produce plenty of milk; and if she had a little meat on her bones, she'd be good between the sheets.

Waste

My begetters are right, a restaurant is no place for a Muslim girl to work. But I can't give it up – the pay is great, and it beats working at Albert Heijn, where I've been employed since the age of fifteen. After six years stocking shelves, working the cash register and slicing bread, I was ready for a change of scenery. I was no stranger to forbidden waters by then, and sneaking around had become practically second nature to me. The most beautiful flowers grow at the edge of the ravine, as they say. This has pretty much become my life motto. In the long run, constantly avoiding risk is dangerous too. It results in a long and incredibly boring existence.

I don't wear a headscarf during my shift; my employer prefers it that way and so do I, so I'm not complaining. Naturally, my begetters are unaware of this as well, so I have to be careful that I don't run into anyone I know. It's never actually happened; I knew when I applied for the job that the chances of seeing anyone from my neighbourhood were next to none. The restaurant is far away and mostly caters to tourists, and it's pretty expensive, so it's not particularly appealing to people of slightly darker skin tones. And, unlike all the other Middle Eastern restaurants in Amsterdam, there are no water pipes on the menu, so my people would never come here anyway – shisha is kind of their thing. A day without a puff is a day not lived.

My begetters have no problem with the fact that I work at a supermarket. To them that's 'a normal job for a woman', as long as I'm not out at night and don't have to refill alcohol or sell it at the cash register. Mother had understood from Imam Blahdiblah that the bearer, buyer, seller and pourer of alcohol are all damned by the Prophet (peace be upon him), so she demanded that I be assigned to the bread department. I also had to make sure that my shift ended before dark so I could walk home by myself. Otherwise, Father or Halil would have to come and pick me up. At least, that was the case until last month, but after a lot of arguing I put my foot down. I was twenty years old and done with being picked up. At first they claimed that it was for my own safety, but then the truth came out: they didn't trust me. They wanted to make sure that I was really at work and not sneaking off somewhere else at night. But since I insisted, with a lot of shouting and stomping, on being allowed to walk myself home at night, I've started working at the restaurant. But I can't be out very late, until a little after ten at the most. My begetters know that Albert Heijn closes at ten o'clock sharp.

During our fight about the whole being-picked-up-from-work thing, Mother expressed surprise at all my complaining. She reminded me that there was a time when it was unthinkable and absolutely ludicrous for a girl to have a job at all; girls were supposed to busy themselves with household chores and prepare for family life. And if you asked her, the way girls dressed nowadays was completely backwards too: the headscarf is worn with jeans, form-fitting dresses and other modern clothing, sometimes even with jewellery, sandals and make-up, whereas it used to be worn with long, shapeless robes. She lamented that so much had changed in the Turkish culture. 'We are losing our connection to our faith and gradually succumbing to Westernisation,' she declared. It all made Mother very uneasy: our religious doctrine was undoubtedly superior, the West was soulless and depraved, but here we were following in the footsteps of the wicked. Our integration – or should I say assimilation – had been too successful, we'd gone too far, conservatism was quickly losing ground to the progressive modern ideals of the West.

While I think Mother is stuck in the Middle Ages, she believes that we're the ones who've lost our way, become totally disconnected, led astray by post-modernism (in her eyes the great murderer of religion, society and humankind) and decadence, all because women are becoming economically independent, leaving the house whenever they feel like it and no longer walking around in potato sacks. To her, these are the essential issues; if you separate the woman from her primary task as a stay-at-home mother and turn her into a man, it won't be long before we Muslims are sliding down that slippery slope like snowballs and ultimately abandoning all of our principles. A culture dies when there's no one left to carry, share, maintain and impose it. I guess progress is a matter of perspective. Women of her generation had so few choices growing up that the amount of choice their offspring have must be utterly astounding, while I compare myself to the Dutch norms and constantly feel like I am banging my head against a wall of restrictions.

At the restaurant, I get generous tips from the tourists, who make up almost all of the clientele. My colleagues, who are all men except for one woman who's morbidly obese, claim that it's because I'm a woman and nice to look at. They all make significantly less that I do, which has often become a point of contention. They call it sexism, which is something that women are usually the victims of, but not in this case, apparently.

After so many complaints from the staff, the boss recently decided that from now on, all the tips will go into a jar and be divided fairly among the employees at the end of the month. Far from fair, if you ask me. More equal, maybe, but fairer it was not; everyone knows that I earn the most, and in this life we all get what we deserve based on our knowledge and ability. But ultimately I was forced to surrender to the tyranny of equality.

What bothers me most is the amount of food we throw away at the end of the day. Whenever there's a party, we throw away pounds of meat and fish afterwards, much of it completely untouched. It goes from the pan to the bin. I ask if I can take some of it home, as my family and neighbours would be grateful to have it. Out of the question. Apparently, 'the refugees', as my boss likes to call his Yemeni workers – most of my co-workers are Yemeni, by the way – have already asked this same question on numerous occasions.

I don't understand, but I ran into the same thing at Albert Heijn. 'If I give you bread you won't buy any bread tomorrow, and the same goes for everybody else,' said Peter, my branch manager.

I find it physically painful to see how much food is dumped every day. At our house, throwing away food is a very sensitive issue; it's a kind of sacrilege. If Mother sees that the milk has expired, she uses it to make dough. If the bread is stale, she uses it to make breadcrumbs for meatballs. If it's mouldy, she saves it to feed to the pigeons and ducks, which isn't much appreciated by the council. They've put up posters all over the place reminding people that bread attracts rats, but nobody in our neighbourhood cares about that. Throwing it away is simply not an option, it's haram, which explains why our neighbourhood was teeming with rodents. Mother would be furious if she knew that any of us had thrown away our sandwich. Imam Blahdiblah said that Allah will punish the wasteful with poverty, for he who does not value the small things in life doesn't deserve great things. But somehow, Albert Heijn has never been struck by Allah's wrath.

Redistribution

Yesterday, I had a curious conversation with Defne. She came over to show off the sweets she'd scored at a classmate's birthday party. There were at least ten of them. She was pretty happy about that, but she couldn't help but express her disappointment over an incident that had occurred: after the piñata was smashed, she had scooped up at least four times as much as the other kids. She'd come up with a pretty savvy strategy: she got her hands on a bag beforehand and sprang into action as soon as the sweets hit the floor. In the end, however, the slower, more easily distracted children didn't get any. So, the birthday boy's mother promptly seized the bag and redistributed her loot to the rest of the kids, so that everyone got the same amount. Defne was thoroughly annoyed; the other kids simply hadn't tried hard enough or thought to come up with a strategy in advance. There was no point in even trying if everyone got more or less the same in the end.

'Most of them weren't even paying attention and were off doing other stuff while I was coming up with a plan. The other kids were just slow. They should've moved their lazy asses a little quicker.'

I can see Defne growing up to be a brutal capitalist. At least capitalists are honest about the ugliness of man. When Mother heard her story, she tried to teach Defne that giving alms to the poor doesn't make you any less rich. And that he who covets lacks much. And that the poor have an easier way to heaven. And that happiness is the art of making bouquets with the flowers you have. And that sobriety is the source of all pleasure. And that greed is a bottomless pit. And that money leads to complexity and that complexity can never achieve the level of simplicity. And that ambition is the absence of satisfaction.

Risk

I've been back at Oma's for twenty minutes and have been ignoring the long list of missed calls from the begetters. I can feel Mother's hot breath on the back of my neck. A few WhatsApp messages appear on my screen. They want to know where I am and what on earth I'm doing out so long after dark. In the winter, it's even worse because it gets dark at five o'clock. They're testing my patience. I'm finding it harder and harder to tolerate the demands being imposed on me. Last week, Mother emphatically informed me, or shall we say ordered and threatened me, as she does, that since I refused to be picked up from work, I would have to tell my employer that I was no longer available for evening shifts. I just nodded, too tired to argue, but now I was in hot water because the clock read eleven-thirty.

If I say that I just got home and that I had to stay late at work due to circumstances beyond my control, she'll be suspicious. I used that excuse last time, and I doubt she'll accept it again.

Three weeks ago, I got home around eleven after being gone all day, and Father had stopped by Albert Heijn to see if I was really there. It was for that very reason that I worked at a branch on the Elandsgracht, far from home, but that didn't stop him. When I got home from The Hague, Father slapped me and shouted that I had no self-respect and that I was a filthy liar. I was also branded a slut because I hadn't had a chance to change my clothes and was still wearing pumps and make-up. With a string of woman-shaming expletives, which Mother was using with increasing regularity, I was smacked from one ear to the other.

'Who knows what you've been up to all day? I don't believe a word you say. You say you're working at the university, but for all we know, you've dropped out. It's not like in high school, where we could go in for a parent–teacher meeting and get some answers. Just look at what time you come home, and wearing *that*, unbelievable. Shame on you, I can see every single curve on your body. Is that what you learned in all those years at the Quranic school? You deliberately ignore our messages and phone calls. Don't tell me you haven't looked at your phone. Do you have any idea how many stubborn, disobedient girls like you have been raped? And after that, their life is over because no one will marry them. Do you want to end up like that?'

In Mother's jargon, 'being raped' and 'falling into sin' are synonymous with being a Muslim woman who, in a moment of weakness, gives into *zina*, or extramarital sex. She calls it 'being raped' because she firmly believes that any righteous girl who gives in to that kind of 'dirty', 'sinful' lust has surely been manipulated by some son of a whore who intends to use her and 'throw her away', or in other words simply not marry her. The crazy thing about it is that she is not the least bit worried about the psychological consequences of a real rape – all she cares about is the loss of purity and the possibility that my future Quranic prince won't want me any more because I've been 'defiled'. Moreover, in our world, a woman is never completely innocent in a rape; if you're foolish enough to walk the streets at night even though your parents have warned you a thousand times not to, if you're stubborn and continue to disobey, you were kind of asking for it. You deserve any blame or social consequences that befall you. We Muslims adhere to the belief that if there's a conflict both parties are at fault. If you decide to publish offensive cartoons, for example, you're partly to blame. In other words, it takes two to tango. And that's an ideology, by the way, not the result of discrimination in the allocation of internships.

This time, Father was furious too. Usually, he was the one trying to calm Mother down and de-escalate the fight. But now that he'd punctured my Albert Heijn balloon, he didn't trust me any more. Apparently, when he stopped in to check on me, my co-workers felt the need to tell him that not only was I not working that day, I hadn't worked all week.

'From now on, I want to see your school and work schedule every week. If you want to meet up with friends, you can do it here at home or show me on FaceTime who you are with and where, and only during daylight hours! I want you home every night, before dark, no exceptions! We've had enough. You're lying to us, we're your parents, we're responsible for you and it's our duty to protect you.'

With the passion of someone fighting for a noble cause and tears streaming down my face, I declared that that was never going to happen, that I would rather die than give up my freedom. That I wouldn't put up with even more restrictions when they already kept me on such a short leash. That I was twenty fucking years old and could decide for myself what I did with my time and when I came home, and that I only lied because they gave me no other choice. That the lies were forced by the truth.

At that point, Mother, who had been indulging in her hot temper lately, got physical. She grabbed me by my headscarf and slapped me, after which I heard Defne scream and start to cry. I wriggled free and fled back to Oma's apartment. I ran into my room and locked the door, which Mother had been known to pick open with a teaspoon.

There was an unread message from Lucas on my phone: 'Did you make it home okay, babe? Want to picnic in the Zuiderpark tomorrow? The weather is going to be great.'

Now, three weeks later, I find myself once again in the same situation. Oma tells me that they're over there steaming, waiting for me to come home, that they just called. She says I'd better go. As usual, Oma had tried to tell them to leave me alone, that they should stop making my life miserable, but once again her words fell on deaf ears.

I hope Defne is already asleep. It's depressing to think of her growing up in such a tense environment. Because of me. That can have a huge effect on a child. Thinking about Defne made me feel cruel. How many times had she locked herself in her room and cried while I battled it out with our begetters? I'd recently stumbled on her diary, and inside she'd written page after page about how she hated it when we fought. She even drew a picture of us mid-battle: three people screaming at one another and her covering her ears.

I'm so caught up in my own troubles that I hardly see Defne any more, I barely have time for her. We used to go on little outings, or I'd take her to the library, because nobody ever did that. The other day I asked Mother why the hell she never took the time to pick up a few books for her youngest child, to which she responded with the kind of primitive reasoning that leaves me utterly speechless: 'One should raise a child to have good character, she gets enough knowledge at school.

You used to read books, and you still read now, and look what's become of you. You live outside of your own family, your own community, you're practically Dutch.'

I also hope that Halil is home so he can stand up for me and help keep Mother under control. He does that for me some-times, and they always listen to him. He does have a penis after all, so criticism from him isn't written off in advance. Unfortunately, he's almost never home in the evenings, he's usually hanging out with friends, so I'd better not get my hopes up. Besides, Halil has already indicated several times that I shouldn't rely on his support, that he has no intention of going against our begetters. He told me to try to live by their rules, that it would save me a lot of trouble and grief. 'Just work in the afternoons,' he said laconically the other day. 'And if you want to meet up with your girlfriends, do that in the afternoon too, and if they call you, just answer or send a picture. It's not that hard, is it? Why do you have to make them so mad?'

Halil doesn't know that I have a boyfriend, so he assumes that I spend my weekends studying or hanging out with the girls. Obviously, he would never approve of my relationship; he'd turn on me in a heartbeat. After all, he doesn't want a wayward *kech* with no self-respect for a sister either. I'd tried to engage him in a debate on the topic a few times, but there was no arguing with him.

'But *you* can go out after dark and stay out late wherever you want. You can go on vacation with your friends without supervision, and work or hang out until midnight. You can go to the beach and wear whatever you want. You don't get called, nobody asks you to send them your location, or video calls you to see where you are and who you're with, you don't have to show anybody your schedule. You don't get hassled about the photos you share online. There are even nights when you don't come home at all, and nobody cares. You're free to go out and party. And on top of all that, you have a girlfriend and they know about it and they have no objections whatsoever, as long as you don't bring her home before marriage. Why don't I deserve the same freedom?'

'I didn't say you don't deserve it, Büsra, you don't get it. You're not going to change our parents and neither am I! They're not going to change, nor are their religious and cultural values. You can argue and whine all you want, but all it does is create friction and negativity in the house, which makes things even worse for you. All I'm saying is that things would be a lot more congenial around here if you just came to terms with the facts. There are rules. Our culture is the way it is. You're a girl and I'm a boy. Sorry, I can't do anything about it.'

Halil thought I was just trying to stir the pot because I didn't want to inherit the silence of all the other women in my situation. Whenever I hoped that Halil might stand up for me, he left me deeply disappointed. He'd rather see me conform than rebel, even if it made me explode. I had expected a more enlightened perspective from someone so highly educated, but Halil wasn't a horse that I could bet on. Maybe he was right. Maybe I should just accept my fate. In that case, I might as well break it off with Lucas because it was never going to work out anyway. It was just a premature romance that looked more like a primary school crush.

'Do you believe in God?' I asked Halil the other day. He shot me a quizzical look. 'Tell me the truth,' I said.

'Well, if there is life after death, then I'm better off believing in God. And if not, it doesn't matter anyway,' he replied.

This was the dumbest answer I'd ever heard. As if God

would actually smile on such a sly crapshoot from a devious, unsuspecting mortal. My brother was so incredibly stupid. I had no use for him.

I decide not to go over there. I put on my pyjamas, get into bed and turn off the lights, my heart pounding. If they storm into Oma's house to get me, I'll be asleep or pretend to be asleep. Might as well postpone the war a little longer.

Rome

The fact that Lucas has managed to stay with me for three years is pretty impressive. He deserves a girlfriend he can sleep with, go out with, go on vacation with, go to the movies with and hang out on the couch in the evenings with. Not somebody who always has to rush home in the afternoon. With me, it's more of a WhatsApp relationship. I had tried to secretly go on vacation with him, but of course I wasn't allowed to go anywhere without supervision, neither in the Netherlands nor abroad, even if I lied and said I was going with a girlfriend.

'The only time you'll ever go on vacation without your family will be with your husband. Get that into your head,' Mother said. I didn't expect anything else from her. In high school, it was the same story, which is why I never went on any of the class trips, unlike Halil, who – again because he had a penis – got to go.

I missed all the school trips, except the big one to Rome that everybody takes at the end of high school. That one is compulsory, and my coordinator wasn't buying the story that I was sick again. What a coincidence, she said. Then she asked me if my parents weren't letting me go, and I said yes. So, she told Father that the trip was strictly mandatory and there would be tests and other assignments that I would inevitably fail if I didn't go. Mother still needed two weeks to think it over and consult with Imam Blahdiblah. In the end, she reluctantly agreed but made sure to warn me (threaten me) two hundred times not to go out after dark and not to leave my room, to keep the door locked, even during the day, and not to associate with any of the boys. And to always remain in the company of female teachers. If the teachers were drinking alcohol, I was to stay away from them. The worst thing about the whole trip in Mother's eyes was that the girls had to associate with 'grown men', which was absolutely forbidden in our religion and the imam had explicitly warned parents about it. 'Complete madness! Girls and boys that age taking a trip together! Sleeping in the same hotel, with rooms right next to each other? *Astagfirullah*, another plan thought up by non-believers.'

The enthusiasm must have rippled across my entire face. The night before we left, I couldn't sleep. I couldn't wait until morning; it felt as if I were pulling it towards me. My classmates always assumed that I just didn't want to go on these trips and that I only called in sick to get out of paying for it, but it wasn't my fault. They called me a 'cheater', a 'faker', a 'party pooper', a 'sad sack', but I was too ashamed to tell the truth, worried that they'd tease me for being this pathetic girl who was oppressed by her narrow-minded parents. There was nothing cool about that. Plus, it would make me different from the other kids, most of whom were Muslim like me but were still allowed to travel or work in the evenings. If I tried to use that on my begetters, I got: 'But they aren't our children, they've got nothing to do with us. Just because they're lost, sinful wanderers without honour doesn't mean we should be the same. If one person jumps off a bridge, are you going to jump too?'

I didn't want to be the only one with idiotic begetters; I

didn't want people feeling sorry for me. I hated that. Even back then. In class, I protected my image by acting tough and mouthing off. No one knew that I would actually kick and scream for days, trying to convince my parents to let me go on these trips.

At school, whenever the class was busy preparing for the trip – discussing the itinerary and all the things to pack – I just sat there quietly, because I already knew that I wasn't going. 'Can you bring a Bluetooth speaker for music, Büsra?' they asked while planning for Paris. If I answered yes, they'd be stuck without a speaker. 'No, mine's broken,' I lied. 'Okay, then you can bring the snacks and Red Bulls.'

The trip to Rome was incredible. I laughed and talked the entire time. It was, without doubt, the best time of my life. To this day, it's the only real holiday I've ever had (since all the summers in Turkey stuck in my begetters' village don't exactly count as a holiday, they were more like torture – but more on that to come). For the first time in my life, I had five days of total freedom.

To my surprise, the teachers didn't really bother us on the trip. I had expected them to be more authoritarian, that there would be all kinds of rules and constant supervision, but we only saw them at mealtimes and on tours, which were technically optional. For example, a group of us decided to skip the Colosseum because the queue was hopelessly long and we had better things to do, like try bungee jumping and take a speedboat tour.

Mr Radstake, the geography teacher, who was as posh and elitist as they come and always wore a suit, the kind of person you really couldn't picture taking a shit, suddenly made jokes like, 'It looks like Mrs Van der Horst got a blow job.' We all stared at him in shock.

'What did you just say?!' Derya demanded. Radstake pointed at Mrs Van der Horst's new Italian haircut, 'Check out her new do!'

'Good one, dude!' yelled Devrim, who was sitting a few rows up on the plane, and gave Radstake a thumbs up. All of a sudden we were addressing each other with the informal you and calling our teachers by their first names, apparently an unwritten rule on class trips. Mr Stokebroek became Erik; Mr Radstake, Joop; Mr Prenen, Ramses; and Mrs Van der Horst, Marjan. After the trip, everything went back to normal. A shame, in my opinion; I found the dissolution of the hierarchy refreshing.

The teachers had left all the trip planning to the students after we had complained that their itinerary was way too expensive. 'Come on, we could do it waaaaay cheaper than that!' we protested when the coordinator told us the price was 580 euros per person. In the end, she gave up. 'Well, guys, if you're dissatisfied with the price, I'll leave the planning to you. It will save me a lot of time and effort. And after all, it's your trip.'

In hindsight, she probably shouldn't have done that. We booked the cheapest hotel in Rome, having collectively agreed that we didn't need any luxury (or shall we say decency) because we weren't going to sleep anyway. We had to pay for the trip ourselves, and we couldn't cough up that kind of money. In the end, we got the price down to 390 euros per person by scouring the internet for the best (I'm talking the cheapest of the cheapest) deal possible. We flew easyJet, which was the first mistake: Kaoutar's suitcase got lost, which significantly reduced her enjoyment of the trip. She called customer service every day, but they gave her the autopilot answer that they didn't know where her suitcase was but that they were working on it. Since she didn't have any of her stuff, the teachers gave her 100 euros to buy something to wear for the next five days, but she wasn't satisfied. Kaoutar, who was very fashion-conscious, argued that 100 euros wasn't nearly enough to buy the kind of clothes she needed. She was the type of person who knew exactly when Zara was coming out with a new collection, and she was also incredibly vain. Apparently, she was some kind of influencer on Instagram and had been planning on taking all kinds of beautiful pictures of herself in Rome for months. Mr Stokebroek refused to offer her any more money and told her that 100 euros was more than enough to buy a few perfectly good basics. Then again, Mr Stokebroek probably bought his clothes at Lidl and clearly didn't understand the magnitude of the problem that Kaoutar was facing.

The hotel turned out to be hell on earth. It stank, the interior was incredibly dingy, everything was broken and there were bugs everywhere. Akram, our class oracle, had predicted it. 'How much you wanna bet that it's nothing like the pictures?' he'd said in class. The pictures on the website weren't just misleading, they were downright fraudulent. The building was practically in ruins; it could almost replace the Colosseum. Everything was narrow, the floor creaked, it was more like the Anne Frank House than a hotel. The wallpaper was from the Mussolini era, and there were those shoebox telephones with the spinning things for dialling numbers.

The teachers immediately booked a different hotel for themselves and left us behind to enjoy our cesspool. Anyone was free to join them, for an extra fee.

'Nah, we're warriors, let them go, we'll survive,' Youssef said.

'Hey, Joop, Erik, Ramses, Marjan, I thought we were friends!' Devrim said as they were leaving.

'Sorry, guys, we're not staying here,' Marjan said, shaking her head.

'No, no, no, it's all right yo, go on, leave us here to rot, go and don't look back!' Mo said. After they were gone, he added, 'Those dirty bastards, they're going to sit in a Jacuzzi and have a massage afterwards while we're practically sleeping on top of each other over here. Every time I bend over to pick something up, I've got to press my ass into some guy's dick.'

'Have you ever noticed that Ramses's left ball is bigger than the right one?' Devrim said. Ramses was our economics teacher.

'Dude,' said Mo.

'Fucking hell, bro,' said Youssef.

'*Tfoe*, why were you looking at it?' Kaoutar asked.

'Say, Dev, why don't we leave you alone with Hasan tonight?' said Derya.

'I'm telling you, I've seen it a couple of times now, look closely next time, his left ball bulges out of his pants, I swear,' Dev said.

After he said this, obviously I looked, and he had a point.

On the first night, all the girls hung out in the guys' hotel room. If Mother were watching us in her crystal ball, she would've had a seizure. Their room was significantly messier than ours.

We blasted out music, munched Italian snacks, and Dalal had got us some Bacardi, raki and Red Bull with ice. As far as alcohol went, I was a total virgin, so I didn't really know what to expect, but it turned out to be nothing mind-blowing. It tasted like petrol (don't ask me how I know what petrol tastes like), and if you drank a couple of shots in a row it felt like your throat was on fire. When we ran out of alcohol, Devrim called on Mohammed to turn water into wine. 'Yo, Mo, the liquor store called, they want to know how that prophet of yours pulled that one off!' he whooped.

'That was Jesus, not Mohammed,' I said.

'Jesus is one of your prophets too, right?'

'How did you guys drink all that booze?' I asked. 'Christ, there was a ton of it.'

'All thanks to Akram, it's in his blood; his dad is on a liquid diet too,' Dev snarled. Akram's father was an alcoholic. Fortunately, Akram was too wasted to be stung by the joke. Most of the group got completely smashed, producing priceless conversations that I and the other respectable, sober Muslims in the room mercilessly filmed and edited into memes, which were immensely popular. With my videos, I at least made sure that later on, when they sobered up, they wouldn't be riddled with guilt, that they would only remember the good moments, clearly, vividly and with tremendous joy.

These memes went around the class for the rest of the school year; every teacher saw them and they were even in the yearbooks handed out at our graduation ceremony. Of course, only those that featured the guys – the girls demanded that I immediately destroy all evidence of their one-time moment of ecstasy before people started gossiping and they 'cried shame and got slapped by their brother'.

Derya had made out with Quincy that night. They were already crazy about each other, everybody knew it, but they weren't officially going out. That was understandable – when Derya danced with him at the Christmas gala (which obviously I was not allowed to attend; Halil was there), the gossip spread like wildfire the next day. '*Oh my God!* Did you see Derya going wild with that black dude? Just wait until Hakan hears about it, she's dead!'

Derya's brother Hakan went to our school but had

graduated the year before. However, he still had plenty of old cronies at the school and quickly heard the high-profile news about his sister. Derya was Turkish and Quincy was Surinamese, perhaps the deadliest of all multi-ethnic combinations, because Quincy was black, and Turks saw their nationality – and by extension their race – as sacred. One way or another, girls who had anything to do with 'blacks', or *'azzis'* or *'zenciler'*, were almost immediately labelled street whores and beaten up by relatives for chasing after a big dick. I'm not sure where that idea even came from, but it implied that men with more melanin couldn't possibly have other attractive qualities. It was a very persistent belief in our community, so any Muslim girl with a black boyfriend was choosing a very difficult road for herself.

In the end, somebody in our class let slip that they had made out in Rome, and Derya got knocked around by her brother. He didn't break any of her limbs this time – he limited himself to a couple of belittling blows – but black eyes and broken bones were sure to follow if she didn't start 'behaving herself' soon. She was out of school for a week due to all the commotion at home, and when she finally returned she didn't want to talk about it and wouldn't even look at Quincy any more. I recently saw on Instagram that Derya was engaged to a guy of her own ethnicity. They looked happy and in love. On Facebook, Quincy is now in a relationship with Charlotte Leeflang. They, too, radiate prosperity.

On the second night, we explored the streets of Rome with hip-hop music blasting from our Bluetooth speaker.

'My feet hurt, I want my bed!' Quincy moaned at around 3.15 a.m. when we still hadn't found our way back to the hotel.

'This isn't the jungle of Suriname, dude, we'll find it, you whiner,' Youssef said.

'Yo, Quins, don't be so lazy, I mean, I know you people are known for that and all, but you could pick up your feet a little,' Devrim said.

'You want to know what else his people are known for?' I added.

'Dammit, Büs, I *knew* you were going to say that, you dirty girl, you. You want that black dick, don't you?' Devrim said. They laughed.

'I told you we'd end up lost if we left it to Dev,' Akram said.

'Dammit, Piet, there you go again.' Dev called Akram 'Piet' after the meteorologist Piet Paulusma, because he was always making predictions and insisting that he saw things coming; it was really more of an affliction. He was always saying things like, 'How much you want to bet that [insert consequence here] will happen if we [insert cause here]?' after which the others would sigh at his alleged clairvoyance.

'Yo, Dev, we may not be in the jungle of Suriname, but this isn't Kolenkit either, I'm tired too, are you sure we're going the right way?' I asked.

'Oh, I bet you could find your away around the jungle just fine, Büs,' Dev said. I sighed. Nobody laughed; we were all too tired.

'Hey, feed me, man. I'm dying here,' said Mo, whose diet mostly consisted of street corner sausages and whose stomach was a black hole.

'Suck my dick, slimeball, you already ate everything we had,' Dev snapped.

Ikram tossed Mo a bag of mini pizzas from the supermarket.

'I'm sick of those things. I want something else,' Mo whined.

'Yeah, me too, they have a really bad aftertaste,' I added.

'Yeah, but you're used to that, aren't you, Büs? Don't act like you don't like it,' Dev snarled.

On day three we went to the beach, which turned out to be more miserable than relaxing. While the guys and girls without headscarves cooled off in the water and basked in the sun, I sought shade with other covered girls. We felt like we were melting. As we sat there with our long sleeves and jeans glued to our skin, we watched the girls in bikinis enjoy their freedom in the clear blue water. We saw them transform into bronzed goddesses before our very eyes as the drops of sweat rolled down our lower backs to our buttocks. Sila didn't wear a headscarf, but she still joined us in the shade. She had sensitive skin and would burn to a crisp. She got sunburnt on the first few days of the trip, so she was already sore. This meant that whenever she made a sarcastic comment, all you had to do was give her a friendly slap and her red skin would glow with pain. 'Ouch! Red lives matter!' she'd squeal.

We had bought one of those flapping things from an immigrant pushing a rickety cart. He'd seen us sweltering in the heat and came over to peddle his inferior wares. At first, he wanted ten euros for the thing, but I'd rather die of heatstroke than spend ten euros on a piece of crap that you could buy for less than a euro in a junk shop. And I told him that too. 'I'm not crazy,' I said in my best English, 'I won't pay that much. I'll give you three euros for each, which is still too much, but that's what I'm offering you,' I said.

He acted like there was no way that was possible and turned to leave, but I knew it was just an act.

'Just buy them, come on, who cares, we're dying here,' said Hasan, who was sitting next to me. He was the only guy not swimming and was always hanging out with us girls. He had always been the entertainer in our group of friends and that was reason enough for the other guys to ridicule and humiliate him; after all, he was practically one of the girls. You could tell that Hasan was gay from a mile away, and that made life difficult for him at our school. I often heard people mutter things like 'fucking *zemmel*' after they found out that Hasan was a *top* or *ibne*.

Hasan was a really sweet guy, and I hated to see him being treated like that. One day a gang of guys decided that hurling insults was not enough. As Hasan was walking down the stairs, somebody pushed him from behind and he hit the ground.

'Ha! What a *zemmel*. I'll bet his ass still hurts from last night.'

'*Tfoe*, now I've got to wash my hand!'

I felt an impetuous rage welling up inside me. I wanted to throw them to the ground, euthanise them, gouge out their eyeballs with a rake, but the moment of barbarism passed. I supressed my urges and said, 'Fuck off, you thugs!' And they ran off hooting and hollering.

It might help if Hasan were a little less flamboyant, more of an alpha-gay, but unfortunately Hasan was more of your typical handbag homosexual (for want of a better description). Before I became friends with him, I was fully convinced that homosexuality was a disease or at the very least a choice, and thought the idea that one couldn't do anything about it was utterly absurd. That's what they taught us at the Quranic school, that homosexuality could be cured. And even if you couldn't be cured, that was your problem; you would just have to deny and stifle your feelings for the rest of your life, and with enough willpower and righteousness you would succeed. Now I know for sure that homosexuality is not a choice; otherwise, there wouldn't be any straight women left.

In Muslim countries, many homosexuals commit suicide. That's understandable, seeing as God is merciless on the subject, as is nature – two idiots with the right organs can procreate while two homosexuals cannot. Or perhaps nature and God are the same? Nature is terrifying, especially human nature. And if nature is God, then that makes me an extremely God-fearing person. But history has shown that the more humans detach themselves from nature, the less they have to fear.

God's judgement on homosexuality was the first scratch – no, dent – in my rock-solid conviction of Absolute Truth.

By the third night of the trip, Ikram was covered from head to toe in violently itchy bumps – bedbugs, apparently. She'd had some kind of allergic reaction and could hardly move without pain and a whole bunch of cream. 'We were so fucking cheap that we ended up in a hotel with bedbugs, no air conditioning, no hot water in the girls' shower, and a toilet that doesn't flush in the guys' room!'

'It was Mo's idea to book this place,' Derya said accusingly.

'So, Mo's the bad guy!' said Devrim, pulling Mo into a headlock.

'Well, to be fair, Mo was the first to state his preference,' I said, 'but he didn't shove it down our throats.'

'Yeah, you'd know all about that, Büs – you've had things shoved down your throat,' Dev said.

'Come on, assholes, we all agreed on this place, you're all a bunch of fucking whiners, don't try to peg all the sins of Israel on me,' Mo retorted.

'I hate to say it, but I predicted this,' Akram said.

'Shut up, Piet, you only say that when your stupid prophecies turn out to be true. But even a stopped clock is right twice a day, so yeah, it's easy to say in hindsight,' said Dev.

'Never again. This place is hell, the staff don't speak English, they don't even look at you when you talk to them, they just bark till you leave,' added Youssef, who started itching the next day too. He also had haemorrhoids, but that wasn't the hotel's fault.

'*Drerries*, the worst is the food. The granola tastes like Whiskas and there's nothing else for breakfast, unless you count them stale crackers and that cheese that tastes like the sole of your shoe,' Devrim whined.

'*Those* crackers, not them crackers,' I said.

'Oh fuck off, Büs.' I was known for correcting people's grammar just to piss them off. I even did it in our group chat, where every other word contained a spelling error. Most of the time, they just ignored me. This is still true, three years later. But now that I'm studying Dutch at university I have more authority.

The neighbourhood around our 'hotel' was overrun with refugees and beggars. If I didn't know any better, I'd say we were in Morocco, not Rome. Not that I'd ever been to Morocco, but I'd heard so many stories from friends that I had a pretty clear picture of the place. I had never seen so many beggars, not even in Turkey, while Italy is a European country and supposed to be better off, or at least that's what I would've expected.

But apparently we were in some kind of ghetto. The girls were constantly being harassed by men on the streets, who hissed, whistled and whispered in languages we didn't understand, though it wasn't hard to imagine what they were saying. The teachers had warned us about pickpockets and scammers. Still, they got us. We saw this lady with a toddler faint in the street so we – along with a few other bystanders – rushed over to help her. When she finally came to her senses five minutes later, she thanked us profusely for our help and left surprisingly quickly, and that's when we noticed that some of us were missing cash and one person had lost their phone.

I couldn't get over how many nuns there were in the streets. The way they walked reminded me of my own relatives. At the Vatican, some people in our class were warned about their skimpy clothing. If the guys didn't put their shirts back on and the girls didn't pull down their skirts, we would be kicked out. It was practically a sharia state.

On top of that, we were constantly being followed by street vendors trying to sell us 'designer' goods. 'Louis Vuitton, *real*, *wallah*,' they claimed. They could tell by the headscarves that most of us were Muslim, so they tried to flog stuff to us in Arabic, but the Turks among us didn't speak any Arabic, and the Moroccans didn't speak any second language at all, except for a few words of Berber slang.

'Yo, Sadaf, what are they saying?' Devrim demanded.

'I'm Afghan, you backwards idiot, we don't speak Arabic.'

'Whatever, like I know.'

'It's all gammela gammela,' said Quincy.

'Yeah, all the same,' said Devrim.

Dev was half Dutch and half Kurdish, and also an out-spoken, fanatical advocate of a sovereign Kurdish state and an unabashed supporter of the PKK, which had led to some pretty heated debates in class between him and the Turks. Let's just say that there were some rather passionate opinions about whether members of the PKK were resistance fighters or terrorists. So, Sadaf said, 'Hey Devrim, where do you come from again? What language do they speak there? Oh wait, I forgot, that country's been wiped off the map.'

'Ooooo, diss! That one hurt!' hissed some of the more sensation loving among us.

'That was a pretty good comeback, I'll give you that. I'm

humbled, truly humbled,' said Devrim sportingly. Then he noticed that some of the Turks among us seemed to really appreciate the joke, so he added: 'Just you wait, what's gone can always come back, man,' to which Derya replied: 'Or what's gone can just stay gone.'

Then I turned to Devrim and said: 'You act like you're going to run off and join the Kurdish army tomorrow. But you're practically wearing wooden shoes, dude. You're as Dutch as the Delta Works and tulip fields.' Everybody laughed. Devrim was as Dutch as train delays, everyone knew that, so his Kurdish nationalism wasn't all that credible. He even had an Amsterdam accent, which he had inherited from his mum in Jordaan. And he was always listening to old Dutch drinking songs, even in the hotel in Rome. His room-mates got so sick of it that they barred him from connecting to the Bluetooth.

'Bro, fuck off with all that Dutch music, *wesh*, does this look like a pub to you *wela*?' said Youssef that night when we were all hanging out in the guys' room, practically in one another's laps.

'André Hazes is a legend. You have to feel his music, it has to penetrate every fibre of your being,' Devrim said.

Then Ayoub said, 'Hey, *wollah teh*, turn that music off or I'm going to penetrate every fibre of your being, *ezebi*.'

All of a sudden, I was startled by a piercing sound right next to my ear. It was the phone in the hotel room. 'Shit, they're going to complain again, I said turn it down!' said Aimane.

'Stop stressing man, chill out,' said Devrim as he picked up the phone.

'Yes? Ah, okay. Yes, we are sorry. Okay. Okay. Yes, we will lower the volume. Good night. Sexy lady,' he said and hung up. We laughed.

'How do you even know if she's hot? Did you see her out there or something?' Youssef asked.

'No idea, just dicking around,' Dev said.

'Before you know it some massive walrus with a bowl cut is going to come in here looking for you,' said Quincy.

'Yeah, just the way you like it, Quins, lots of meat.' More laughter.

'Naaah, not too much meat. Are you crazy? You think I'm some kind of butcher, everything in moderation.'

'Whatever, man, if she shows up you'd bang her. You've been dry for a while now, Quins.'

'Nah, I can handle a lot, you know, but I'm not looking for a lady so round that she rolls down the street if she falls. That'd scare my *tollie*.'

'Trust me, dickhead – if you want, you can stick it in anything, except maybe in a dude. But when you're in prison, you'll even do that.'

'Helllloooooooo, we're still here, all this *tollie* talk is making me nauseous,' I said, pointing at the girls.

'Yo, Büsra, why don't you shut up? What, are you going to act all holy now? You talk like a truck driver when you're not around the girls, you two-faced snitch. It's like being on a revolving stage with you: in one scene you put on your habit and in the next you pull out a three-piece anal kit and a dildo,' Devrim said. They all laughed.

'I don't do anal,' I said. They laughed louder.

'Oh, so you do take it the other way?' Emre wanted to know.

'Man, shut the fuck up, you know that we're just joking, right?' said Mo, who occasionally stood up for me.

'Girls aren't supposed to make jokes like that, brother, come on,' Emre said.

Some of the girls and a few of the boys nodded in agreement.

'True, but you know Büs, she's a special case,' said Akram.

'Knowing you, you've probably fucked and sucked all the black dick in the country, pervert,' Devrim quipped.

'No way! I go for blonds,' I said. Most of them laughed. Nawal, Kübra, Mahsume, Hind and Kaoutar looked at me disapprovingly. They found my dirty talk completely unacceptable for a young lady, but they were proper Muslim women.

Emre also found my behaviour unacceptable, and he had let me know on more than one occasion. 'Yo, behave yourself, Büsra, come on, we're just kidding around here, but have a little self-respect, you know. What kind of Turkish girl talks like you?' he said with a serious look. 'Look, I don't want to get up in your business, I'm not your brother or your husband or anything, but you're really lowering yourself with this kind of talk.'

As if he would have the right to interfere with my life if he *were* family. Emre and I had never really got along. He was your typical humourless hypocrite who thought guy talk was only for guys and liked to preach to girls about vague concepts like 'self-respect'. He was a nice person and all, and he probably meant well – after all, he, too, was a victim of his own upbringing – but that didn't mean he could reprimand me. It was hard for me to joke around with Turkish guys, or just make friendly conversation for that matter – even at work. Most of them were like this and immediately assumed that you were trying to flirt with them. Somehow the Moroccan guys were more sociable and open to normal conversation. The other day my cousin actually brought this up, which was revolutionary. I was actually a little shocked. I rarely heard people in our community hanging out our dirty laundry. She said: 'When I take the kids to school, I have no problem greeting the fathers of the Dutch children and striking up a conversation, but that never happens with the Turkish dads, which is weird, it's like there's an unwritten rule that men and women don't talk to each other, it's actually really awkward. Why can't a Muslim man and a Muslim woman have a normal conversation with each other? We always have to make assumptions,' she complained, and rightfully so.

'You were supposed to turn that music down, dickhead, that's what that lady said,' I hissed at Youssef.

'No way dude, they can suck my cock. This place is gross, they're lucky we're still paying to sleep in this shithole. There's not even hot water in the shower or air conditioning, and it's fucking hot outside,' Dev said.

'We can't even flush our own shit, we have to keep using bottled water to get it down, pretty soon we're going to have to call a truck to haul it away,' said Mo.

'Yeah seriously, we took cold showers this morning. Good thing it's summer, otherwise we'd all be sick,' said Dalal.

'And I'm still covered in bumps from the fucking bedbugs!' moaned Ikram.

'Yo, toss me something to eat!' Mohammed shouted from his bunk bed at Devrim, who was closest to the table with the snacks. 'I haven't eaten anything all fucking day.'

'Oh yeah? Those pizzas on the terrace ate themselves, then?' said Kübra.

'Oh that, yeah okay, just that then, but I need more food, I'm a hungry boy, you know.'

'Here you go, fatty, don't eat it all, leave some for me too. If we end up trapped under the rubble when this place caves in, you've got alternatives. We haven't,' Devrim said as he tossed him some sandwiches, crisps and waffles.

'When have you ever seen Mo say no to food? He eats like a vacuum cleaner,' Hasan said.

'Boys, boys, without mine and thine, the world would a heaven be,' said Mo with his mouth full.

'Yo, Mo, if you eat it all, I swear I'll come fuck you in your sleep with my colossal cock, which is still whole by the way because my parents didn't put me under the knife as a baby like you Mohammed-heads do,' Devrim said.

'Yeah, whole and dirty with all that nastiness growing under your dirty foreskin. Besides, we can last longer if we have to. You're done after three moans,' Emre said.

By the sound of it, Emre was no longer a virgin and not trying to hide it. If I did the same, he would call me a *kech*.

'So hey, Emre, how do you know that? Weren't you just going on about self-respect and not joking around about sex?' I asked.

Quincy laughed. 'Wow. What did you think? He worn it out from peeing? Emre shoves it into anything that breathes, don't even get me started,' Quins said.

'Brother, that's normal, we're men, that's how we are, we're filthy animals, but as a woman you shouldn't be like that. You don't want to bring shame on yourself and your family.'

I'd be surprised to ever hear Emre make a coherent argument. The tricky thing about the norms and values of Muslim guys is that it's hard to pin them to a coherent set of rules. But talking about norms and values undermines them if there's no corresponding behaviour. The ease with which some people put their hypocritical decency on display is undeniably some kind of vicious provocation.

'All that stuff about hygiene and foreskins makes no sense. Anybody can keep themselves clean, you don't have to cut things off. I mean, yeah, if you cut your toes off, I guess you won't have to worry about athlete's foot any more,' I said, resuming the debate.

'But still, you can last a lot longer,' was the response.

'Why don't you put your money where your mouth is? How about a little competition? Let's go find ourselves a couple of Italian prostitutes and we'll see who can last longer,' said Dev.

'Yo, *tfoe*, now that you mention it, I'm suddenly reminded of that fucking hairy ass of yours and my appetite is gone, man. There's no way I'm getting hard with anybody with that image in my head,' Mo replied, and everyone laughed.

'You know what, lick my Kurdish ass hair. A real man has hair,' Devrim said.

'Gross, what's all this about?!' said Kaoutar.

'Do you have ass hair?' I asked Devrim.

'You bet. Every man has ass hair, Büs, don't act like you didn't know that, pervert,' said Dev.

'Every man?! You think everyone is a gorilla like you are? Only Turks have ass hair!' said Mo.

'It's true. I don't have ass hair,' said Youssef.

'Me neither,' said all the Moroccan boys at once, while the Turkish guys remained suspiciously silent.

'I'm a Kurd, not a Turk,' said Devrim.

'Your dad is from Turkey, so, like it or not, you're a fucking Turk, and your hairy ass cheeks prove it. You can tell someone is a Turk based on that alone, it's like your trademark,' said Mo.

'Perhaps this explains why, according to statistics, Dutch paedophiles prefer Moroccan boys to Turkish ones. Apparently, paedos aren't into hairy asses either. Thanks for clearing that up, I'd been wondering about that one for a while,' I said.

'I know what else you've been wondering about, Büs, you dirty girl,' said Devrim. Everyone laughed.

No one really understood why I was the butt of all of Devrim's sex jokes. After all, I was a properly headscarved girl who had never been caught fooling around with a boy. Besides, I hadn't told anyone in the class that I was dating or in a relationship, so they just assumed that Devrim was a blowhard who was making those comments to fuck with me, that they had no basis in reality. That's what I'd led them to believe. Devrim was always saying stuff like that with zero regard for the facts, so it made sense. But the truth was that Dev wasn't just a blowhard; he had caught me red-handed making out with Lucas at The Hague Central Station a few months earlier. Apparently, Dev had been visiting his sister in The Hague. He had snapped a picture of us mouth-to-mouth and WhatsApp'd it to me on the train with the message 'Nice work!' and a string of thumbs up emojis, then 'Ur good!' while I was still staring down at my phone in a state of shock.

'I always knew that you weren't as holy as you looked, with all your dirty jokes. I had you all figured out,' he texted, followed by numerous emojis. The day had finally come. I was kind of relieved that it was Devrim who saw me, because any other guy at school or in my class would've told everybody and soon the whole school would know, including Halil, who was two grades below me. Devrim was kind, free-thinking and not the type who would try to ruin my life. I called him immediately, begged him to delete the photo and tell no one. My hands trembled as I held the phone to my ear. He said he would. I knew I could trust him.

'Calm down, Büs, breathe!'

Despite my relief, I was still stressed all day because I couldn't help but think, what if it wasn't Devrim who took that picture? What if he did forward it to somebody? I had to be on my guard; I could no longer assume that The Hague was safe. Since this incident, Devrim assumed that I was an all-rounder, a *moetjoe*, somebody who, out of fear of her own community, leaves the city so she can get it on with Jan, so to speak. I never set the record straight by explaining that the guy I was with was my steady boyfriend. That was none of Devrim's business.

'*Tfoe* man, imagine you marry a Turkish guy, you're all excited for the wedding night, and then he lies down on the bed, takes off his boxers, you look and suddenly you see his hairy fucking ass cheeks, and you think did I marry a goat or a Turk!' Mo exclaimed, laughing hysterically at his own joke, as always. A few others chuckled along with him.

'Okay okay, but ass hair can be removed, while there's no cure for a lack of character. Moroccans have to deal with that for the rest of their lives,' said Emre, who always felt called to uphold Turkish honour.

'Ooooooo,' echoed around the room.

'We may have ass hair, but at least we're not shitty people. You Moroccans would sell your own mothers for a little drug money and steal whatever you can get your hands on, don't even talk. At least the Turks are hard workers, you people are as lazy as they come. But whatever, that's what you get around here,' said Devrim, who was suddenly siding with the Turks. Around that time, the Moroccan mafia had left a decapitated head of some guy named Nabil in front of a lounge near our school as revenge against an enemy clan.

'Ooooooo,' they said again.

'What are you laughing at?' Mo asked Quincy. 'At least we've got our own culture, religion and folklore, you blacks don't even have that. You don't even have your own language. Your own surnames! You guys are still owned by the *tattas*, you have their names, pray to their gods and speak their languages! What kind of black dude is called Quincy de Vries?!'

Another 'Ooooooo.'

'True,' said Quins, and after three seconds he retorted, 'but at least I can point out the land of my ancestors on the map,' he said looking at Devrim.

'Ooooo! That was low,' people shouted.

'Fuck all of you, everyone in this room can drop dead for all I care!' then Devrim started singing at the top of his lungs with Ciske the Rat blasting from the speaker.

'Dammit, here he comes again with his depressing ass music,' Mo said. Youssef stuffed his head into his pillow, Aimane threw his Adidas slider at Devrim's head, but he managed to dodge it.

'Yeah Dev, sing your heart out, man, don't rob us of this pleasure,' I said, after which I got a banana peel thrown at my head.

'Put some normal music on, dog!'

The music changed to French hip-hop.

'And besides,' Quins continued, 'my ancestors may have been brought here as slaves, but yours chose to leave their country so they could get some lowlife shit job over here. I don't know which is worse, being enslaved or coming here knowing that all you're going to do is fill the gap between what used to be legal slavery and robots that haven't been invented yet.'

'Oooooooo,' everyone said.

'Okay, enough, we've been thoroughly dissed, man,' said Youssef.

'Not me, dude, my parents left their country because of war, we owned a bunch of jewellery stores back in Afghanistan,' Sadaf said.

'Yeah, but that's because your people aren't right in the head and are always blowing each other's brains out for dumbass reasons like cause one guy prays a little different than the other. So, don't act all tough, sweetheart,' Devrim quipped.

'You're one to talk, dude, your country isn't even geographically detectable,' said Sadaf.

'Whatever, why don't you come up with something original for once, dickheads? Besides, I'm half Dutch, and you filthy monstrosities don't have shit to say about that of course because then you'd be puking on the hand that feeds you. Back in your countries, you'd be shovelling goat shit in the sandbox all day and getting ass fucked by some farmer with two front teeth and black toenails. You'd be sitting there like a broody chicken giving birth and milking cows in that godforsaken inbred village of yours just barely scraping by. The only bright spot in your life would be when your cow gives birth to a calf so you can sell it for a few quid, and you'd be down on your knees thanking Allah for that.'

'Why ass fucked?' I asked.

''Cause your cunt would be all saggy and *finito* after so many babies, and your man needs something tighter,' Dev said.

'You'll have the same problem if you keep getting so much dick, Büs.'

'Right,' I said. Emre dropped his head in his hands and shook it back and forth.

The next morning, we were supposed to go to St Peter's Basilica; the teachers were already waiting downstairs, but the boys were apparently in a state of deep hibernation. I went into their room and was immediately accosted by one of the most abominable odours I'd ever encountered, emanating from parts of the body where the sun doesn't shine. 'Get up, you pigs! We're not going to wait around for you all day!' I shouted, holding my headscarf over my nose, a vain attempt to prevent the heinous stench from seeping deeper into my nostrils.

'Yo, Büs, you wearing a Gucci belt now? Rich bitch,' said

Ayoub with a yawn. I had borrowed Ikram's belt that morning because I didn't have one myself.

'No man, I'm not into brand-name crap, this is Ikram's.'

'Büsra's a right Gucci hoochie,' said Devrim with his eyes closed, still giggling with a hangover from the night before.

I let out an audible sigh and started yanking off their blankets and pillows to rouse them out of bed.

'I . . . tell Erik we'll be right there . . . I'm going to shower . . . Under the . . . Ugh, I can't talk. I'm up here searching for words like Holloway looking for her kid.'

I had no idea what Dev was talking about, but that happened a lot.

'You sick bastards, I heard you gossiping about us last night, I was sitting there with a glass against the wall listening to everything you said. What do you mean Büsra will be an escort in five years?' I asked Dev.

'She who listens through the wall, hears her own shame. Sorry dude, we were predicting everyone's future career and you were unanimously assigned that profession. But don't take it personally, I'd do it myself if I had a cunt.'

Just then, Aimane walked into the room, prayer rug in hand. I suddenly noticed that his bed was empty and already made. He was the only one who was dressed, clean and ready to go; he hadn't been drinking, after all. 'Where did you come from?' I asked.

'I was praying in a broom cupboard.'

Otherness

This morning, Lucas opened his father's mail in my presence. It was a letter from the Friends of the PVV thanking him for his donation. We knew that Koos voted Conservative, but that he actually donated to the right-wing, anti-immigrant party was news to his son. 'He's gonna do what he wants, I don't care any more. I've given up trying to talk to the man about this. He can't see past all those idiots he hangs out with. To him, Muslims are just a bunch of Gargamels storming into innocent Smurf villages with a net, like these giant octopuses with suction-cup tentacles ready to suck the life out of you. I'm telling you, Pim Fortuyn was the only reasonable politician this country ever had, that man had real vision. He said you had to accept, respect and integrate, and see the newcomers as your equals, but that it was also time to close the border.'

'Whatever, this is a democracy. It's not like the PVV could ever put its views into practice. I'm not worried. Besides, even if they do get votes, they'll never lead this country alone. Dutch politics is based on mutual ideological dilution,' I replied.

'But still, it does matter, because if I have to curse you out every time you go out the door and tell you I'm going to kill you some day, even if I don't even have a weapon on me, you wouldn't like that. And that's what those idiots do, they have no appetite for constructive solutions, they'd rather just stand on a corner grumbling and sighing. If only we'd never let them in – that's their mantra. It's a prayer with no end, a train with no end, one long Black Pete debate, that's what makes it so tragic. And that's what my old man is giving his money to. Pretty pathetic, huh? But what can I do? It's his choice, his money.'

Koos was the first PVV supporter I had ever seen up close. Before that, I thought that particular segment of the population was the underbelly of society, consisting of the most heinous racists alive. Just a bunch of bitter, thoughtless hotheads who had found the perfect scapegoat and liked to blame all their problems on people of a slightly darker skin tone. Until I met Koos.

The first time he saw me in his house with his son, he was confused. He saw me in the living room. I wasn't wearing a headscarf, but I was clearly not of Germanic descent, which he didn't find problematic, by the way. Curious at most. We got to know each other a bit, and I couldn't help but notice that he had a heavy Hague accent. I occasionally had to ask him to repeat himself. He struck me as a good-natured, funny person. He was a big guy, fat, but in a nice way. It looked good on him, very manly. I could see where Lucas got his stature from. I quickly learned that in The Hague you pronounce the last syllable of certain words differently – an -er became an '-ah', -en became '-ih', and the ij sound, so common in Dutch, became a sort of 'eh'. Even the r was different. Sometimes they pronounced words in such a way that I couldn't attach any particular rule to it. But outside of these rather small deviations, I also got the impression that they had a language all their own.

At our first meeting, Koos asked the standard questions that one asks a potential daughter-in-law: how long had we known each other, where had we met, and so on. He noticed that I was from Amsterdam. He seemed genuinely interested and said that he was happy for us. Until I got up to leave. That's when things got a little tense. I put my headscarf on and went to say goodbye. He stiffened at the sight of me. All of a sudden, he was completely tongue-tied and looked at his son. I decided to extract myself from the thorny situation and walk away. Later I was informed that, to put it mildly, Koos did not appreciate the fact that I wore a headscarf and didn't want to see me in his house ever again. I didn't understand. Before I put my headscarf on, there was no problem at all, and now all hell had broken loose. Because of a fucking piece of cloth that I wrap around my head. But could I really blame him? People find the strangeness they're used to less unusual than the ordinary they don't know.

'Oh just let him rant, don't let it get to you, of course you can still come over. What's he thinking? It's my house too. If he wants he can take it up with me, there's nothing he can do about it,' Lucas said over the phone in his best Hague accent, which was considerably lighter than his father's. In their neighbourhood, having an aversion to the headscarf was not unusual. Xenophobic sentiments had been fermenting in Loosduinen for a long time. I got dirty looks just walking down the street. There were a few times when I got water thrown over my head from a balcony or beer dumped on my head. Fortunately, the glass wasn't full, and thank God they didn't throw anything heavier. Sometimes passers-by would call me scum or mutter that I should go back to where I fucking came from. I have to be honest, it wasn't the most opportune emigration destination for me either, which was precisely why I didn't want to 'go back'. In The Hague, you've got the pacified tribal conflicts between the diplomats, and the real conflicts in the streets.

Lucas would flip out when I told him about it; he offered to pick me up at the station, but I didn't want to trouble him, so I lied and said that it wasn't happening any more. Whenever we held hands on the street, we got more dirty looks. He was probably seen as some kind of race traitor or Islamic collaborator, no idea. And it wasn't just in his neighbourhood but everywhere we went. Everyone looked at us. Always. Everywhere. We were a walking circus, which wasn't entirely incomprehensible. We were a sight to behold. I was called a *kehba* or a fucking *kech* from passing scooters, by people wearing fur coats, Gucci hats, white socks and slip-on sandals. When we were in the tram, all kinds of men and women of North African appearance would shoot me nasty looks. Sometimes a man would address me in Berber or Arabic, and I'd tell him I was Turkish and couldn't understand a damn word he was saying, and everyone would look up in surprise. I was often mistaken for Moroccan, even at work. Those scooter gangsters probably took me for one of their own, or at least as a fellow Muslim, which was fairly obvious, after all. As if I didn't have enough trouble with my own ethnic group.

I could handle the dirty looks; they didn't bother me after a while, but Lucas found it increasingly disturbing. He could get really furious, especially with the most obvious and provocative starers. He couldn't stand racist halfwits, he said. I told him that if I saw a blond, tattooed hunk walking arm in arm with a girl in a headscarf, I'd probably stare too. Couldn't we just ignore it? But he couldn't.

The second time I was at Lucas's house, Koos saw me in the living room without my headscarf and sat down next to me. 'Büsra, tell me, why the hell do you wear that rag on your head anyway? You're such a pretty girl!' And that's how our first real conversation began. I explained to Koos that there was no need to be offended, that I wasn't your typical Muslim believer, that I was more free-thinking, that I only wore it because it was customary in my culture, but that I could take it off whenever I wanted, even next to him, which wasn't technically allowed, but I wasn't much of a rule follower. I told him he didn't have to worry, that I wasn't out to get them. I felt as if I needed to prove myself in some way, but I wasn't sure how. How could I explain without confusing him that I wore a headscarf even though I didn't really want to? That I was a Muslim even though I didn't agree with most things Muslim? That I hated my parents but I couldn't leave them? That I did everything in secret while also knowing that eventually I would have to choose: either run away or conform? That I was caught up in a war and was constantly postponing the final battle because I didn't know what to do? That I could run away and win the war, but that would mean never seeing Oma and Defne again?

As time passed, Koos became more understanding of my situation, though he remained sceptical for a long time. But after that day, he didn't make any more comments about the way I dressed. We started to get along. One day I asked him if he hated foreigners, seeing as he voted for the PVV.

'No, of course I don't hate all foreigners, come on, and that's not what the PVV stands for at all, that's just what the media wants you to think, sweetheart! The PVV is just a down-to-earth party that wants to solve problems, it's as simple as that. Take the Schilderswijk in The Hague, for example. Look how much that area's deteriorated in a short amount of time. It's one problem after another. You wouldn't be seen dead walking around there. All the other politicians look the other way, but not Wilders. That's why I support him. If you behave nicely and adapt to our culture, you're more than welcome here as far as I'm concerned. Look at you! You're a perfectly nice, bright girl, people like you aren't the problem – you've actually got something to offer this country!'

His argument was suspiciously similar to my begetters' argument about all the Syrian refugees who had settled in the Turkish metropolises since the war. My own family was outraged by the fact that there were more Arabs in Istanbul than Turks. My cousin Mert had recently visited Turkey and told us that he couldn't believe how many Arabs there were. They were everywhere, he said, it didn't even feel like Turkey any more. Among Turks, making xenophobic comments about foreigners was more of a rule than an exception. Turkey simply doesn't have the economic means to feed millions of Arabs – that's the go-to argument. Moreover, the Turks felt that they were being culturally and demographically under-mined. Syrians were known to have lots of children, spoke their own language, took over entire neighbourhoods and quickly barbarised them with all kinds of Arabic shop names. At one point, the Turkish government even banned Arabic on windows and billboards. Then there was the fact that crime had gone up, and it turned out that a lot of the perpetrators were, in fact, Arabs, which left people foaming at the mouth any time another Turkish woman was raped or assaulted by a refugee. Both left-wing and right-wing Turks agreed: the Syrians were problematic, and they had to go; there were too many of them and they were too disruptive.

Koos said that was exactly how the PVV in the Netherlands felt, that it could no longer look away from the prob-lems caused by the rampant immigration of a disruptive, low-educated ethnic group. The prison demographics alone spoke volumes. It turns out that PVV supporters and Turks have more in common than they like to admit.

Three times in three years, Lucas picked fights with total strangers for making derogatory comments about us being together. All three of them were white, because they tend to be more upfront about their hate, whereas those of darker skin tones just would just spit or shout from their scooter or car and drive off. All three times, it was a man who had insulted or scolded us to our faces. No, actually that was two of the times. The third time, it was a guy who just stared at us for a long time with this sly grin on his face and finally shouted, 'Hah!' and spat on the ground – that was it – but Lucas saw it as a call for confrontation. There would've been a lot more situations like this if I hadn't grabbed him by the arm and dragged him away. Normally, he was a gentle person, but if you stepped on his tail, he'd snap at you, and in those moments I didn't recognise him. He'd become blind with rage. Phlegm wasn't exactly his forte. In one of the fights, he took a violent blow to the face. It left him in pain for weeks, and he needed medication to regain natural movement of half his face, but the damage to the other party was downright disastrous. The guy walked away with two black eyes and maybe a few broken teeth and a broken jaw. In the other two fights, Lucas didn't sustain any significant damage; he was a boxer, after all. After those primitive altercations, I became more hesitant on the street. I no longer wanted to hold hands, hug or kiss in public. I was afraid that one day things would get out of hand, and I would be partly to blame. Lucas didn't understand my logic; what did I have to do with it? 'Well, it would be my fault for not adapting to a situation that I knew would otherwise end a certain way. I mean, if you can't change the situation, it's up to you to change yourself.' A ridiculous argument, in his opinion. Apparently, he didn't know how the world worked yet.

The most recent altercation happened three weeks ago, when we were walking back to his house. 'Fucking race traitor!' this guy muttered when he walked by and saw us holding hands.

'Well, look at that, another moron for the collection.'

'Are you talking to me?' the man asked.

'Yeah, I'm talking to you, do you see anybody else around here who matches that description?' Then Lucas grabbed the guy by the collar, which startled me.

'Come on, I'm not in the mood for police, let him go, please, let's just keep walking!' I begged. We'd talked about this before, and I made him promise me that he would restrain himself, for his own sake. He knew I hated it and that my entire week would be ruined if he got into a fight, so he let the guy go and we hurried off. 'Camel fucker!' he shouted after us, and I pulled Lucas along.

When Koos and Bianca, Lucas's mother, heard about our little incident, they got all riled up as well. Koos told Lucas that he should've asked for his help, that they could teach the guy a lesson. I knew that there was a time when Koos would've probably taken the other guy's side, but he had known me for years by then and his ideas had changed. He had come to see my headscarf for what it was, a piece of cloth, and had learned to look beyond it, at who I was as a person. There we were, a Muslim woman in a headscarf and a right-wing PVV voter in one of the most right-wing, blue-collar areas of the Netherlands, and yet we belonged together, we were family, we'd been eating and laughing together for years, we shared our joys and sorrows. Nevertheless, he had made it perfectly clear to his own daughter, Tessa, that she better not even think of coming home with a Muslim guy. The men were different, he said. The women were all right, but his daughter should make no mistake, there was no way he'd ever let a Muslim man in his house.

Paradise

Whenever I laughed a little too long at Koos's jokes while watching TV and started to snort, he would do an exaggerated impression of me, which made me laugh and snort even louder. Those were the best moments. Whenever the two of us laughed together, Lucas would grin from ear to ear and take me into his arms. 'I love you, Büsra, you know that?' he'd say, glowing with happiness. Other times he'd say, 'Sometimes I wonder what I ever did to deserve you.' When I asked him what he wanted for his birthday, every year he said the same thing: 'More of you. I don't want anything else.' I'd pull him into a deep embrace, and as always when we hugged or kissed, I could feel him growing big and hard. Even if I just gave him a peck at the door, the first thing he'd do was grab my hips and pull me into a passionate kiss, which he was really good at – not that I had anything to compare to, but still, I knew he was good. Naturally, my body was chemically drawn towards his. 'Easy tiger, I just got here,' I'd say to cool him down as I pushed him back into the living room, where I'd greet Koos, Tessa or Bianca. Then he'd grab me and pull me into his room. 'No, first you help me, there's plenty of time for chit-chat later, this is an emergency, I've been missing you for so long.'

It helps that he's also particularly aesthetically appealing. He has long dark blond hair that falls to his shoulders, totally irresistible in a bun, blue-green eyes, full dark brown eyebrows that frame the colour of his eyes. He is tall and undeniably muscular but not too muscular, just right, with the sexiest arms you can imagine. When he's naked, he looks like a Greek god, a perfect statue, you could polish him up and put him in a museum. From every angle, he was a sight to behold, a picture of beauty. He was so damn delicious, an incredibly tasty creature, inside and out. And sexiest of all was his voice, deep and masculine, and his prominent Adam's apple, which drove me insane. The first time I spoke to him on the phone, I was immediately in love, because his voice was so right. He could have the most beautiful girls on earth, and judging by the photos of his ex-girlfriends, he had. But he was mine, and that felt like the biggest trophy in my life.

Today, everything went the same way it went for the past three years: he took me into his arms as soon as he opened the door, dragged me into his room, which was right next to the door, threw me onto the bed and locked the door behind him. Then he pulled me onto his lap like Sinterklaas and asked how the train was, how my day was going, how I was doing, whether I'd done anything naughty, how much I'd missed him. As I answered each of his questions, he ran his hands all over my body. I always made a point to wear clothes made of soft, thin fabric, because I knew he liked that. I almost never wore jeans. Usually, I had on a tight skirt and tights, and an equally tight top that accentuated my enormous breasts without exposing them. He undid my bra and took my soft breasts and hard nipples into his hands and squeezed, sometimes softly, sometimes hard, so occasionally I'd say 'ouch' while I was talking. Then he would twist my nipples. It hurt, but it also made them hard. He touched every inch of my body; every nerve ending in my erogenous zones was activated by his sensual fingers, his firm hands, his kisses. After that, he'd want me to bend over his legs while he sat on the edge of the bed. He'd pull my skirt (usually one of those stretchy pencil skirts) up over my ass and pull down my tights so he could feel my soft, laser-smooth legs. He'd pull my thong aside without taking it off and plunge his fingers into my very wet, deep pink parts to prepare them for what was about to come, as he listened to me talk and bombarded me with more banal questions about my day.

He could really turn me on: those kisses pressed intermittently into my neck, the way he'd position himself behind me and press his rock-hard cock against my ass. I shivered as he ran his nails ever so slightly over my breasts, giving me goose bumps.

There had been times when I'd asked him to stop, told him that I just wanted to lie quietly in the bath with him, or finish watching the movie, or finish cooking, or finish telling my story, but he couldn't stop, he wasn't capable. He couldn't focus until he was fully satiated, and that never lasted long. It was a constant hunger that had to be satisfied. Sometimes we had sex as many as eight times in a single afternoon. I'd be exhausted on the way home. We were both chronically horny, we couldn't help ourselves, we became magnets the second we saw, touched or smelled each other.

Sometimes he came too quickly, before I did, like this afternoon. Then he'd be disappointed and ashamed, while I just laughed, enjoying his humiliation. 'I don't get it, with you I can't help it, I swear I've never had this with any other girl, you're ... You're too much, you're too fierce, you're too feminine, too round, your hips drive me crazy, your ass carries me away, your breasts hijack my mind. You have the most beautiful shape, you're so soft and sensual. And that moan of yours, the way you breathe, the way you look at me . . . I can't resist, it's beyond my power,' he explained.

'I forgive you, baby, don't worry, you're doing a great job,' I said, stroking his head as if he were a little boy who couldn't tie his shoelaces. In missionary position, he was able to hold out a little longer, but as soon as I turned around, it'd be all over within a minute, guaranteed. Once I figured that out, I stopped flipping over, in an effort to save my own orgasm, but he'd turn me eventually and I'd quickly feel his hot cum glowing inside me, some dripping down my thighs and some rushing deeper into my body. Yet another fruitless attempt at conceiving a life. The guy could spew truckloads.

I now know that circumcised dicks are far less spectacular in terms of production and projectile. And that's not all I know. I know that some men come very loudly, while others don't make a sound. Some tremble and sweat when they come and others don't. Some are inexhaustible and can hold out for fifteen minutes or more, while others find twice in one day a lot to ask for. Some have a micro-penis that you couldn't jerk or suck off even if you wanted to because it's barely as long as your hand, or even smaller. Some can fill a tablespoon with their sperm and others an entire cup. I know now that there are big guys with surprisingly small penises, and average guys with elephantine dicks. That some can get rock hard with very little effort, while others always need a little help and rarely get harder than a boiled egg. Fortunately, Lucas was a testosterone bomb.

It didn't take long for me to realise that my ass was my strongest weapon. All I had to do was turn around and gently brush it against him and he was trapped, totally mine. He would automatically grab me and pull me into his crotch, and within seconds I could feel him growing. Sometimes I'd go after him while he was deep in a video game, on the phone, cooking, exercising or studying. If we were in public, he'd get mad. Furious even. 'Don't. Please.' I didn't care, I was having fun; I could get him hard anywhere and everywhere, and he'd have to walk around like that all day. It was a game to me, and I loved the romance and eroticism of it. What a shame that so many women miss out on this, I often thought. I felt sorry for Muslim women. Experience is the only way to free ourselves from guilt.

If I got him all riled up without finishing the job, he'd blackmail me. 'Just you wait, you're in for a serious punishment,' he'd say.

'Oh yeah? I'm waiting. What are you going to do?' I'd tease.

Once we got home, he made good on his threat. He'd lift me up and throw me down on the bed so he could have his way with me. Any resistance on my part was crushed under his huge arms with their bulging blue veins, which became extra visible against his pale skin. I had fairly light skin myself, but mine had a warmer glow to it. He was impatient and gave me no time to undress. He jerked down my tights and thong in a single pull and yanked my skirt up over my ass. With his other hand, he'd flip me over and rub his swollen cock across my wet, buttery cunt. I'd moan as his balls touched my clitoris, which had become hypersensitive to all touch. I turned towards him, kissed him passionately, occasionally sucking on his lower lip with a suggestive look, almost begging. Then I'd push him on his back and spoil his cock with my voluptuous lips. I licked, kissed and sucked at a leisurely pace. Sometimes I'd let out a soft moan so he could feel the vibration of my voice as I encircled his cock with my lips. I never shoved it down my throat immediately. I did the same with his balls. I'd kiss them tenderly, occasionally sucking, as I slowly guided my lips towards his shaft, circling it with a moist, soft, hot tongue. Slowly, gently, I'd start to glide my lips up and down it, until I finally had it in my mouth and began to suck. If I tried to use my hand, he'd push it away. He wanted only my lips and my tongue. The blowjob never lasted long; he'd grow impatient and clumsily pull himself on top of me so he could enter me fully. But I wouldn't let him, not until he'd tasted my juices with his tongue.

He would speed up when I started to moan, then pause and slow down again, delaying my climax. I could feel his hot breath inside me. He'd lap up all the wetness between my legs and roll his tongue across my labia, inside and outside, piece by piece and then all at once. Sometimes he'd squirt whipped cream into my pussy and greedily lick it up. When he finally started gently sucking in my vagina, swirling his thin, soft tongue around my clit before moving it across my entire cunt, I knew I wouldn't be able to hold out much longer. Especially once he inserted his finger while gently sucking my clit. He was great with his fingers and knew exactly where to put them at exactly the right moment. Trembling, groaning with pleasure, I'd press his head deeper into my pussy and come. Afterwards, he'd immediately climb on top of me and envelop me in his arms. I loved being in his familiar grip. His dominating, virile body and the fire in his eyes that betrayed his animal lust excited me. It invariably became a hunter–prey relationship, I was devoured, and before I could do anything about it, I found myself locked in his grip, already moaning towards a second climax from his panting thrusts, from all his tongue and finger work. He could never fully surrender to me, and even if he did so when I asked, he'd get impatient and end up restraining me once again so he could dive back into my soaking wet insides. There, he'd twirl his finger and make a 'come hither' motion, first with his finger and then with his tongue. 'You're small and I'm huge, we're perfectly symbiotic,' he'd say as he kissed my insides. Sometimes I'd be so paralysed after sex that my muscles didn't work any more, usually because I'd been tense, especially when he penetrated me from behind. Those thrusts were harder, and it felt like the only way to absorb them was to tighten my muscles, to take cover. 'I can feel you all the way in my stomach,' I'd say. I didn't have anything to compare to, Lucas was the only person I'd ever been with, but he considered himself particularly well endowed and my pleasure confirmed that. Smoking increases the risk of impotence, I read on the pack of Marlboros on his nightstand as he saturated me from behind. It reminded me of the little leaflet that came with the pill that said it could lower your libido. I wondered what we'd be without his cigarettes and my contraception.

If I moaned too loudly and there were other people in the house, he would press his hand over my mouth and continue undisturbed, stimulating all eight thousand nerve endings in my clit before moving on to my vulva. We never used condoms. 'You need to feel me, and I need to feel you, we have to melt into each other, let's not fight it,' he said. All I can say is thank God for the pill, which I secretly took every day and kept rolled up in a sock.

Having an orgasm was the greatest pleasure I had ever experienced in life. I finally understood why Islam went on and on about all the sex and virgins in paradise. I would sign up for that too.

If I resisted his advances and insisted on going out into the living room to chat with his parents or sister, he would lift me up off the ground. I was immediately defeated because I was no match for him physically. He was 6 foot 3 to my 5 foot 3, and so much stronger than me. Sometimes Bianca would shout at her son from the living room to leave me in one piece. In those moments, I wanted to die of embarrassment, but Lucas didn't care. Sometimes he'd even start kissing me in front of his parents, and then he'd announce that we were going to his room to play table tennis. To me, it was like he lived in some kind of libertine nudist camp, and in the early days of our relationship, my cheeks would turn bright red.

After the wild sex, we always took a bath or shower together. As soon as I was naked, he'd wrap his irresistible arms around me, and before I knew it I'd feel his hard cock pushing against me, first between my legs and then quickly inside of me, since he could tell by looking at me that I was far from unwilling.

The first time we actually did it was anything but bliss. We had already tried five times on five different days to deflower me, but it didn't work. It just wouldn't go in. I was impenetrable, like a brick. I started to doubt whether I had a vagina at all. And the pain when he tried to force it was unbearable. We had almost resigned ourselves to the fact that it just wasn't going to happen, that he was way too big for me or that maybe I had vaginismus, as Google suggested. I felt intensely shitty. Like I wasn't a woman. What if I could never have sex? Everyone has to deal with loss at some point, but I didn't know you could lose something you never had. I wanted it so badly. I was determined not to give in to this fate. 'You are going to penetrate me right now, perforate me if you have to, keep going, even if I scream and cry, you're going to rape me!' Lucas looked at me nervously, confused. 'Are you sure about this?' he asked at least three more times. 'Yes, very sure, and you're not going to stop when I say stop, because I'll never forgive you if you do.' This was followed by a painful session, a lot of blood and two days of limping.

'Why are you limping?' Father asked when I came home that night. 'Muscle pain,' I said.

The other day, I tried to resist him to see what he would do if I pushed him to the limit. With a sullen look on my face, I told him I wasn't in the mood, that my stomach hurt and I had a headache. I watched him wilt in front of me like a fish on dry land. He begged for mercy.

'Please, baby, I'm really struggling here, I need you, I've missed you so much, please. Your body, it just drives me crazy, I'm sorry, I can't help it, I'm helpless against this desire.' He began to weep like a slave begging his master for a sip of water. He ran his fingers up and down my body and into my thong. It's true, I was well proportioned. I got it from Mother.

'No, no means no, okay? I said I didn't feel like it. Control yourself for once, or do it yourself, you've got a hand, haven't you?' I snarled. I was a pretty good actor.

'Come on, I'm not going to jerk myself off when my beautiful, horny princess is sitting right here beside me. I want you so fucking bad, I see that ass of yours and I feel your hips and I get all restless. You're torturing me, more than you know,' he whimpered. He embraced me firmly from behind and pressed his rock-hard cock against my ass. I pulled away. Finally, when it became clear that I wasn't going to budge, he grabbed a book to distract himself. I relished the scene. It was the first time in my life that I'd felt power over a man. Never before had I had one so ensnared. With power comes great pleasure. Mother was right, men thought with their penises, and that could be used against them. But whereas Mother considered this a good reason to cover yourself from head to toe, I did the opposite. I used it to seduce them. I used all powers at my disposal. I worked him until his balls turned blue, until he was about to burst. How weak they are! Total suckers, every last one of them. You should've seen him, begging, pleading, irritable, burning with desire. A heaving pile of misery. We women, we who were created from their rib, we are the ones who can push the limit, not them. We don't become blinded by desire; at most we become more driven.

After half an hour of agony, I laughed and told him I was joking, that I didn't really have a headache. He didn't think it was funny. 'I'll teach you not to play those conniving little games with me again.' I was mercilessly punished for my fun. He ruthlessly pinched my nipples and thrust himself inside of me until it hurt. He slapped my backside so hard that it left a red handprint on my skin. And just as I was about to climax, he would pull out or quit the game entirely. He wanted me to feel what he had felt. I locked eyes with him, made it clear that I was not going to give up, that I wanted him, but then he demanded to know what exactly I wanted, told me to whisper it into his ear, otherwise he'd stop.

'Please,' I said.

'Please what? What do you want me to do? I don't under-stand,' he toyed.

I couldn't stand it, so I decided to take matters into my own hands, literally. I sent my fingers to just the right spot in an effort to redeem myself. But he slapped my hand away, twisted my nipples with his fingers, which was all at once painful and intoxicating. Then he spanked me hard. 'You want it, you got it,' he said. I felt his hardness penetrate my hot, wet insides, and moaned to high heaven. We were two souls of one body. We needed to kiss and satisfy each other, as if our lives depended on it.

After I came, I wanted to go again, but my body couldn't take it. I was, after all, the weaker sex. One thing was clear: God must have loved women more. Not only did we have double the nerve endings downstairs but also our orgasms could last up to fifteen seconds, unlike those of the more privileged sex, which only lasted five.

I often lamented that in Islamic cultures, the greatest control you could have over a woman was over her sexuality. But it had finally sunk in: it's actually women who have control over men's sexuality.

After another tempestuous lovemaking session we were lying in bed and watching a Sunday-night show when he looked at me intently. 'Could we just record this moment, copy it a thousand times and pull it out of a box whenever we need it? Will you stay with me for ever?' Victor Hugo was right when he said that the pinnacle of happiness is the certainty of being loved. These were small, elusive moments in which everything fell into place, wind-still moments of pure joy and contentment. The kind of moments that fill you with a sense of peace about what you're doing with your life. When you know intuitively that it's right, that this feeling is right. The most beautiful experiences in life are not the loudest but the softest. There is so much motion in the world because we have grossly overestimated its value. And there is so little stillness.

Was it really possible to store a fleeting moment of happiness in your soul so you could reach for it when times were hard? Could you cherish life's joys and use them like petrol or batteries?

Every time he said this, I became riddled with anxiety, overwhelmed by the thought that whenever you are afraid of something and want to slow things down that's only going to accelerate them. Pleasure combined with fear is far more oppressive than grief. A part of me must have died at that moment. I knew that this was as good as it could get, that one day it would all be a memory. There was doom on the horizon, and I was setting myself up for a let-down.

When we got hungry from all the sex, we went out to eat. Lucas took a picture of me with a mouthful of fried fish. He always did that. He took pictures of me with sauce on my cheeks, a burger in my mouth, looking like a wet scarecrow after being caught in the winter rain, my mascara running down my face and my hair falling out of my headscarf. He filmed me whenever I lip-synced to songs on the radio. I didn't appreciate him capturing my ugliest moments, but he thought they were funnier, more 'authentic'.

Exogamy

I'm at The Hague Central Station, waiting for the train to Amsterdam. Lucas is sick; his parents are in Spain. He's got an ear infection and can't stand or move without his head throbbing and losing his balance. I made him some soup and gave him my love, but unfortunately I had to get going. It was getting late.

'If only you could stay here with me tonight,' he had said woefully, with a desperate look on his face. I promised him I would call in sick to work tomorrow and come back early in the morning. That was the best I could offer. But I hate not being able to be there for him when he needs me. 'Just say you're sleeping over at a friend's house, baby, please, your parents won't mind. I really you need you,' he pleaded. Obviously that wouldn't fly, and if I did it anyway they would be video calling me all night. And when I finally did get home they would never forgive me and be even more suspicious. They would also demand to speak to the girlfriend in question to verify that I'd really been at her house and check my WhatsApp messages just to make sure. 'Truth is good, but proof is better', that was Mother's creed. If you asked my parents, there was really no reason to spend the night at a friend's

126

in the first place and, on top of that, it wasn't safe. What if a brother or father or some other man entered the house? And who exactly is this girlfriend? What if she slips a pill into your drink? No one could be trusted, especially non-Muslims and non-Turks. They would need to get to know this girl before I'd be allowed to set foot in her house, but for now I wasn't going to sleep over anywhere, not even at my own cousin's. Things could go awry. In every family, there are men. 'Men have appetites they can't always control,' Mother said.

'You act as if men are a bunch of apes cut off from civilisation, with no ability to think or reason,' I said, irritated.

'Well, they are, even if it doesn't seem like it. Don't be fooled, every man thinks with his penis.'

Nietzsche said that woman was God's second mistake. According to Mother, it was man. I don't even want to know why Mother holds this view of men. It's because of those blessed lectures at the mosque. It's because of the gossip she hears from other women, which she always makes sure to share with me in the hope that I will get scared and adopt her views. She'll repeat the story of the girl who was tutoring at someone's house and got raped, or of the girl who worked in home healthcare and got raped by the son of the elderly woman she was taking care of. Or of the girl who met a guy on the internet – always the evil bogeyman in Mother's stories – and got drugged and raped, something like that. I don't know. I have heard those stories so many times that I want to drop dead every time she opens her mouth to tell one again. They make me sick. They're like a cloak of depression dropped over my shoulders. With Mother, the unlikely only rarely has to win out over the obvious in order for it to be true in all cases.

Lucas eventually stopped complaining and resigned himself to my situation, accepting the limits. He knows how things work, but I can't help but notice that he's starting to struggle with the fact that our relationship has been this way for years, and I can't say when it will ever change or when I will introduce him to my begetters. It's just not an option in any foreseeable world, but that's hard for him to accept. I considered getting my own place so I would have more freedom, but they wouldn't have it. Mother said that she would punch herself in the face if I moved out and brought shame on the family. And she was crazy enough that she probably would. On top of that, she said she would call the police. When I told her that that wouldn't make any difference since I was a legal adult, she said she would call all our relatives to come and stop me. And if I still left home, despite everything, I would never see their faces again. Not Oma, not Defne, not Halil, no one. And I would give her acute paralysis. If I wanted that on my conscience, then by all means ...

They would never accept Lucas, and if I pushed him on them anyway, they would make my life miserable and find some way to punish me. It wouldn't even matter if I lied and told them that he had converted to Islam: to them, a converted Muslim was a fake Muslim. 'They can give up their faith again whenever they feel like it,' Mother said one time when I asked her what she thought of converts. This would never happen with a born Muslim, she claimed. I didn't ask her for statistical evidence. And I don't think she's ever actually met a convert. She just knows. 'As long as a person's family isn't Muslim, they'll always lead their child astray – and their grandchildren,' she said. 'Also, you can never know for sure whether the conversion was sincere or if they only did it to get married.' I can't argue with her there, but then of course you run the risk of refusing a sincere convert. Not that Mother would mind that. To her, the crux of the issue is the origin of the person's family, as would become clear later on in our discussion. 'And even if the person turns out to be a perfect Muslim, you're always better off with a Turk, someone who knows our language and culture.'

This is different with Moroccans, by the way, who care more about religion. With us, your nationality is your second religion, which is something that Moroccans often don't understand. They're not nearly as patriotic as we are. Moroccan identity mostly comes down to Islam, whereas Turks have, in addition to Islam, all their non-Arab idiosyncrasies and their distinctive language and culture, which are sometimes held even higher than religion.

I'm also not sure that the sanction for my extramarital relationship will stop at disownment. I have no idea what they are capable of. According to my relatives, it's up to women to uphold the honour of their penis-bearing relatives, and they do this with their chastity – in other words, their cunt – which they must 'preserve and guard for its rightful owner', who will one day unveil it. If a woman succeeds in this, the family's honour is consolidated. If not, all is lost, and the woman must be inexorably avenged for her unpardonable sin. Honour crimes may follow. The Islamic scriptures offer no concrete points of reference for such treatment, it's more a regional and cultural practice. In fact, Islamic scriptures explicitly forbid honour killings – only a sharia judge, not individual persons, can order a sinner to be stoned or whipped to death if there are enough witnesses – but many local scholars couldn't care less about that. Honour crimes also happen in non-Muslim communities in the Middle East if you're deep enough in the tribal quicksand. But, as mentioned, Muslims don't always stick to the pure teachings of their faith, and people in these communities believe such crimes are mandated by Islam.

In the Netherlands, police deal with roughly five hundred honour crimes per year, twenty of which involve murder. In Turkey, that number is roughly two thousand, and those are just the cases that are reported. Honour crimes take different forms: assault, abduction and, in extreme cases, killing. The mildest variant – and the most common in the Netherlands – is social slaughter and total boycott, as in completely humiliating the sinner, shaming her, belittling her, subjecting her to psychological pressure and sometimes resorting to verbal and physical violence. In most cases, the woman is thoroughly slut-shamed by her family, acquaintances and neighbours, and no one is allowed to interact with her any more. According to our religion, a woman's father must approve of her partner in order for the marriage to be considered valid. A mother is allowed to give her opinion, but she doesn't have any real say. Without the father's consent, you'll never be truly married in the eyes of God, even if you exchange vows before the law. Man's law is, of course, secondary to God's law and has no real value in the eyes of Allah.

Exactly how much danger you are actually in and how the honour crime will play out is different in each family and depends on how many crazy male relatives – uncles, cousins, brothers – you happen to have in your vicinity and their willingness to either let it go, forgive you or punish you. If they so staunchly believe that they'll be able to silence their conscience out of unconditional loyalty to their religious ideals and are also able to come to terms with the idea of attacking another person's freedom and individuality for the sake of the community, things can get pretty dangerous. Either way, I recommend that you stay far away from people in whom determination and conviction converge. Ambition is the mother of both great success and deep disappointment. When it comes to ambition, it's quickly all or nothing.

I myself am blessed with an orthodox family in which such things are considered entirely unforgivable. I already got a taste of this when my cousin ran away from home two years ago. She was in love with a man who was in fact Turkish but who was not approved. Her father didn't get along with his family. Moreover, he already had his eye on another candidate for his daughter, one who came from a more Quranic, traditional family. Apparently, he had already secretly promised his daughter to them years ago. She didn't know about this – he said that he wanted to hold off on the wedding until she was done with school. This wasn't because he valued her education, by the way; he was saving up her student loan money to buy real estate in Turkey. He had registered her at a different address so the government would think she wasn't living at home and thus send her extra funds, especially given that her father was officially unemployed. In our world, pledging your daughter to another family was as important as the wedding itself, and a real man puts his money where his mouth is. Withdrawing from such a transaction would mean a huge loss of face, which was out of the question.

Therefore, my uncle had a huge problem on his hands when his daughter didn't listen and came home with another man. His moral reputation was at stake, and with it his entire social existence. The man he had in mind for her was far more orthodox in his religious practice, which is crucial for a happy marriage, and most importantly, he was already family. He came from the same village in Turkey that 'we' came from. This made him a safe choice and guaranteed that his daughter wouldn't 'fall into unknown hands' (in other words, that his daughter would continue to benefit his own circle and not that of some total stranger who was trying to 'profit from somebody else's daughter', because a woman is, of course, nothing more than a cunt for a man to profit from). My own begetters thought my uncle was absolutely right: having in-laws from your own family or your own village was much more appropriate than having total strangers you knew nothing about. If they were in your family, you knew if they could be trusted, but a stranger could leave your daughter after a while, or the bastard could cheat on her or conceive children with someone else (or maybe he already had, you never knew) or he might treat her badly and be completely ungrateful.

But Betül, my cousin, she was stubborn. One day she packed her bags and quietly left. She moved in with her boyfriend and, rumour has it, they were even properly married. Not that it mattered; Betül's marriage was considered invalid by the family and the community, making her a whore. She was living in a state of *zina* – having sexual relations with a man outside of marriage. Her partner was subsequently threatened with a knife by her brothers (my cousins) and her cousins. It was only a threat, seeing as my cousins weren't so dumb that they were willing to go to jail for something like that and throw their lives away (I presume), but they did give him a good beating. After that, my uncle demanded fifteen thousand euros from his unwanted son-in-law. Turks call that *baslik parasi* or *süt parasi*, the money a man pays to his prospective father-in-law. Just for being his daughter's father. Again, this is not a custom based in scripture, but in conservative Turkish circles people consider it spiritually permissible to sell their own daughters. Father paid Grandpa ten thousand guilders for Mother when they got married. The amount can differ depending on the father and the daughter. If the daughter is pretty and fleshy (as in big tits and wide hips) and a lot of men have already asked for her hand, the price goes up. If not, the price goes down. It all comes down to value for money, like any product on the market: it's dictated by supply and demand. Nowadays, hardly anyone adheres to this tradition, except people who have remained rigid and old school despite having lived in the Netherlands for a long time. People like my uncle. Father likes the custom too and has already made it known that he plans to ask his future son-in-law for money when he requests my hand – oh, how I can't wait to be sold.

Anyway, my cousin's husband was cowardly enough to fork up the cash, hoping that my uncle and the rest of the family would forgive them. He thought that the gesture would allow his wife to reunite with her family, who were surely feeling pretty guilty by then. But nothing could've been further from the truth. He had fallen right into their trap. He received no gratitude whatsoever – rather he was scolded and cursed. They were never forgiven. I haven't seen Betül since and nobody ever talked about her until six months ago when she called her mother to tell her she had breast cancer. She too – it seemed like all of a sudden everyone was getting cancer: Aunt Kadriye, Jill (Lucas's fifteen-year-old cousin), Gülsüm (a co-worker), Emine (the sister of Nawal, a friend from high school), Yusuf (a boy in my neighbourhood) and now Betül. I'd seen more hospitals than I ever wanted to see again. She was looking for support, but she wasn't going to get any. My aunt really wanted to visit her, but my uncle wouldn't allow it. He didn't want to hear another word about it; she was no daughter of his. She was the one who had chosen to turn her back on her family and go her own way, and now she'd just have to be strong enough to go it alone. This was no reason for him to soften up or forgive her sins, this was God's punishment for disobeying her father. To him, her getting cancer was the ultimate confirmation that God punishes disobedient sluts, both here in this world and in the hereafter. If only she had married the righteous man he had found for her instead of the dog she was with now. The man didn't even pray, and his mother didn't wear a headscarf.

After a few months, Mother reported that Betül had sent her brothers a text message that the tumour turned out to be benign and they were able to remove it. I wondered how this fitted into my uncle's Allah-punishes-sluts analysis, but to be honest, I didn't want to know.

Betül doesn't live in Amsterdam any more, and her father has torn up all her photos. She probably has kids by now and is enjoying a happy life with her husband. I hope so. I tried to look her up on Facebook and Instagram, but I couldn't find anything.

But what really made my blood boil was what happened after this whole incident occurred: two years later, the same thing happened to Betül's brother, my cousin Tayfun. He wanted to marry a woman his parents loathed. 'Over my dead body!' they'd said for months. She was from a leftist Turkish family, true Kemalists heart and soul. Her family looked anything but devout, they dressed in Western clothes and the parents were divorced. On top of that, the girl didn't even wear a headscarf. In the summer, she wore short dresses with plunging necklines. Until then, this was absolutely unheard of in our world. Tayfun's parents were so staunchly conservative that the men and women sat separately when visitors came over. The women wore large headscarves and long robes, and the children all went to Quranic boarding schools. They didn't even own a television – they thought it was devilish because all the shows had half-naked women in them and people living in sin. How could they accept a daughter-in-law whose family drank wine and raki and utterly ignored the divine precepts ordained by scripture?

134

My uncle couldn't get over the fact that the prospective in-laws were divorced, let alone all the other things about the family that offended him. 'In families where divorce is considered normal, children learn that it is normal and one day they are sure to end up divorced themselves,' he claimed. This girl couldn't be tamed. She was too free-thinking and independent. Such women would file for divorce in a heartbeat. They didn't care about honour, community, tradition or shame. They didn't fear God or live by unshakeable norms and values. She would rebel at any restrictions imposed upon her. Girls like her considered it normal to have male friends even after marriage, they posted photos of themselves on the internet, they went around 'half naked', they wore make-up and perfume whenever they went out, they laughed and chatted with their male colleagues in the cafeteria at work, they would lie 'naked' (that is, in a bikini) on the beach, they would go out at night without their husbands, keep working after they had kids and just dump them off at some day care, and even go out partying at some godless club. What was my uncle to do with a daughter-in-law who definitely wasn't going to raise his future grandchildren to fear God and would probably trade in his son for another man after a few years?

In the end, Tayfun turned out to be just as stubborn as his sister, but despite all the disputes and disagreements he was not disowned. His choice was tolerated, albeit reluctantly: he was, after all, a man and didn't need his father's permission to be properly married in the eyes of God. That was only the first case of the unequal treatment of Tayfun and Betül, two siblings who had committed the exact same crime in the eyes of the exact same parents. As if that wasn't bad enough, something even crazier happened: two weeks after Tayfun's wedding, news arrived that they had already divorced. This was completely unprecedented; we'd never known anyone to be divorced so quickly. Two weeks is a pretty short marriage by any standards, but in our community it was completely unheard of. I never found out what exactly the reason was, but the gist of it was this: the in-laws couldn't stand each other; they'd got into a violent argument, and Tayfun and his wife had each sided with their own family, and things got out of hand.

When I heard this, I thought: there's that idiotic weak-minded bullshit again. In our circles, it wasn't that unusual for people to end up getting divorced due to irreparable friction between their families. In fact, I would venture to say that this is the number-one cause of divorce, something you don't often hear among Westerners. In retrospect, though, I have my doubts about this story. The two families didn't get along from the start, so why had things suddenly turned so violent?

You should always be a little suspicious with conservative Turks. When a scandal occurs, they tend to keep their explanations short and superficial in the hope that it will all go away, but their brevity can also be a way of dodging further questions so they can maintain their moral high ground. After all, Quran-abiding Muslims live for their honour – if they lose it, they'll be outcast. It's the beating heart of their social existence, their *raison d'être*: one must display unshakeable moral integrity at all times or otherwise be disgraced. There's no room for error, uncertainty or doubt. But, in the end, stubbornness is an iron chain around the neck of a boorish mind.

It's all about how things look on the outside, how you present yourself, putting your best foot forward all the time, that's the quintessence of life. Anything personal, frank, intimate or human is taboo and could become the cause of a scandal. There are so many taboos in our culture that they could just call it 'tabooism' (not to be confused with Taoism).

There's one thing I've never understood. People who want to uphold their honour end up making life unnecessarily difficult for themselves. They frantically cling to hypocrisy, appearances, their outward roles, and in so doing wrap themselves in a straitjacket of righteousness. Eventually they're living in a cage of their own making. Perfectionism is, in virtually all cases, an obstacle, and anyone who strives for it will ultimately get their hands dirty. How wondrous are the people who commit themselves to eternal dissatisfaction.

Anyway, my cousins and I put our heads together and pondered this divorce situation, and reached the following conclusion: in the Muslim community, the only possible grounds for such a quick divorce would be if the woman turns out not to be a virgin on the wedding night. And given that girl's modern, free-thinking family, she was probably no Mary. And knowing Tayfun and his level of indoctrination, he couldn't handle it. Tayfun was handsome and likeable, but he was raised in a household with extremely narrow-minded, ultra-conservative and downright medieval worldviews. Chances are he had internalised at least some of his family's ideas – for example, the whole cult of virginity thing – and was thus intellectually mutilated.

But what I really can't get my head around is that even after his grave mistake, Tayfun was forgiven by his parents and the community. If a woman did such a thing, she'd be doomed for life. All that stuff about honour, godliness, reputation, virtue, unforgivable sins, non-negotiable duty, shame, gossip . . . suddenly none of it mattered. Tayfun had a dick and was thus, despite his failings, no lower in the pecking order.

Obedience

Mother calls. I got home way too late again because I was taking care of Lucas. It was midnight, almost one o'clock, before I was home. Someone jumped in front of the train, which happens a lot, causing a delay. I answer and say that I'm home, that she doesn't have to worry. But she's already in a rage. I shouldn't give a shit what they think, I should just do whatever I want, refuse to pick up the phone just to drive them crazy, I'd secretly enjoy it.

It is true that I've stopped answering their calls. I refuse to be accountable to them any longer. But I'm not doing it to drive them crazy, as she says. Actually, I think she's the one driving herself crazy with the thought that she's losing control over me, that I'm becoming increasingly recalcitrant, sovereign, empowered, that my battle for freedom is unfolding before her very eyes, and that she has no idea where I go and what I do. It kills her to see that I'm not an extension of her and that I never will be, that I'm following my own path and all she can do is sit there with her tail between her legs and her hands in her headscarf because she doesn't know what else she can threaten me with. I'm as slippery as an eel. When I say I'm on my way home from work, all she can do is take my word for it. She's a ticking bomb. Suspicion and despair can drive a person towards the improbable, or even the completely absurd. Maybe I should be on my guard.

I say I'm tired, and hang up. She screams like a maniac that she won't put up with this behaviour any more, that I should come to their apartment and settle this once and for all. I'd better go before she gets even madder and storms into my room. I wipe off my make-up and change clothes. I pull on pyjama bottoms and a bathrobe. All I want is to not give a fuck, to just walk over there in the clothes I was wearing, to not have to constantly worry about their judgements, their aggressive tone, their moral blackmail, but I'd rather spare myself the headache. I have a report to type up for class tomorrow. I grab my keys, open the door and walk the two steps to their apartment.

Defne is already asleep. She's got school in the morning. They don't seem to care. As soon as I walk in the door, they both start yelling. Mother takes the lead, as always. In most reactionary families, it's usually the father who's in charge, but at our house it's Mother who's the Islamic Stalin, the Khomeini with a cunt, the Muslim-fascist despot, sharp as nails and utterly ruthless, unwilling to budge a fraction of an inch. Moral fearlessness is a fundamental trait that all leaders – large and small, good and bad – seem to possess.

And she has no sense of tolerance whatsoever; the word wasn't even in her vocabulary seeing as it requires adding the water of ignorance to the wine of wisdom. Ambition is intolerance. Tolerance requires mental brawn, which she certainly doesn't have.

Father knows that he's better off supporting her regime, otherwise he'll have to listen to her moaning day and night. He rarely opposes her. Occasionally, he'll mutter that she might be exaggerating but that I should still listen to her because she is wiser than I am, and I'm supposed to respect and obey her unconditionally. These are just standard Turkish statements, totally unfounded and arbitrary. What makes her wiser? Her age? Her motherhood? Does this mean that she has 'life experience' and thus deserves respect? What experience does Mother really have? She worked in the Anatolian countryside ankle deep in cow dung until she was twenty-five only to be married (well, technically sold) off to Father, who offered the highest bid and promised to take her to Holland so she could be emancipated from her peasant's existence.

As soon as she got here, she had me, and a whole new world opened up for her; she found herself occasionally having to leave the house and mingle with Western society, a world she didn't mind benefiting from economically but which she was ideologically against.

At the mosque, they teach you that you shouldn't adapt yourself to meet the demands of the decadent and depraved. Although they might seem blessed by the Creator, their prosperity has been stolen, acquired through the oppression and exploitation of others. You shouldn't let yourself be seduced by their hollow ideas, which are nothing more than whispers of the devil. Naturally, you were allowed to adapt a little bit: you could learn the language, be kind to your neighbour, and contribute to society by working and paying taxes (as a man, of course), but beyond that your loyalty was to the Islamic world. You had to cling to 'the cord of Allah': no matter what, your religion, community, language, norms and values were more honourable and more worthy than those of the infidels.

On Fridays, Imam Blahdiblah's message usually went something like this: 'The Netherlands is a godless country. It has done away with its own God and now it wants us to

140

do the same, so that we too will become culturally depraved. This country is a paradise for homosexuals, they've turned whores in windows into tourist attractions, and intoxicating substances like drugs and alcohol are not only legal, they are culturally embraced. They cannot control their wives and daughters, who roam like cattle, willing to go to bed with anyone and everyone, as if the bed is nothing sacred, as if sexual intercourse is nothing special, they'll allow a total stranger into their most intimate places. Moreover, the Netherlands is the lapdog of Israel and America, and its own foreign policy record is anything but clean. The injustice that these people have carried out and are still carrying out against our brothers and sisters, we shall not forget! Truly, God sees all! All of this goes directly against the message and the moral boundaries of God and His Prophet, peace be upon him!'

Mother again launches into a monologue like a broken record, full of offensive, degrading slurs. True to form, she demands to know what she has done so wrong as a parent and why I'm so stubborn. She says I'd better watch out. How on earth could I even think that it would be okay to come home so late? She simply cannot fathom why a young lady like myself would spend so many hours outside the house rather than doing more appropriate things like staying home and baking biscuits or watching couples bicker on Turkish television with her on the couch or going to lectures at the mosque where an imam answers questions from the audience like how many times you have to recite a chapter of the Quran over a bottle of water or a pack of muffins to make it holy so that it might help heal a sick person (once again, the same logic applies: if it works, it's an act of God, if it doesn't, it's not) or drinking tea with relatives or neighbours who drop by for a visit.

I understand why she doesn't trust me; I always come with

the same excuse, that I was at work, even when I've spent the whole day at the beach with Lucas. That's bound to get noticed at some point. So, she came up with a solution. If I really wanted to work in the evenings, she would allow it, but Father would pick me up as he did a few months ago. It was, after all, pretty strange that I didn't get home until one o'clock in the morning.

At that point, I can't control myself any longer. I'm tired of constantly defending myself, and being subjected to a steady stream of taunts and humiliation. I'm not going to sacrifice the little bit of pleasure I have from my relationship too. I don't want to go back to the days when I had to leave Lucas in the afternoon and head back to Amsterdam so that Father could pick me up from work without noticing that I'd been gone. I start calling her a sick psychopath, a control freak, a narrow-minded philistine, a stupid donkey from some backwards village in Turkey who knows nothing about the rights and freedoms we have here. I make her out to be an inferior human being, which I will later regret – I actually need to restrain myself, because all I'm doing is giving my opponent yet another opportunity to play the martyr later on when she complains about me behind my back to neighbours and relatives, which she will have ample opportunity to do, and of course only highlights these things. After all, the tone can overshadow the message and make the other person unwilling to accept it or consider it worth taking seriously at all. In our culture, especially, the tone makes the music. And of course, Mother would use the opportunity to flaunt my sins and exaggerate everything I said, taking my rebuttals and indignation out of context, concealing her own transgressions and misconstruing my words as profound insults against her person in order to make her own narrative sound more convincing.

But if you need to exaggerate like that, to single out the very worst of what I said in a moment of high emotional tension, and to leave out the rest, maybe it's because you don't find your own story all that convincing. Mother is truly a special breed. Even devout relatives, neighbours and acquaintances think she went too far in demanding that I be picked up from work. But she couldn't care less. She took it as a compliment that she is apparently one of the few women who still takes the teachings of the imam and, by extension, God, to heart. She was racking up extra points with Allah for going against the grain and remaining true to her conviction.

Anyway, this misstep of mine pales in comparison to the sins of my enemy. With trembling voice and hands, I declare that if she dishonours me one more time by calling me a slut, she will never see me again. And if she decides to take draconian measures to restrict my freedom even more, I'm leaving this family. I mean it. I glare at her with a penetrating look in my eyes, so she knows I mean it. Devout Turks are not amenable to words alone, no matter how meaningful they may be. She has to hear me think it.

Suddenly she's quiet, her face serious. She looks at me wide-eyed and turns up her nose, more out of disapproval than necessity, as if she's just caught a whiff of an unpleasant smell, and then she mutters, 'I tell you, Ismail, this girl is lost. She's turned provocation into an art.'

She asks me in a hushed voice, her eyes half-closed, why she's being met with such a violent reaction, if I have something to hide. What's so wrong with a father or a brother picking me up from work, why would this make me threaten to leave home for ever? Why would I be so upset about that? Wouldn't it even be nice to have someone to walk home with? My reaction could only mean one thing: that I wasn't going to work at all. I was taking them for a ride, stringing them along, but she's too smart for that. From now on, she's going to stop by the store to make sure I'm really there. She doesn't believe a word I say any more. Distrust and control are the most reliable forces of people who wish to maintain the balance of power.

I walk away and slam the front door behind me. I feel a bizarre kind of adrenaline pulsing through my body, in the area around my heart. I count to twenty – somehow that helps. Then I go back to my room at Oma's. The smell, there it is again. The dirty wipes and cotton balls that I used to remove my make-up are still lying there. I toss them in the little bin on my desk. I put my earbuds in and turn the volume up as loud as it will go. The first song on my playlist is my favourite, 'I live my own life'.

My jewellery hangs above my perfumes. Gold and silver earrings, countless rings and necklaces. Unfortunately, most of it disappears under my headscarf. I only wear the necklaces and earrings when I go to Lucas's or when I work at the restaurant. Mother invariably has to make a comment when she sees me enjoying my baubles or putting effort into an impeccable appearance, as I tend to do. I believe in enjoying the beautiful things in life, myself included.

'You're ridiculous to spend so much money on that stuff, can't you just dress normally, fear God!' or 'How dare you pray with all that perfume on, are you crazy? It has alcohol in it' (she still thinks I pray), or 'One day I'm going to chuck all that make-up of yours over the balcony, it's haram, you should be ashamed, you're a Muslim woman!' or 'You can't pray wearing make-up or nail polish, you must wash yourself and wearing make-up invalidates that!' or 'Didn't you hear what the imam said? If you wear perfume and walk by a man, the angels in heaven will make note of your sin!'

144

She had already thrown away my cosmetics a few times in the hope that I would stop using them, but I kept right on buying them, I didn't give up. By now, she's resigned herself to the fact that I own make-up. If she sees me going out with a made-up face or runs into me on the street, she can't help but violently shake her head and make some snide remark so that everyone will know that she can't stand to look at me. Father has forbidden me to wear it too, but fortunately he's always at work. Most of the time he just hears Mother complaining about it. But if he does see it, he can become pretty cantankerous. He thinks make-up is for prostitutes and automatically associates it with porn. He doesn't see why I have to wear it to school or work. The few times I got caught, I tried to laugh it off, but they weren't laughing. Sometimes he would try to win me over with carefully chosen words, without mentioning God: 'You see, make-up is worn by women who have something to hide, and it doesn't make you any prettier. You only think that because society wants you to think that, because you see it on TV and in commercials. Everyone is more beautiful in their natural state.' But eventually he couldn't help but add, 'That's how God created you! Wanting to change that is a terrible sin, it doesn't suit a modest woman.'

Once again, his reasoning doesn't add up. If make-up makes me uglier, then wouldn't that be a good thing since I'm not supposed to seduce men? Isn't that why I wear a headscarf and all those baggy clothes in the first place? So, what's the problem exactly? But when I mentioned this, they only got more furious and made me out for a pedantic bitch, who wouldn't listen. Naturally, they didn't have any reasonable rebuttal. I was driving them crazy; I was pushing their buttons. But that feeling was mutual.

Father may not have been as devout as Mother, but he was

all the more obsessed with morality and decency. Girls were supposed to be virginal and subdued so that one day they'd find a good husband, otherwise they'd end up alone and be a disgrace.

If you ask me, demanding modesty in women is pretty shitty. Nothing good comes of modesty, and it's only ever admired when it's false. I think it's insane to cover up your feminine beauty. Though it's probably a good thing that all those God-fearing women keep themselves covered and chase after righteous partners rather than those who are successful, handsome, kind or funny. It makes for less competition for all the women doing their best out there. I, for one, prefer to use every feminine charm at my disposal to hook the best catch. In my opinion, you're crazy to spend your whole life covering yourself in cloth and ultimately settling for someone who only cares about God. I don't see any wisdom in that. Only stupidity. And I'm not stupid.

To be honest, I hate my begetters. All they're doing is standing in the way of everything I want and stand for in life, but I feel guilty about leaving Oma and Defne behind for ever. So indifference has become an unattainable goal for this wannabe cynic. I'm not going to kid myself; they will never accept me for who I am. At the end of the day, they're uneducated, displaced and constantly exposed to the strictest interpretation of Islamic scripture by organisations that will allow any hothead to spew his intolerance – with government subsidy. My begetters, who have no critical faculties whatso-ever, eat it up like cake. Somehow they're highly susceptible to the indoctrinating worldviews peddled by those scumbags. Not that I blame the organisations. Error out of self-interest is one thing, but error out of stupidity is worse. I'm mostly angry at their many followers. And the people who subsidise them, including the Dutch government. But I can't stand up to them alone and make them see things differently. I have no one to back me up, not a soul on my side. Except Oma, but she doesn't have a say.

Given all the variables, there's a part of me that understands why my begetters are the way they are, though, for the time being, I can't forgive them for the way they have oppressed, blackmailed and restricted their adult daughter's freedom. But what I really can't understand is that there are young people from my own generation who were born and raised here in the Netherlands who think the same as they do. I had hoped that the older generation's failure to achieve any kind of enlightenment might convince young people to do things better.

Nobody else has these problems, it seems; they've all resigned themselves to the rules. Nobody else struggles with the headscarf. Nobody else secretly has a white boyfriend. Nobody else wants to lie on the beach in a bikini in the summer. Nobody else argues with their begetters day in and day out. Nobody else has so many questions about the laws of religion. I'm all alone, but how, why? Where are the other people like me; why is everyone so utterly similar? Why haven't I ever met a kindred spirit? I know that, were one person to actually be unique, that would be an exceptional occurrence. But still, sometimes I get the feeling that nobody's in the same boat with me. To truly judge a person's originality, you have to take into account all the similar people who came before them. I have. And I don't see many allies.

Music is forbidden, dating is forbidden, all forms of extramarital romance and the excitement and turmoil that comes with it are also forbidden, going on holiday without a male relative to chaperone is forbidden, having friends of the opposite sex is unacceptable, getting dressed up and wearing make-up is inappropriate, going out at night is forbidden, posting photos on social media is frowned upon, watching 'dirty, immoral' films and series is forbidden (and I'm not talking about porn here, just a movie with people kissing), lying on the beach or swimming in the sea in the presence of men is forbidden, images of human beings are forbidden, celebrating birthdays or any other pagan holidays is forbidden, working alongside men is forbidden (at least according to the Quranic school, but most Muslims are okay with it) and don't even think about going to a party or a festival.

So, what's left to enjoy in life? Or is life not meant to be enjoyed? What am I, a houseplant? Should I just go to school and work and pretend that I have no feelings or desires whatsoever, while all around me I see the boys I grew up with indulging in their freedom? Should I enter into a marriage with all the sex rammed out of it before it's even begun because my begetters have paired me with a humourless, bloodless, Quranic prick who barks at me every time I step out of line because he was raised to believe that women have to be tamed? And then what? Accept my life as a broody hen like all the women around me? Until I'm worn out? Is that what I'm supposed to live for? For God, family and fatherland? Does God delight in my tragedy? If so, then why does He make rules that beg to be broken? In general, the purpose of rules and regulations is to determine whose interests take priority when conflicting interests arise. But what interest does the other person have in me following these rules? The idea that the individual is subordinate to the group is professed by those who are willing to sacrifice the group's interests for their own ambitions. But what are God's ambitions? Fear is the driver of ambition. What is God so afraid of?

I was seven when I learned that singers, dancers and

actresses were all going to hell. A woman's singing and dancing could be arousing for a man, and the only man you were
allowed to arouse was your husband. Even professional ath-
letes were damned for wearing tight clothing on international
television. The teacher at the Quranic school told us that
according to the Prophet, peace be upon him, a woman should
cover herself in such a way that a man can't tell whether she
is young or old. She said that women are the most difficult
test that men will face in this world, and that's why we were
to avoid all contact with the opposite sex and interact with
them only if it was strictly necessary.

If our lesson ended at the same time as the boys', we could
still leave, but we had to look at the ground if we ran into a
boy in the courtyard or in the corridor as we collected our
shoes from the rack.

Around the age of fifteen, I started receiving lessons on
marriage. I was told that I would have to obey my husband
because he was just a little higher in the eyes of God and the
woman was made of his rib. If your husband was dissatisfied
with you, you wouldn't go to heaven; his satisfaction was
your ticket to the afterlife (and satisfaction, especially within
the confines of marriage, would be a scarce commodity). The
Prophet, peace be upon him, said that if he were to appoint
a second entity for a wife to kneel before after God, it would
be her husband.

The husband was appointed by God to handle the money,
and the wife's job was to take care of the offspring and support him. Love would come after marriage, or it wouldn't,
you didn't know, but as long as you chose a man of God, you
would be happy.

When I asked the teacher how you could choose a marriage partner without dating him first, she said that dating

didn't work anyway. You could never really know a person in advance. On a date, he or she could pretend to be a completely different person, so you were taking a risk either way. The only one you could trust was God. Besides, dating was forbidden. The only way that you would be allowed to meet before marriage would be if you, as a woman, asked a male family member to chaperone. Meeting privately was out of the question.

I didn't ask how you could know whether the guy would be good in bed. That doesn't matter either, she would've said. In our world, marriage was based on mutual understanding and tolerance, not on love or attraction, which were inherently fleeting. Love was at most an afterthought, nothing more than an improperly cultivated Western concept. Marriage was about finding someone you could trust, someone who would stay with you and remain at your side in the face of adversity, in sickness and in health. That is why so many Muslim couples are the result of arranged marriages. The two candidates meet each other a couple of times before the wedding, always in the presence of their parents, and after they're hitched it turns out that they can both breathe, are somewhat physically appealing (as in, not deformed) and are able to hold a conversation. That's how all the people in my family were married.

Nowadays, the younger generation do the searching themselves. The woman still needs her father's blessing, but at least she can choose (within the non-negotiable frameworks) who she will marry.

Enlightenment

In class, we'd discussed *Candide ou l'Optimisme*, which made me reflect on my own situation. I've had a problem with certain aspects of Islam for a long time, especially the rules imposed on me by my parents and the horrendous Quranic school, where I've wasted far too much of my life. On top of that, the love of my life is not a Muslim, which is absolutely unacceptable for a woman of my faith, though men can marry non-believers if they want to. But beyond these factors, I was also having doubts about core issues, like why God would create a world and fill it up with so many people who were doomed to spend eternity in hell. Eternity. I can't even fathom it. Isn't it just a word that people use figuratively? I mean, if you promise to love someone for an eternity it's sweet and all that but obviously nonsense. Nothing is permanent. How could you expect me, as a twenty-year-old university student with half a brain, to believe that all the non-Muslims in the world are going to hell? Did people actually think that? How did they convince themselves of that one? You'd have to be completely insane. And why would you want to send people to hell at all? And some of the most intriguing people at that! I thought you were supposed to do unto others as you would have them do unto you. Aren't moral principles secretly nothing more than attempts to limit your possibilities?

If God is almighty, why would he have created us to worship Him? Surely he doesn't need our worship? Why even bother keeping yourself alive or trying to earn a living or stay healthy when the poor, the sick and children will automatically go to heaven when they die? If suffering is so meaningful and important, why try so hard to avoid it?

According to the teacher at the Quranic school, we were created to worship Allah, even though He didn't need anyone to worship Him, that's what Allah decided, and if you disobeyed you would go to hell and stay there for eternity, drinking your own piss and regrowing your skin so that it could be burned all over again. I think a penal system is an important measure of a society's civilisation, and God has made it clear where He stands in that regard.

If you weren't born Muslim, it was your job to discover the true teachings of God and convert, because ignorance was no excuse, especially not in times such as these when knowledge is so readily available.

In my opinion, truth must be incontrovertible knowledge; delusion is merely conjecture. That cannot be true. Delusion in ignorance. And if a deluded person lives in their own delusion then they are not capable of knowing the truth. But surely they could figure this out themselves? Surely you don't have to be super smart to work all this out? Isn't truth marked by the fact that our knowledge of it is uncertain?

Maybe the world just wants to be deceived. Maybe understanding is disastrous. Maybe foolishness is what makes life liveable because truth isn't in our best interest. Idiots and fools are probably happier than the wise. And truly deep thinkers are often mentally ill. Doesn't the fool enjoy the best fate?

Is that why people are so willing to follow false prophets? Wouldn't we all be helplessly lost without our refined capacities of self-deception? Is that why it's always the most insincere people who have the audacity to openly question the sincerity of others?

Maybe this is why we as people have made it our goal to constantly forget that life is meaningless. Maybe cultures and religions are just products of our desire to forget our own mortality. Therefore, if we were immortal, we would also be cultureless. And thus we can assume that the immortal gods are cultureless.

The greater the fear and misunderstanding of death, the greater the need to forget or ignore our own mortality, and the stronger the culture and religion. The believers are the ones who cannot accept a miracle for what it is and constantly demand an explanation. Believers are cowards. People who love life so much that they can't bear to think that one day it will come to an end; people who, when they do find the truth, are so startled that they have to hide it away again. People who attempt, on a massive scale, to question the only certainty in existence. But the fact is, the only way to be happy is to truly accept your own mortality. And also the randomness of life. Those who deny the whims of fate will never learn to anticipate them and will never find comfort in resignation.

One learns a lot more from searching for truth than from already knowing it. Of course, it's comfortable to think you already know everything you need to know, otherwise you might become restless or confused, but what's even better is overcoming the fear of not knowing and finding out that there is a hell of a lot more to discover. Making sense of our experiences – that is the art of living. The thirst for truth comes at the expense of knowledge of reality. It's important to entertain new ideas that extend beyond the limits of your knowledge. Good philosophy, unlike theology, has the power to reduce both hope and anxiety. And there is freedom in that.

Just as they were afraid of the truth, which is why they had to lie even to themselves, so was I afraid of their silence. After all, certainty is the firing squad of religion. And that fear is what compelled me to speak out.

Stories from religious scripture are supposed to give meaning, which explains why they are so absurd. Nowadays, people allow themselves, against all warnings and common sense, to be deceived. Of whom, then, are they the victim? Why do people let themselves be so easily manipulated by something like morality? Morality can be a good thing if it teaches you how to deal with reality rather than prescribing what reality should be.

The other possibility is that there is an unimaginable number of people who are unimaginably stupid. I don't know which is worse.

I also didn't really understand what made God so merciful, but I didn't dare to think about it. One time, I gathered the courage to challenge a teacher who was telling us about the horrors of hell.

'But that's awful, isn't it?' I asked cautiously, and she promptly replied that we shouldn't look at it that way, that our measly human minds couldn't possibly comprehend the wisdom behind the law of God, that we were doomed to follow our desires and emotions, which were inevitably tainted by all the rubbish the atheists were teaching us in this country. We mustn't fully submit to our own logic; we just had to obey. Any notion that it might be unfair were whispers from the devil that could be avoided with frequent prayer and by filling our hearts with the fear of God.

What an excellent system religions have; even your thoughts are censored, so that not even they are toll-free. George Orwell's Thought Police were nothing compared to that.

And then there were all those rules that just didn't sit well with me. For instance, I just could not understand why a headscarf and a long robe were so necessary or why I wasn't allowed to have a boyfriend before marriage, which was still a long way off. Or why that person had to be Muslim – that meant a lot of really great people were off the table.

So, over the years, I began to profile myself more openly as a progressive, free-thinking Muslim woman who didn't necessarily agree with all the rules of religion and who preached the importance of seeing things in the spirit of their time and context. I was a kind of orientalist. I'd heard about it from leftist Turks on YouTube. They viewed religion this way as well. I was relieved: I had finally found a group that I could join, that I could identify with. At the Quranic school I had felt like an outsider until then.

One day, when I proclaimed at the mosque that I actually disagreed with the headscarf and didn't want to wear it, that I thought it was unnecessary in this day and age, and moreover unfair, because the boys were allowed to wear whatever they wanted, even when it was hot, I was harshly admonished by the teacher. If I didn't recant this statement and repent immediately, I would automatically fall away from the faith. How dare I say such a thing? You couldn't just pick something and say you disagreed with it, who did I think I was, a co-legislator with God?

'We Muslims believe in all the texts and all the precepts that Allah and His Prophet, peace be upon him, have provided for all of humanity. We do not participate in that modern chatter of certain sick souls who call themselves Muslims but claim that the headscarf is no longer necessary or that we should consider homosexuality perfectly normal. We must distance ourselves from this. Don't expose yourself to their nonsense, they're just a bunch of riff-raff with an identity crisis who are ashamed of their own religion. They want to mimic and please the West, but they continue to shamelessly call themselves Muslim while they jettison just about everything Islam stands for and accept all things Western, which is what the Prophet, peace be upon him, warned us about: beware of the hypocrites. They are far worse than the disbelievers. There are entire books written about them. At least the unbelievers show their cards, the hypocrites are traitors from within, cloaked in our own uniform. Has our Prophet, peace be upon him, not been crystal clear about homosexuality? About covering your beauty? About the role of men and women, and their rights and duties? What do we care about the views of feminists and gays?'

Her rage came from deep within; my rebuttal didn't sit well with her.

Left-wing Muslims argue the exact opposite to people like my teacher at the Quranic school, namely that our religious doctrine can coexist with feminist achievements, freedom, equality and other modern principles. They claim that the rules are products of their time and that as an individual you are allowed to mould and shape your religion, that you can pick which rules to follow, despite the fact that scripture makes a clear distinction between Muslim and non-Muslim, male and female, slave and master. Despite the fact that certain things are explicitly stated in the doctrine. Otherwise, the Ottomans wouldn't have had any harems or been able to turn their prisoners of war into sex slaves. Otherwise, they would've had no problem abolishing slavery.

Progressive Muslims are thus walking in the footsteps of cultural Christians, who, over the course of the last centuries, have gone through a sort of civilisation cleanse. They avoid the tricky questions ('that's not really part of Islam') or they say it's not their Islam, that it's just what the extremists believe. But if the religion started in Mecca, how on earth did it spread to places like Spain, Pakistan, Somalia, Turkey, Iran, Aceh and other non-Arab areas?

However, conservative Muslims argue that you cannot brush off extremist ideas as not being part of the Islamic doctrine and condemn those who say they are. In my opinion, the conservatives win the argument here since there hasn't really been a reformation. After all, our faith is presented as a perfect religion that's not bound to time or place – that's what I was taught as a child and what the imams still preach today. In the schools recognised by all Sunni Muslims, extremist interpretations still exist and are still, in many ways, supported by scripture. The schools in which these interpretations reside still haven't been challenged or changed by theologians, only by individual Muslims who try to distance themselves from them or remain silent and choose not to practise them, as the vast majority of Muslims in Europe and secular countries do. So although there has been tacit reform in Islamic practice, upon closer examination, this reform still isn't theologically supported or recognised by religious leaders, which allows radicalisation and fundamentalism to persist among people who are open to it. Muslims who disagree with what they see as tragic and outdated Islamic principles have left it entirely up to the individual to interpret, select and contextualise, and to know when not to take things too literally. But this isn't a logical or sustainable approach – how can you trust that everyone will actually do it? There are plenty of less intelligent and more fanatical people who simply aren't capable of this kind of critical thinking and see certain texts as an encouragement, so it remains a smoking gun.

If an imam or a mosque wants to follow a different path, like the one in Germany that allowed men and women to pray together or the one in France that opened its doors to homosexuals, they are sure to get bullets and letter bombs in their mailbox. That's just the modus operandi. They'll be threatened by people who see these new practices as attempts to water down the doctrine, and the people who support them will be made out to be hypocrites and heretics. After all, the doctrine has no flaws, and if you happen to find some and bring them to light, you are a non-believer. This still happens here in Europe, and especially in the Middle East. Turkey has seen its own share of violence: in 1993, a hotel in Sivas (the birthplace of my begetters) was set on fire because Alevi intellectuals had gathered there to discuss *The Satanic Verses*. On 4 September 1990, writer, atheist and critic of Islam Turan Dursun was murdered by Islamists in broad daylight for his ideas. If religious fundamentalists are a problem, one could argue that maybe there is something wrong with the fundamentals. The whole business of it stinks. But the question isn't so much whether things could, in theory, be reformed, because even if the possibilities are there (you can, after all, interpret a text any way you want, which explains why there are so many different types of Muslims) the fact remains: if every subversive convulsion is met with violence – and all it takes is a couple of transcendental idiots out there who, for whatever reason, aren't satisfied with what the material world has to offer – reform still isn't possible in practice.

The undeniable value of stupidity lies in its ability to connect large groups of people.

Atatürk, a revolutionary statesman and founding father of the Republic of Turkey, was the first to call for reform, and not without success, but he wasn't a theologian and is really only known within the Turkish context. Moreover, that was a reluctantly imposed secularisation from above and not an evolution within the population itself; the intellectual promise of the Enlightenment wasn't nestled in the hearts of the people. For secularisation to succeed, it can't just happen at the level of the state, it also has to occur in people's minds.

The most controversial texts in the legacy of the Prophet (peace be upon him) are about faith as a sociopolitical factor, about carrying out jihad in order to install a sharia state based not on the laws of man but on the laws of God. Jihad expansion is about the only thing that Saudi Arabia hasn't managed, by the way, and is what sets it apart from ISIS, the Taliban and al-Qaeda.

In Muslim-majority countries, theologians still bicker about issues such as political Islamism versus democracy, but most Muslims in the Netherlands have no clue about these debates; they prefer a kind of feel-good Islam that falls more or less within the right-wing Christian norm, even if they don't realise it. They know they're supposed to keep women submissive and wrapped in a headscarf, make sure their daughters and sisters remain virgins and second-class citizens, eat halal meat, reject gays, fast during Ramadan and refrain from drinking alcohol, but they couldn't care less about political issues because their relatively sweet version of Islam is drenched in the amniotic fluid of democracy, while in Turkey meanwhile, Sultan Erdoğan, who enjoys the unconditional awe of all Turkish imams, is walking a fine line and poses a serious threat to secularism. He has been known to praise Ottoman glory, emphatically promote the Muslim identity and invest tons of money in religious education, which has leftist Turks foaming at the mouth because all of this jeopardises Atatürk's achievements, which were, incidentally, mostly thanks to the Enlightenment.

Atatürk rammed secularism in like a suppository; those who objected, such as those few imams who continued to stubbornly advocate fundamentalism and prefer the caliphate, were eliminated. Atatürk aimed to establish a modern republic, abolish the caliphate and undermine religious dogmas, which were rampant among the people at the time, so that science and economic progress could flourish, and women could be emancipated. An organisation was needed to settle all matters related to religion, including what would be taught in the mosques and what content would be included in religious textbooks, and this became the Directorate of Religious Affairs, also known as the Diyanet. This ensured that there would be no confusing voices preaching fundamental Islam to the people, and that all leaders, both secular and spiritual, would be singing the same tune. In general, the Diyanet talked only about the spiritual, socially acceptable aspects of Islam: help the poor, fast during Ramadan, pray as much as possible, brush your teeth, count your blessings, water the plants, don't litter, put your dirty socks in the laundry basket, don't kill insects – in other words, no funny business, that was the mantra. It offered a home-and-garden kind of Islam. Through this organisation, Atatürk sought to give the brand new nation state a cultural-religious identity, one that wasn't necessarily Islamic, more oriental. These days, right-wing believers like to refer to such people as 'cultural Muslims'. And it's true that admiration of something, in this case doctrine, goes hand in hand with a sharp judgement. They don't believe in admiration, only blind worship.

Many Turks claim that Atatürk is the reason why, of all the Muslim-majority countries, Turkey is by far the most modern, civilised and liberal today. But they also worry about the current discourse in which politics and religion are becoming increasingly intertwined. Politics is about the question of what is right, but it takes a right and just society to handle moral issues. If the norms and values of most Turks are shaped by religion, then their politics will be intrinsically entangled with religion, which is, by definition, bound to a clear code of ethics regarding good and evil. And where do you draw the line? Can a political party be 'inspired' by religious values? Religion in politics is clearly evil if it results in a theocratic agenda, but does the same apply to fundamental moral issues? For example, can't a Christian party oppose abortion on religious grounds? Is it okay to be in favour of polygamy? Are you allowed to use taxpayers' money to build more Quranic boarding schools and pay off imams?

I myself have developed an inherent distrust of religion that I simply cannot overcome. Religion has tremendous power, yet many people in the Netherlands have lost sight of this. The idea that something is outdated can be surprisingly outdated.

Religion aestheticises life, it hems the horizon of our existence with mythology, imbuing even the most banal activities with meaning and spirituality. For many, it is a hunger that needs to be satisfied. In that way, it is also an intoxication, with an effect similar to drugs. It is powerful, it can make a person intensely happy because it appeals to our primal need to achieve unity with being. You give up your individuality by participating in something bigger than yourself. And that's what makes it so dangerous: you sacrifice your autonomy, turn off your brain and submit unconditionally to the transcendent. The effect is stupefying – whereas the loner swears by drink, the masses have their prayers, verses and slogans. It leads to fanaticism, self-sacrifice and herd-like behaviour. If you are religious, you are not a person; you are deliberately trying to become a kind of caricature.

I have a healthy respect for the power of religion, but at the same time I feel profound aversion and mistrust because it's such an irrational force that can so easily lead to destruction. If someone derives personal satisfaction from their faith, I don't have a problem with it provided that it's under secular conditions: religion is personal, something to be confined to one's personal life. People can be homophobic, people can be patriarchal – all that falls under the right-wing norm. But as soon as there's a totalitarian appeal accompanied by a demand for submission and a need for public order on the basis of religion, then it's a different story. When that happens, religion becomes an existential threat to a free, open society; it hijacks the mind and becomes a danger to the freedom of others. Anyway, I'm speaking in the abstract here; things are more complicated in practice because religion merges with ethnic and cultural identity. It belongs to the tradition in which the population exists. It has been profoundly shaped by the outlook, norms, values and worldview of the culture in which it is practised. It is something that, even for those who are not particularly religious, has become inextricably intertwined with our existence.

Even the private–public distinction is blurrier in practice, as it is a demand imposed by secular society and not immanent to religion itself. The idea of a devout community with internal social control is crucial to the maintenance of any culturally relevant form of faith. But that does not correspond with the secular notion that it all has to remain in the private sphere.

This explains why some Muslims become indignant when

you criticise their political views. Somehow, politics has become entangled with religion, and religion, in turn, with culture, identity, and even race and origin. An attack on Erdoğan or a degrading cartoon of a sacred figure is viewed as an attack on Islam itself, and thereby an attack on Muslims and anyone born Muslim or who is part of a Muslim community. It's a chain reaction and rarely perceived as separate components, though it's certainly possible to have a love for the Middle East and its people and cultures without being a fan of its religious views or certain political leaders.

None of this seems all that difficult to me, but I get glassy looks from people when I try to explain it.

Democracy

When I was twelve and in my sixth year at the Quranic school, I was sitting in class on a hot Sunday, completely covered in layers of fabric, everything except my hands and face, when someone knocked on the door. In walked a blonde, spindly woman in her early fifties with short, buzzed hair, dressed entirely in red with a symbol of a rose on her shirt. She made sure to take off her shoes, conforming to the rules of the house of God. She had a stack of leaflets in her hand and another load bulging out of her shoulder bag. The teacher didn't look up; the guest was not unexpected. First, she explained that this woman had come to deliver leaflets that we had to distribute on the home front. We were supposed to tell our families to tick this party in the upcoming elections. The woman with the shaved head – quite a sight among all the headscarves – smiled, perhaps a little petulantly, since, after all, she couldn't understand a word our teacher was saying. For all she knew, the teacher was introducing her as a piece of pagan scum while she stood there smiling like an idiot. Personally, I wouldn't take the risk of smiling while someone introduced me in a foreign language, but that was her choice.

I glanced down at the leaflet that had been pushed into

my hands, or should I say, leaflets, because she had given me four of them. Four copies of the exact same brochure. 'Give them to all your relatives.' She probably assumed that I had six brothers and five sisters who were all of voting age. It was from the PvdA, the Dutch Labour Party. Under a photo of several women wearing headscarves, written in big block letters, were the words 'VOTE LOCAL'.

If they were so progressive they would have helped me escape those insufferable lessons or at least told the government to stop subsidising them; they would contribute to efforts to rein in indoctrination instead of cultivating it, instead of courting the conservative immigrant vote by assuring my begetters and people on the street that they'd get them their mosques. If they were truly so forward-thinking they would support me in my freedom to take religious doctrine a little less seriously.

Religious criticism should be a leftist soapbox; in that sense, they were nothing more than salon socialists.

After the leaflet lady had gone, we continued the lesson. 'God has given man the right to give his wife a corrective slap,' the teacher repeated. 'Of course, there are many conditions: for example, she should first be verbally admonished and then the couple should sleep in separate beds. Violence should only be used in cases of emergency when there is truly no other way. Experts agree that there should be no broken bones, that any violence should be purely instructive and a means of clarifying the household hierarchy, seeing as the man is in charge of his wife and children, like a shepherd over his flock. Scholars diverge on how far the violence may go, but they unanimously agree that this right must be used with discretion. To abuse it would be a terrible sin, as the best man is the one who treats his wives well. That said, women can become quite hysterical and unreasonable, and sometimes physical sanctions are the only option.'

The marriage between the Dutch left and the Muslim orthodox community in the Netherlands is bursting with unfathomable incongruities. The conservative Muslim community is, for the most part, an imported equivalent of the Dutch Bible Belt, a kind of oriental right-wing Christian party, with women who cover themselves and pray behind the men in the mosque. It's against abortion, against gay and trans people, against gender neutrality, against freedom of expression in the form of satire, against blasphemy, pro-circumcision, pro-nationalism, with an our-people-and-our-faith-first mentality and distinct gender roles. It's a world where women stay at home peeling vegetables while the men bring home the money, where people are sceptical of modernity and entirely anti-feminist. What in God's name does a community like that have to do with the all-inclusive left and its rainbow flags? How could you possibly vote for Erdoğan in one country and the socialist Labour Party in another?

I am angry
But seek peace
in looking away
So I can let it rest
I want to fight
with the teacher at the mosque
where she still sits
in peace and harmony
I want to fight
with Mother
And no longer

Let myself be enslaved
I want love
I want hate
I want everything
I want nothing
I want Mother to learn her lesson
And put down the aggression
I am happy
I am mad
Nonchalant
And concerned
I get all riled up
I seek middle ground
Until I give in
And swallow again
I search and I search
For myself and people like me
Who are still surrendering
And I curse and I search
For the children
and their future
And what will soon be theirs
And I think and I search
I search like hell
So hard that I sweat
And it eats away at me
I ponder and I search
and waver back and forth
Endlessly measuring
I search for Allah
And the reason for my surrendering

Barbecue Crisps

At some point during my youth, I figured out that there were friends and neighbours who didn't have to go to Quranic school. They were Muslim too, but different; they believed in moderation. They had a mother who didn't wear a headscarf, went to the beach in the summer and couldn't read Arabic. Being wise means knowing which areas in life require moderation.

Every Monday, they told the kids at school what they'd done over the weekend, fun things. I was jealous. All my days off were spent at the Quranic school, I never had anything adventurous to say. My cheeks turned red when it was my turn to share; after telling the same story so many times I felt pressured to recount something more interesting. The others had played football, gone swimming, barbecued, been to the movies or watched one at home on the couch, taken bike rides and gone out for chips and ice cream, or to the zoo or an amusement park.

So, one day I decided to make something up. I said I'd been to the movies. I'd heard other kids talk about it a lot but had never actually been myself. We hardly ever went on family outings; my begetters were too suspicious. I can think of just a few times that we went somewhere, and then it was only because we'd received a city pass from the council in the letterbox with a free ticket or discount for something. After a lot of begging, we finally convinced Father to take us to the NEMO Science Museum, and Mother took us to the swimming pool once. It was fantastic; Halil and I were so excited that we didn't sleep a wink and stayed up all night chatting in our bunk bed, him on the bottom, me on the top.

But then the teacher asked if I wanted to tell the class about the movie I saw, and my face turned red as a beetroot. After a lot of stammering and stuttering, sighing and puffing, I got out of it by saying that I'd forgotten what it was about. She probably thought I had some kind of learning disability.

At Quranic school, I mostly learned the domestic rules of our faith and about the life of the Prophet, peace be upon him, which consisted mostly of battles, I noticed. It was always about battles, war, struggle and distress. All the teachers were fervent Erdoğan supporters and obsessed with Turkish politics, but they also ventured into the realm of geopolitics from time to time, at least to the extent that they had to do with Muslims, and liked to talk about topics such as the eternal struggle between Israel and Palestine and the war in Iraq. In their view, the world was divided into two camps: the *ummah* and the rest. This was curious, however, since suddenly all the Muslims in the world would be seen as one solid block, while Mohammed's legacy has deteriorated into countless clusters and schisms that are all out to get each other and could literally drink one another's blood. The Islamic island kingdom can hardly be called an archipelago; if you put a God-fearing Turk and a Palestinian in the same room and made them talk about the fundamentals of the Islamic doctrine, there would most certainly be disagreement – the same goes for a Turk and a Turk, for that matter. We are born schismatics.

169

We were often shown terrifying images of Muslim suffering in Gaza, Iraq, China and Burma that became seared into the back of my mind and caused me physical pain. The teacher, who incidentally couldn't speak a word of Dutch and, like many mosque employees, was living in the Netherlands illegally and sleeping in the mosque, explained that the images were proof that non-Muslims would always be hostile to us until we lost our faith. I found the images repulsive and utterly shocking; they kept me awake night after night. Pictures of people and children being cruelly beaten, a Rohingya baby in a puddle of water being struck with electric shocks over and over again by Buddhist extremists. He screamed his lungs out every time the power surged through his veins. Those images will remain forever engraved on my retinas. A lady shrieking as she recounted how her husband had been tortured by US soldiers in Abu Ghraib prison, that she herself had been humiliated, raped. I became furious at all the enemies and governments that did nothing to stop it, the Netherlands included. 'The Christians' actually considered it beneficial, the teacher said. I accepted all of this without question.

Fortunately, I went to a public primary school, where they took a different approach to education. I felt great affection for the teachers there – they weren't Muslim, but I knew they were allies who would never condone all the horrible things happening to Muslims around the world. They made this clear when I blatantly asked them about it. I wasn't the only child in the class who asked these kinds of questions. It didn't take them long to realise that these issues were on their pupils' minds: 'Are you a Christian, Mr Erik?', 'Why aren't you a Muslim?', 'Do you even like Muslims?', 'Israel is bad, isn't it?', 'Do you respect Muslims?', 'Did you vote for that guy who hates Muslims and talks about headscarves?', 'Do you want Muslims to go away?', 'What do you think of America?'

Aside from the resentment and impotence I felt from all the images of torture I'd seen at the Quranic school, I mostly felt afraid. After all, my loved ones were Muslim, I was Muslim, wouldn't that mean that sooner or later we too would be tortured and humiliated? So why didn't God stop it? Apparently, we couldn't count on him, otherwise he would have helped those people. Just because we believed in God didn't mean He believed in us.

That's not the only way they instilled fear in us. For instance, we were also shown a picture of a severely disabled and deformed girl who, we were told, had thrown the Quran on the ground and said she no longer believed. Less than an hour later, she was completely paralysed. The doctors had no explanation or cure. The moral of the story was that you should always hold the Quran above your waist and never put it on the ground or in your lap; that would be a huge sin, something for those clumsy Christians who put their Bible under their chair in church.

One time I dropped the Quran in front of the teacher and stood there speechless until she said that I would be forgiven if I kissed the book three times and pressed it against my forehead. I made it six just to be sure.

The relaxed, down-to-earth, relatable attitude of my atheist teachers at school began to temper my suspicion towards non-Muslims, or the 'Christians', as I assumed they were called. They weren't the least bit zealous and rarely adamant in their answers, unlike the teachers I encountered over the weekend. The Quranic school teachers were sometimes even moved to tears, which made me uncomfortable and gave me goose-bumps. The godless public-school teachers, on the other hand, were mostly light-hearted and funny; they seemed more concerned about the fact that *we* were so concerned about all this.

'God doesn't exist, you guys, those are just a bunch of stories made up by people, I promise. Don't worry about it.' I secretly found that very nice to hear, much nicer than all those temperamental rants we had to sit through at the mosque, nicer than all the emotions shouted through a megaphone. It seemed to emancipate me from the feeling that I had no choice but to share in the pain of a massive group of people from all over the world facing all kinds of obstacles and tremendous suffering. Ms Hatice said that we should pray day and night for our 'brothers and sisters' in misery, but I didn't want to think about babies being murdered for being born Muslim day and night. It made me sad and, above all, angry. I didn't know who to turn to with all that pent-up rage, those intense, heavy feelings of injustice and victimisation, except to God before bed, but was that really enough? If I stewed over that for a while and then went to pray, I couldn't sleep afterwards because of all the grief and doom hanging like a dark cloud over my mind and soul.

This is why I can't stand it that Defne attends a religious primary school; she's being robbed of any chance to ever think critically or hear other points of view. Every day of the week, and again at the weekend, she hears nothing but religious doctrine. When I was growing up, there was no Islamic school in our neighbourhood, which allowed me to come into contact with other perspectives and celebrate the Dutch holidays. 'But Islamic schools produce excellent results' is often the rebuttal you hear from Muslims in the media. Yeah, so what? They're only looking at the collective, not the individual. How many students get accepted into elite high schools doesn't say much about who they are as people, all it shows is that they're good at studying. But who are they as human beings? What values do they stand for? Intelligence is not a one-dimensional concept. An excellent test score is worthless if you can't appreciate the freedom of others.

At school, I was in a diverse class with children from many different walks of life and family backgrounds, from both hemispheres. For instance, I knew that Anjali did not eat beef at Christmas dinner because she was Hindu. I knew Harmanjot was not allowed to cut her hair because she was Sikh. Her father and little brother had long hair too, usually braided and wrapped in a white turban. I also knew that every Sikh had the same surname, Singh. All of them. And all the women used the prefix 'kaur' before their last name. That seemed pretty impractical to me.

I knew Himano was half Dutch and half Surinamese and believed in the Christian God, just like Jeremy, Latoya and Junior, who were all black, and oddly enough all without a father. Then you had Nick, who was half Turkish and half Dutch, and an Alevi Muslim. He didn't have a mother because she was a heroin addict and lived somewhere else, in another city, and had no contact with her son. 'That's what you get when you marry a Dutch woman. They are so unreliable,' Mother had said once in reference to Nick's father's marriage. Nick was my best mate in primary school. Whenever the topic of mothers came up at school, for example on Mother's Day or even when the word came up while reading aloud, he would start to cry inconsolably, tears streaming from his green-gold-blue eyes – the same colour as our betta fish at home – and he would run out into the corridor or to the toilet to pull himself together. I would go after him and rub his back; the teacher didn't mind. This happened a lot, I remember, but it never got annoying; we were always nice to him. When he cried, he

173

was absolutely silent; when the teacher tried to talk to him, nothing came out. He just wanted to stand in the corridor and cry. Not talk. He's now a drug addict himself.

Some of the kids ate ham during the break and were allowed to have barbecue crisps when someone handed them out on their birthday. From fellow Muslims, I had learned that that particular flavour of crisps contained pork so if anyone ever offered them to us we knew right away that we had a pagan on our hands. If Himano or Jeremy refused to trade crisps with us, preferring to keep their own flavour instead, we would close ranks and pressure them into it.

'But these crisps are against our religion, and it's not fair that we can't eat any crisps and you can!' In the end, they'd always give in. After all, there were more of us than there were of them. It was the same with certain snacks. At first it was just the bacon-flavoured ones, but soon all the Red Band gummies landed on the haram list because somebody's mother said they contained 'pig'. In primary school, we Muslim kids learned that almost every sweet contains 'pig', and so we could only eat lollipops, crisps and chocolate. Eventually, the Katja brand came out with these vegetarian sour strips, which all the Muslim kids bought. Before that, the pagan kids had a pretty sweet deal – we would always go to them to swap our sugary stash for crisps – but once the new Katjas came out, the game was up.

There were times when I got stuck with a bag of barbecue crisps too, but I didn't eat them or try to trade them because I didn't want anyone to feel obliged to swap with me. The non-Muslim kids had made it known that they weren't fond of the forced barbecue transactions. Ms Aliza – a tough, no-nonsense Frisian woman whose doggedness made her the school Gestapo – asked me why I wasn't eating my treat. Even a normal question sounded combative coming from her; her corpulent figure and commanding presence inspired awe and you became extra accommodating. I'd even sensed this from Father during the report-card meetings; on the way home, he couldn't help but express his astonishment at her size.

'Um ... because there's pig in there, and Allah doesn't allow that,' I said.

'Nonsense, there's no pork in these, it's just pork *seasoning*. It's got spices to make it taste like pork, but of course it's not real pork, that would be impossible!' Her story sounded plausible to me; I'd already been wondering how there could be meat in crisps. I carefully opened the bag and tasted one. 'Pretty good, right? Just eat them, it's fine, really.' So, I kept munching away until Hajar walked up.

'Oooooo, Büsra eats pig, look!' she shouted for the entire class to hear.

'Eeeew, disgusting!'

'*Tfoeee!*'

'What, so you're not a Muslim now?'

'You're going to hell!'

'Noooo!'

I got a crisp stuck in my throat.

'Ms Aliza said there's no pig in them,' I shouted in my defence, though I was noticeably hesitant.

'Yeah, duh, because she's not a Muslim, of course she says that, stupid,' said Amin.

'And you believed her,' shrieked Hajar, 'How stupid can you be?'

'My mum is smarter than she is. She's a driving instructor and she earns ten times more than the teacher,' Hamza exclaimed.

'You really are a sucker,' said Harun.

'Boys!' Ms Aliza shouted, joining the debate. 'Everyone can eat whatever they want here, I don't want to hear any more of this! Enough! Büsra, just eat your crisps.'

Sure, easy for Ms Aliza to say, she wasn't the one who would be called a pig for months if she finished the bag. I threw the crisps away. Ms Aliza looked at me in disappointment.

Infidel

I was fourteen when I read the autobiography of a Somali-Dutch woman who had been circumcised. I was floored. I asked the teacher at the mosque why this had happened to her and whether it was truly mandated by scripture. She said that it was, but these days it wasn't being done correctly. Originally, the idea was to reduce the foreskin of the clitoris, not cut it away entirely, because according to certain lore this would provide the woman with more pleasure.

I just nodded, but in reality I was completely shocked. I had expected her to say that it only happened in Africa, something I'd heard from left-wing Muslims on YouTube.

Around the age of seventeen, I decided to start emailing imams with questions about things like whether all the demands my parents imposed on me were justified, why when a boy is born you're supposed to sacrifice two sheep in celebration and only one for a girl, why a woman's testimony is worth only half a man's, why almost all Islamic leaders were men, why polygamy is legitimate only for men, why scripture states that martyrs will receive seventy-two virgins in paradise, why it was deemed acceptable to marry your cousin, and what was the deal with that verse in the Quran that said that one day the trees would betray the Jews hiding behind them? Why did the Prophet (peace be upon him) destroy the temples and statues of non-believers? Weren't we called to tolerate pluralism within Islamic societies and grant our subordinates the same rights that non-believers had in society? What about that verse that said if you kill a Muslim, you'd pay for it in blood, but not if you killed a non-believer? In paradise, men could have sex with all the women they wanted, including their earthly wives, without any jealousy or envy. They'd never get tired and could fuck all day long. But there were no verses on how many virgins women would get and whether they too would be able to go all day long without getting tired. Why was that? And that whole no jealousy thing, did that apply to women too? And what about that verse where the Prophet (peace be upon him) had someone executed for blasphemy (when in reality every religion is guilty of blasphemy against other religions)? Why was the Prophet (peace be upon him) married to a six-year-old, and more importantly, why didn't the average Muslim have a problem with this, or why did they come up with nonsensical explanations like girls grew up faster back then? Why in certain countries are girls circumcised in the name of holy scripture? Why does the doctrine approve of slavery and wars of expansion? Why is it okay to hit your wife? Why can't a woman file for divorce under Islamic law? Why did women need their father's permission to marry but men didn't? Why did outspoken apostates have to be killed? Why did imams in Saudi Arabia claim that women shouldn't be allowed to drive a car? Why were these points never addressed, and instead the topic was always switched to how the Prophet (peace be upon him) is so understanding, full of love for truth and justice, so gallant, courageous, conscientious, orderly, patient, honest, generous, witty, entertaining, warm, sensitive to love and affection, faithful to his given word, humble and benevolent, sincere, kind, civilised in his ways, intelligent, well dressed, considerate, empathetic, independent, culturally sophisticated, open-minded, ambitious, disciplined and impeccable in his behaviour? Why was it only endless praise?

The answers I received from the imams were mostly evasive, with a lot of beating around the bush. They advised me to read entire books. But I felt entitled to a real answer instead of being told to bury myself in twenty-four-volume sets that weighed as much as I did and were written entirely in Arabic. After I made it clear to them that I wasn't going to do that and that I expected a real answer, even if it was just a confirmation or rejection of the authenticity of the texts, they all confirmed that, indeed, there was nothing in scripture about women receiving multiple men in paradise. So no, they wouldn't get them. Because women were, by nature, different from men. And that was true even in paradise. Aha. The same went for the other questions: they confirmed that what was written in scripture was true and that the verses I mentioned were indeed authentic, none of it had been made up.

Their only defence was that there were conditions for such measures – for example, an unfaithful spouse can only be stoned in a sharia state and then only if there were four witnesses (three in cases of homosexuality), and that a man is allowed to beat his wife only if there is absolutely no other way.

As if that put things in a completely different light.

Homeland

Today we leave for Turkey, as we do every summer. Unlike every other family, we're flying, because every one of us, except Mother, suffers from an extreme form of car-sickness. We're headed to Sivas, the birthplace of my begetters.

Most Euroturks own beautiful houses in Turkey and spend the rest of the year cramped up in chicken-coop apartments in their adopted country. We were no exception. In Sivas, we have a large terrace where we can relax in the sun. Unfortunately for me, however, the neighbours can see it, which means that I'm not allowed to sunbathe, take off my headscarf or show any skin – in other words, I can't enjoy the sun, which is pretty much the only thing a holiday in Turkey is good for. In the evenings, our relatives come over, and we sit out there and listen to music while the young men pass around the water pipe. Halil can't go a day without shisha; he even smokes back home in the Netherlands. He's been spending too much money on it lately, he complained the other day. It has become an addiction. In the Netherlands, a water pipe costs twenty euros in a Turkish lounge and only ten (and sometimes less) in a Moroccan lounge because apparently the Moroccans have other sources of income and are thus able to offer it at a lower price, or that's what I've been told. If you're smoking shisha on a daily basis, and most guys do, it adds up quickly. In Turkey, water pipes and cigarettes are a lot cheaper; you can buy a pack of cigarettes for €1.50 and smoke a water pipe for as little as one euro, which is probably why everyone smokes there. At least, that's how it seems when I look on the streets. I recently heard that it's gradually becoming more expensive because the government is starting to tax it. They're also banning all drugs, which seems like a good thing to me. Sometimes Erdoğan and I are on the same page; some things are forbidden with the best intentions.

I have never been to any other Turkish cities or other countries on holiday, apart from the school trip to Rome. When tourists at the restaurant where I work tell me they've been to Istanbul, Bodrum or Marmaris, all I can say is that I've seen pictures online. They don't understand, especially since I usually tell them I spend six weeks in Turkey every summer. I once tried to convince my begetters to take us to Istanbul, but they weren't interested. They thought it would be a waste of money since we already had a house in Sivas, and moreover that's where all our family lived. This was, of course, the main reason for our so-called 'holiday' in Turkey: we weren't there to enjoy ourselves, we were there to visit relatives. And there were a lot of them. So, I asked them if I could go with a friend, but that was out of the question. Two girls in the big city without a male chaperone – unthinkable. So I asked if Halil could take us, but that wasn't allowed either. They couldn't imagine my little brother having to spend several days in the company of one of my female friends. That wouldn't be appropriate, two adults of the opposite sex spending so much time together. After all, if I were to go on a trip with a girlfriend and her brother tagged along, they certainly wouldn't approve. 'We don't need any more crazy antics out of you two, with your impertinent manners,' Mother said.

When we get to Schiphol Airport in Amsterdam, the first thing we have to do is check in our suitcases. As always, we have way too much stuff with us. I'm seized by my agonising fear of flying. It absolutely terrifies me even though I know that, statistically, it's the safest way to travel. But our emotions don't always work that way. As a notorious Soviet dictator once said, 'One death is a tragedy, a million deaths is a statistic.' Humans can be irrational. Myself included. I wasn't the best at outsourcing control of my life at twelve kilometres above sea level. In a car, you could see the ground, you could trace the road with your eyes and see how it extended to the horizon; that made it a very different experience. It's not that I'm afraid of death, by the way; death is, after all, an inescapable part of life, perhaps the only real part, and it is our ability to regularly ignore that which we know for certain that makes life bearable, but I find the thought of spending the final minutes of my life knowing that I'm about to crash or drown along with three hundred total strangers in a state of total panic incredibly unpleasant. Who is that pilot anyway? I don't know anything about him, or her for that matter. What if he recently became an alcoholic or he's having a bad day, or what if he's fresh out of school and we're his guinea pigs? What if birds get stuck in the engines? What if this plane is new, and it happens to have some kind of design flaw due to the negligence of some underpaid worker? What if that worker is under the influence of terrorist ideologies and saw an opportunity to sabotage this flight?

Father, sensing my fear, lays a hand on my shoulder and tries to comfort me with the old saying: 'When your time has come, your time has come.'

'But what if the pilot's time has come and we're just going down with him?' I retort. He doesn't know how to respond. So much for his arbitrary Islamic credo.

In Sivas, there are all kinds of well-known chains, restaurants, cinemas, amusement parks and swimming pools. It's a nice place, we shouldn't have anything to complain about. The annoying thing is that after a few days, we've seen everything there is to see and still have six weeks to go. Summer after summer. There's no beach nearby, so swimming and sunbathing aren't an option. Not that I'd ever want to in a burkini, a kind of bathing suit that covers a woman's entire body, even her hair, so she can swim in public. So, every single day, me, Halil and Defne do the same thing: we go into the city centre, get a cheap bite to eat, have a drink on a terrace somewhere, sometimes there's live music, and then saunter home with the sun beating down on our heads. In Sivas, I'm always struck by all the young people begging or selling things on the street. Many of them walk around all day with tray of *simit* balanced on their head. Every time you sit down on a bench, children come up and try to sell you sunflower seeds, chewing gum or packs of tissues. It's not unusual to be approached by a far-too-skinny child with a scale asking if he can weigh you for a lira. Children and teenagers push rickety carts full of knock-off brand-name clothing and other junk, and shout at the top of their lungs in the hope of attracting customers, especially when there are Europeans around.

I despise my holidays in Turkey. I get bored out of my mind, and everything annoys me. Hordes of people come over to the house every day, and they always greet me with an enthusiastic kiss even though I hardly know them. All I know is that they are somehow related to Father or Mother and that's reason enough for me to greet them warmly, pretend that I'm having the time of my life and say that I'm so happy they've stopped by. But the truth is written all over my face. I hate it. I hate playing the perfect daughter who has to run into the kitchen to prepare all kinds of biscuits and pastries and tea for them, and then be forced to endure their endless chatter for hours on end. All they ever talk about is other people, people I don't know with stories that don't interest me or add anything to my general knowledge or quality of life; on the contrary. It's always about other people's sons and daughters who are still single and looking for a partner because they're already in their late twenties, and you know, you really have to start looking by then. Or which children have managed to pop out a couple of kids of their own. Or who's having marital troubles, or the in-laws they can't stand for some petty reason or another. Sometimes the topic turns to politics and that's even more excruciating. The tone quickly becomes impassioned, followed by shouting and swearing about Erdoğan's opponents, whom they refer to as national traitors, nest polluters and ass-lickers of the West.

I often have to replenish the baklava and Turkish delight on the table at least three times per visit. And the tea up to twenty times. Every time someone's glass is almost empty, I have to make sure to pour a new batch before they ask for it. If you forget and a guest has to reach for the teapot themselves and ask for more tea, I have failed as a hostess, and Mother will look at me with disgust.

I sometimes manage to escape by pretending to be busy in the kitchen or by playing games with Defne, which offers some distraction. I'm also always too hot because I have to wear my headscarf and a long dress with long sleeves in the house, in the middle of the scorching Turkish summer, in a house full of people drinking hot tea. This goes on throughout the entire holiday. Every day, new people. Yet another man with a moustache, another lady with a headscarf. They always ask how I'm doing and if I'm still studying and for how much longer. Make no mistake, these are not questions of genuine interest, they're part of a larger plan. They see me as an adult woman, ripe for marriage to one of their single testosterone bombs who would like nothing more than to impregnate me in the near future. Mother gets excited by all their interest; her daughter is in high demand. The more eager they are, the more honour for the family. This proves that she and Father have succeeded in manufacturing an attractive, agreeable, servile, mature and healthy woman. Mother can't wait to marry me off, then her life will be fulfilled. She will have launched a valuable product onto the market that can serve her own circle and strengthen family ties by bringing forth a new generation. Sometimes she'll come rushing in to tell me that X number of women asked if they could come and ask for my hand or if I could already be betrothed to their son; it didn't matter that I was still in school, that didn't have to be an obstacle. If they succeed in betrothing (or shall we say, chaining) me, they're guaranteed not to lose their control over me. I'll be claimed, like a beach lounger someone has laid their towel on. They'll wait until I graduate, but after that comes the wedding, and as soon as possible.

Mother can't stomach the fact that I constantly refuse. She always tells me that it's a missed opportunity because so-and-so's son is so well off, which means that he has a job and a roof over his head and is a fervent Muslim. Sometimes I'm amazed by the candidates my begetters think are suitable for me. Here I am, studying Dutch literature at a respectable university and they expect me to marry a painter (and not the Rembrandt type), a construction worker, a weaver, a plumber or a taxi driver. Sometimes I get mad and ask them how they could possibly think it's okay to pair me up with someone who's completely uneducated. Of course, this is met with dismay. Who do I think I am, how dare I look down on the uneducated, what difference does it make as long as he's a righteous, honourable and pious person? I had my priorities all wrong. Once again, I'm hit with their straw-man arguments: 'There are lots of low-educated people who are far better human beings than those with fancy degrees', 'It's their character that counts', 'That stuck-up attitude of yours will get you nowhere'. If, at that point, I try to respond, I'm completely ignored and told I don't understand anything anyway. Even my demand for someone with a reasonable level of education, which is fairly innocuous and justifiable and, in my opinion, also essential in a fucking marriage that you're probably going to spend a long period of your life in, was too much for them to handle. I didn't know what I was talking about and should just shut up with all my worthless, haughty opinions. I felt like a stupid, incapacitated object, as I had so often felt in my life. They expected me to prostitute myself out to the patriarchy rather than seek my own happiness.

On days like that, Mother would ask me for the four thousandth time if I was absolutely sure that I didn't at least want to meet the man whose begetters had shown interest in me, no strings attached. 'He's from our family circle, he prays five times a day, has a job and his own place. What more do you want? You can't refuse everybody, soon there won't be so many good candidates left, they'll all have found someone else.' When her proposition was met with a hostile, sometimes furious, reaction, she'd back off. Only to start on about it again the next day. She is well aware of the fact that I don't want to get married yet. I've made this clear to her before. Besides, I'm madly in love with Lucas, but of course she doesn't know that. 'After you graduate, you really need to get married, otherwise you'll be overdue,' she often says. In our world, a woman is 'overdue' if she's not married by twenty-five, seeing as that's about as long as her beauty will survive. And, on top of that, people will start to think there's something wrong with me. Mother will do anything to keep those kinds of suspicions at bay. Soon people will think I'm infertile, have some kind of disease, am no longer a virgin, or that I'm too arrogant and difficult to ever make an obedient wife or take care of a man. For these people, there is no other conceivable reason that a woman over the age of twenty wouldn't want to marry a righteous man with a decent income who asks for her hand. Reasons such as not wanting to get married, building a career, desiring independence, preferring whatever spontaneous romance might come your way over a formal arrangement, and prioritising self-development are all way over their heads. They don't believe in love. 'Love comes after marriage,' Mother always says. 'Love doesn't fill an empty stomach.' Then if I say something like love is so much more beautiful than an arranged marriage, she dismisses it as naive nonsense. She says I'm young, that I know nothing of the real world, that I've watched too many series and movies. On top of that, the Dutch have indoctrinated us with all kinds of crazy ideas at school. She claims that one can fall in love with the worst person, that there are plenty of examples where this was the case, that as a girl you're not capable of seeing things in a man that your begetters can see, and are thus completely unfit to choose your own partner, just as children are unfit to choose which food is healthy for them – if it were up to them, they would eat junk food every day. 'Young women are like children, naive and insecure. It's for your own good and happiness. I'm not doing this for myself.' She swore by Allah that the girls who choose their own partner are the unhappiest in the world and after a few years they all want a divorce. That the West indoctrinates us with its pernicious ideas that do nothing but weaken and destroy society because everyone is far too individualistic and fixated on themselves and their own happiness, which is why there are so many divorces. Pursuing one's own happiness is, in Mother's eyes, a philistine endeavour. 'It completely destroys the home. Freedom and individualism do not make people happy; those are not the poles around which life revolves. Just look at all the lonely elderly Dutch people rotting away or all the depressed women with cats and dogs instead of children, or the thirty-somethings with all their unfulfilled nesting urges. There's an anti-child culture among white people. They see children as time-consuming elements that stand in the way of their own happiness. That's how they see their elderly too, whereas in our culture children and the elderly get all the care and attention in the world. Individualism is a threat to the survival of a nation and the human race. It marginalises the notion that we are all citizens, children of God and bound to our communities.'

Then follows a series of stories about relatives, acquaintances, neighbours and random people from Turkish television, all used to support her argument.

'You, as a young woman, are sure to fall for the sweet, slimy words of the first dirtbag who tries to pick you up. You shouldn't. Beautiful words, a beautiful body, beautiful eyes – it's all fleeting, what matters is how loyal he is, whether he's honourable and God-fearing, and whether he earns enough to support a family.'

I nod silently. And heave a deep, internal sigh.

Asymmetry

Halil is on the terrace, video chatting with his chick, who is in another city in Turkey with her family. He doesn't think twice about it, with our begetters in the same room. What does he care if they hear him? It's not like they disapprove.

When I asked them why Halil is allowed to have a girlfriend, Mother replied that she's not responsible for someone else's daughter, and if she wants to spread her legs, that's her problem. 'If she and Halil don't end up together and her parents or brothers show up on our doorstep, I'll just tell them their girl should've kept her knees together, that's just how boys are, you can't tame them, they'll eat where they can eat, it's the woman's responsibility, she should have enough self-respect to say no and not come crying afterwards when she feels discarded. It's up to her guardians to look after her and raise her right, so she doesn't go astray.'

They say they miss each other; Halil asks her about her day. 'You're not allowed to wear a bikini on the beach, just wear a bathing suit with one of those wrap things,' he says. 'Yeah, exactly, a kimono, or whatever you call it.' His girlfriend doesn't wear a headscarf, but Halil still comments on her clothes. She can't wear just anything. He thinks a bikini is unacceptable in his absence, he doesn't want every guy who walks by fantasising about her. Our cousin Mustafa is on the terrace too. He's swiping on his phone and occasionally shouts something along the lines of: 'Now you're a sight for sore eyes. I'm coming for you when I get back in the country, you sexy Sophie you.' Mustafa is a chronically horny chick magnet, he's on every dating app there is and even the ones still in development. Badoo, Tinder and Happn – and those are just the ones I remember from his summary. The tragic thing is that he's had a girlfriend for years, and I know her. She has no idea that he's still chasing after everything with legs in the Amsterdam metropolitan area. That said, I do find myself sympathising with him sometimes; there's no way he'll ever get his wifey-to-be to bed before marriage, she's as prudish as they come. So, it's going to be a while yet. Of course, the hypocrisy is that he would never forgive his girlfriend if she did the same.

Our cousin Abdul is hanging out with us too. He lives in Turkey and finds it incredibly annoying when we speak Dutch in his presence. We try not to, but it still seeps in unconsciously. I always feel awkward around Abdul, he's in love with me and can't stop staring. My grandmother in Turkey has already asked several times if I would be interested in marrying him, and I constantly assure her that the affection is not mutual. Oma has been saying that Abdul and I should be married since we were kids, that we would make an excellent match. Abdul must get a stiffy just thinking about it. And I get all blotchy on my neck and throw up a little in my mouth.

Mustafa and his girlfriend can't get married yet; he has to meet all of the girl's parents' conditions before he'll ever be approved. For starters, he has to have a house and a car. And be able to pay for more than half of the wedding.

First, they'll have to get engaged. Then, there will be a henna party, which is basically the same as a wedding but only for women. Little bags of henna will be handed out and the melancholic music will start to play, marking the bride's departure from her childhood home. Turks are a deeply passionate people – just look at our soap operas. I tried to imagine what would happen if you were to translate one of those soaps into Dutch, and almost died laughing. The sober Dutch wouldn't be able to stomach all the tragedy, drama and passion. Then, the bride and her mother will embrace each other like there's no tomorrow and weep their eyes out in the centre of the circle surrounded by their nearest and dearest to say farewell. After that the henna is handed out in fancy little bags to the rest of the guests. Traditionally, they're supposed to smear it on their hands, but nowadays that's just a formality and you can throw it away when you get home. It's not all tears though, that part only lasts for a minute, there's also dancing and eating. Then comes the wedding, usually the day after the henna party. The most beautiful party halls in Amsterdam and Zaandam are rented, usually a whole year in advance, because you're not the only person who wants to get married. Halls like De Koning and Rhone Party Centrum in Amsterdam are generally booked up all year round. The cost including catering is around twenty thousand euros. On top of that, you have to rent a stretch limo or a jeep to pick up the bride from her parents' house, and don't forget one of those traditional Turkish bands to travel with the bride from her house to the party hall and, when it's all over, on to her new home. The men in the musical formation will start playing dance music on the street in a way that you wouldn't exactly call discreet. The couple's relatives will dance and hoot their car horns, and the Moroccans also like to scream. The local residents look on with fascination, especially the white and black neighbours, who watch spellbound from their balconies. Sometimes they're in awe, but sometimes I see them growling, grunting and snarling. In many cases, there is also an excessive number of Turkish flags hanging from the balcony of the bride's home. Nowadays, some people will hang a Dutch flag as well, just for good measure. And relatives hang flags on the wing mirrors of their cars too, so they flap down both sides of the convoy that follows the bride and groom to the wedding venue, horns honking. The whole way.

But before the bride steps out of her parents' house and the convoy can begin, she's stopped by one of her brothers, uncles or cousins. Some man from her family. He tells the groom and his family who are waiting outside that the bride is ready to come out, but 'the door won't open'. This is part of the act. The man, who is part of her family, 'isn't just going to let her go'. He expects money from the groom before he'll allow her to leave. The generous groom, who would naturally do anything for his wife, reaches deep into a sack and hands over the prepared sum. It shouldn't be too little, otherwise people will say you're stingy. If he's smart, he'll have done some preliminary research and brought an appropriate amount. It's often five hundred euros, but it varies per family. It can be up to a thousand, depending on how wealthy the groom is. If the recipient isn't satisfied with the amount, he can say 'the door still won't open' a few times, signalling to the groom that he better fork out a little more. Thus, it's always a good idea to start low since there's a pretty good chance that the bride's family will demand more. This generally happens at the engagement too, by the way. Whoever is cutting the red ribbon between the rings, usually the father or brother of the bride-to-be, will suddenly proclaim that 'the scissors won't cut'.

Eventually the bride comes out and they all make their way to the wedding hall, which is already at full capacity and not just with immediate family members. Even people who are not at all close to the couple, people they only know via a friend of a friend or who are just casual acquaintances of their begetters, are there. At our celebrations, the general rule is the more the merrier, so anyone who has ever said hello to your begetters or their begetters gets invited. The same goes for anyone who has roots in your family's hometown and their children and relatives; they all count as family. Therefore, the average party generally has more than eight hundred guests. The last one I went to had 1,100. The Moroccans make do with significantly fewer: they're fine with 150 to 250 visitors, otherwise things are bound to heat up. Since Moroccans don't necessarily collect money from every single person at the wedding, whereas the Turks do, the couple often has to pay for everything themselves and that can get really expensive. A Turkish couple can cover most, if not all, of the costs with the gold they receive, but I'll explain this in a minute.

At some point during the party, when the couple cuts the cake, they push a piece into each other's mouths and photos are taken. Interestingly, there are wine glasses and bottles of Moët on the table, but it's just apple juice. It's purely for the photo, to make it look 'elegant' and 'chic'. It's a bit strange actually, that you'd want to be photographed with alcohol even though you despise it as a substance. I've never under-stood it, but that goes for a lot of things.

Towards the end of the party, the couple's relatives form a circle. The bride wears a red ribbon around her waist that symbolises her virginity, which she has successfully preserved for her husband. The bride's father or brother then proceeds to untie the ribbon and gives her a long hug. It's his way of

193

showing his gratitude for protecting the family's honour up to that point and that he will allow her to give herself to her lawful husband on her wedding night.

During the party, the couple receives money or gold from each guest. The way this happens is fairly ridiculous, but I promise I'm not making it up. A person is hired to stand on stage with a microphone after dinner. He – it's usually someone with a penis – announces that it's time for gifts and asks the guests to come forward by group, starting with the front tables. The couple stand side by side, ready to collect their presents. They're both wearing a red satin ribbon. People line up to congratulate them. They give a hug and four kisses; the women to the bride and the men to the groom, assuming it's a mixed wedding. If it's not a mixed wedding, then the whole thing takes place in two separate halls (more on that shortly). Then the guests pin cash or gold coins to the ribbon. By the time everyone has been down the line, the ribbons are completely full and sometimes several replacement ribbons are needed. Then the bride walks around like a mannequin in a jewellery shop. Or the wife of an oil sheikh. The closest relatives are expected to give the most. At the very least a thick gold bracelet, a colossal necklace or an amount equivalent to a thousand euros. Each gift is announced by name through the loudspeaker: 'Two gold bangles from the bride's uncle, Ahmet Kaya. One thousand euros from the groom's best friend, Ali Aydin. Five hundred euros from the bride's grandmother, Ayse Kaya.' You have to sit there and listen to it for at least an hour, or longer if they don't pick up the pace. Even those who aren't directly related or who don't have a lot of extra money lying around still give unspeakable amounts. Literally unspeakable; it's considered somewhat 'disgraceful' and lowbrow to give money in an envelope rather than on the ribbon, and even then the man with the microphone will still announce that so-and-so has given an envelope. All of this is filmed, by the way; there is a cameraman there for that specific purpose. Of course, the entire wedding is filmed, but he makes sure to zoom in on this part so that the couple and their begetters can watch it again when they get home. Then they'll know what everyone has given and be able to comment on whether or not they find the amount acceptable. It also helps them know how much they should give when someone else's child gets married.

In other words, the cost of the wedding is partly paid off by the amount the couple has collected by the end of the evening.

Weddings of more devout families take place in separate halls. This is more expensive than mixed weddings, as two halls must then be rented.

Children of both sexes go with their mothers to the women's hall until the boys reach puberty and start to exhibit masculine traits. Sometimes things can get a little awkward at the entrance. When is a boy too old to follow his mother into the women's hall? Some boys have a full-on beard at eleven, while others still have peach fuzz at sixteen. Most of the time, the decision comes down to the amount of facial hair.

These days, it's increasingly common for weddings to be mixed, something that was unthinkable in my childhood. Just the other day, Father said that he actually likes mixed weddings because you can enjoy the party as a family. Mother still considers them entirely unacceptable and baulked at Father's outrageous remark. So, he thought it was normal to see women dancing lavishly with men on the dance floor? She called it a highly dishonourable, immoral development and was disturbed by the fact that it was becoming increasingly commonplace. You were supposed to have 'protective jeal-ousy' for the women in your family. This is why I was never allowed to dance at a mixed wedding, only at segregated weddings. Mother doesn't even remove her long black cloak in mixed company, nor do any of the other strait-laced women at the mosque.

Hell

We stand on the pavement in front of our house in the city waiting for the taxi to Kümbet, the begetters' village. The heat beats down on the buildings, mountains and paving stones in the distance.

Halil is dressed for the occasion: he's wearing a palm tree-patterned tank top with light blue shorts. I've done my best to look as summery as possible, but that's pretty hard when you're not allowed to show any skin at all. The only other option is one of those desert dresses, but that's not really my style.

Lately, I've been having trouble understanding the point of the cloth I wrap around my head every morning. It's supposed to cover my beauty, but of course that's ridiculous. Was it really going to protect me from all the wild testosterone I would encounter outside? I can see how a burka or a long, concealing robe might hide your charms, but a headscarf? I highly doubt it.

Repetition and habit can make the weirdest, most absurd practices seem like the most normal things in the world. Everyone – including Mother – knows full well that a headscarf doesn't conceal a woman's attractiveness. It's just a cultural symbol in disguise; you wear it because your mother, your aunts, your grandmothers and your cousins wear it too. You wear it to show that you believe in the right god.

You wear it to quietly set yourself apart from unbelieving women, whom you see as fruit without a peel, lollies without a wrapper, as the online imams like to call them. Any fly can drink their nectar, and they will quickly rot away because they have no layer to protect them, but a woman who covers herself remains fresh. And once that fruit is ripe, it is peeled by its rightful owner for his ultimate enjoyment. I used to want to be a fruit with a peel. But not any more. Besides, I'd already been peeled for a while by then.

The only thing I bought while we were in Sivas was a necklace with Atatürk's signature on it. That signature could be found on everything here: jewellery, phone cases, shirts, caps and notebooks. His ideas were alive and well among the leftist youth; many even had a tattoo of his face or name. When Father saw the necklace, he demanded to know why I was wearing it.

'Just because. I stand by the things he achieved.'

'Like hanging imams? Imitating the West and banning the headscarf and other religious clothing? Converting the Aya Sophia into a museum? What things? Do you support those things too? Shame on you! You're wearing the symbol of a ruthless, alcoholic bastard who didn't possess an ounce of faith and ripped the devotion out of people's hearts! Take it off! I don't want to see it again, why don't you get your facts straight about him first before you start wearing brainless symbols that you don't understand, don't be so short-sighted! You wear a headscarf – he hated headscarves! And there you are with his signature around your neck. You're a walking contradiction. You idiot.'

198

The way he put it, you'd almost think I'd chosen to wear the headscarf myself. I had no desire to argue with my begetters about their rigid sense of identity; it was like screaming into the void. So I took off the necklace and threw it away. You wait, I thought at that moment, if I'm ever free from all this I will have that signature permanently engraved on my forearm. Me, of all people. Or on my forehead, even better.

I'd had it with the holiday. I was homesick for the Netherlands and desperately needed a good night's sleep.

The first call to prayer in Sivas is at four in morning, and it wakes me up every night. At home in Amsterdam, we had a digital clock that made the call, but in Sivas the minarets take care of that. And it is deafening. The imam in our neighbourhood has the voice of a crow and my begetters thought it was an excellent idea to buy a house right next to a minaret so that we could hear him five times a day, so that his voice would rattle deep in our corneas and in every fibre, cell and atom of our being. Sometimes the windows shake, it's so loud. In those moments, I realise how nice it is to live in the Netherlands, where you aren't confronted by the dominance of the state religion five times a day. For ten minutes you hear chanting, at 4 a.m., 1 p.m., 6 p.m., 10 p.m. and finally at midnight. Five times a day, the *ezan* mocks the disbelief of infidel Turks. And if someone has died – it doesn't matter who, could be any resident of the city – there's a special call that's extra-long and intense. After all, memento mori. Just as hypochondria is an all-consuming desire for illness and decay, so is religion a desire for death.

If you're lying down during the *ezan*, you're supposed to sit up straight out of respect. If I'm sprawled out on the sofa reading, Mother will come in, scold me for being a disrespectful dog and force me to sit up until it's over.

199

Every year, there comes a day when we make the journey to my begetters' village. And today is that day. I'm not the least bit happy about it. It's hell on earth, even worse than the city. I spend a couple of days there each year, and each year I'm struck by just how awful it is. It's a primitive place, as if you've travelled through time and landed in the Middle Ages. Let's just say that it is not entirely suited to the needs and desires of the modern being. There are no paved roads, the houses are all run-down, and the people look even worse than the houses. Only the animals seem happy. At least they're protected from unscrupulous, cash-driven farming practices. Almost everyone is a farmer, which explains why every house has a stable and hordes of chickens in the front yard. The cattle graze all day in the open air and are free to roam in the mountains. Now, I know there are people out there who find the idea of a digital detox appealing, but let's just say it's not for me. Every year, this becomes abundantly clear in Kümbet, where the lack of internet connection drives me to the brink of insanity. And you can't just take a shower; you have to heat up the water first on some kind of stove. If the water gets too hot, you have to wait for it to cool down, then wash yourself by scooping it up with a plastic cup. On top of that, the squat toilet is outdoors, so if you need to pee in the middle of the night, you have to go outside, where you're surrounded by the sound of crickets and vermin. The toilet is full of snails and other critters; sometimes there's even a dead mouse in front of the pot, or you find yourself face to face with the beady eyes of a rat. Once, when I was thirteen, I went to the loo in the middle of the night and was spied on by a fox. After that, I learned to hold it until morning. Even if it gave me a bladder infection.

We've barely been in the taxi for half an hour when I start

to get car-sick. I ask Allah why me, why this agony? My face is all rosy, unlike my mood. I pull the box of Primatour out of my bumbag and take another pill. I'd already taken one before we got in the taxi, as did Father, Halil and Defne. The disharmonious state of one's health gets passed on to one's children, creating a long line of suffering. In addition to car-sickness, I had also inherited Father and Oma's itchy ears. I'd seen the doctor about it several times, but there was no cure. It was an odd ailment for which they had no explanation. They said it must be some kind of allergy.

I can feel yesterday's meals bubbling up in my body. I look out of the window, trying to take my mind off it. I watch the colossal, breathtaking mountains pass by and shrink into the distance behind me, disappearing on the infinite horizon. New things appear; they grow and grow, and then shrink again, just like everything else before. This goes on for hours. There's not a cloud in the clear, blue sky.

Three hours later, we arrive in the village. My thoughts have been reduced to sludge. I feel nauseous, and as soon as we step out of the car I see Father throwing up a few metres away. Every half-hour someone has puked; what must the taxi driver think? Mother complains that she had to endure the sour smell of vomit for the entire ride and look at our greenish-purple faces. I didn't ask for this, so she can take it up with God.

A tiny stray kitten springs at my feet and looks up at me sweetly. Kümbet, and Turkey in general, is overrun with stray cats, even in the cities. The same goes for dogs, or rather one type of dog: the Kangal, also known as the Anatolian shepherd. I'm terrified of them. And because the terrain around Sivas is so mountainous, they're everywhere. Traditionally, they're used to protect sheep from bears and wolves. They work together, the begetters explained; some dogs stay with the flock while others chase after the wolves over long distances. In the Netherlands, Kangals are used as guard dogs.

Defne picks up the stray kitten and pets it. 'Mummy, look how cute! Can I take her home? Please?'

'No, animals have no business in houses, they belong outside,' she says firmly. Mother is fundamentally against house pets; she thinks keeping an animal is selfish and therefore sinful. Moreover, they're unclean. How can one pray and prepare food in a house if there is a creature walking around that pees, poops and sheds hair everywhere? And if you're suddenly licked by an animal before prayer you'd have to wash yourself all over again.

Mother also taught me that you can't kill bugs or pick flowers, you have to let them live. If I didn't know any better, I'd think she was some kind of vegan or hippie. 'The Quran says you shouldn't even kill an ant,' she'd say. Well, that is true, but the Quran says a lot of stuff. Islam is, in principle, a religion of love – with a 'but'. That love all goes out the window on the eve of Eid al-Adha, when she spends the entire day hacking away at a sheep or bull on the kitchen table. Surely, those animals have more consciousness than insects or flowers. Mother is full of contradictions, as is her ideology, which is known for rejecting all forms of ambiguity.

Normally I'd say that contradiction is the hallmark of every living human being, but that's a different kind of contradiction, one that arises from doubt, regret and reform, the mothers of all wisdom, not from adamance. Mother never doubts. And the absence of doubt is the absence of spiritual growth. This was thus a backward form of contradiction. Staunch believers are extremely decisive, as are psychopaths for that matter, because they're not bothered by the need to consider other people's interests or entertain doubt. Mother is an exclamation mark; Father more of a question mark. A question mark is an exclamation mark that looks down uncertainly to see if it's in the right place, whether it's on thin ice. When it's relieved of this uncertainty, it too becomes an exclamation mark.

I hear a loud bellowing. The sun is going down and the cows are returning to their stalls. I see a shepherd off in the distance attempting to keep the cattle in line by slapping them when they veer off in the wrong direction. One of them has to impertinently take a crap right in front of me; the smell of it is revolting. There are cowpats everywhere, no one cleans them up and the whole place smells like shit. After a while, they dry up and people store them in the cellar for winter.

The cows know their way around. Even after a cow has been sold to someone else, it'll still keep coming back to its old stables and get aggressive with its former owner to avoid having to leave. It's a tragic sight; I've witnessed it several times. Usually, the new owner is called over to pick it up, but the cow still refuses to go; it will moo so loudly that it's more of a screech, and then come the tears. The former owner hates to send the animal away like this, but he has no choice but to beat it with a stick, otherwise it will never learn. After a few hard blows, the cow doesn't come back any more. It understands that it's no longer welcome, that it's not wanted; it accepts its fate as an outcast. I could learn from those cows.

I walk to the house where we're staying. It's a bit of an eye-catcher in the village; it's bigger, cleaner, prettier and, above all, sturdier than the rest. It towers over the other buildings but not as pompously as the new mosque. My grandparents, unlike the other elderly people in this town, have a pretty sweet deal; they sent their six children off to Holland and in return they got this house. There were other parents in the village whose children went abroad, but they didn't live there any more, they had followed their kids to places like France, Germany, Belgium, Italy and the Netherlands. Or otherwise moved to the city. My grandparents were the only ones who had deliberately chosen to remain in their village despite their growing wealth; they didn't see any reason to leave town just because they had more money. Or, as they put it, here they had the world in a box; all the incoming euros had guaranteed them a carefree life and they could live here in a state of *très bien être*. I can't help but wonder what on earth they do all day; it must be unsettling to have had to fight your whole life to survive and then suddenly receive a sack of gold from your children. It's like hitting the jackpot, but what in God's name are a couple of devout elderly Muslims going to do with a jackpot in fucking Kümbet? Now I know why Mother spends half the damn day video calling with her parents.

Grandma and Grandpa were never going to move to the Netherlands, that was haram. According to the village imam, as a true believer you shouldn't emigrate from an Islamic country to a non-Islamic country because, over time, all the corruption you would encounter there would have a negative effect on your devotion. It would, like it or not, engulf you and corrupt your soul, obscure your sense of truth, confuse your heart. Well, I've got to hand it to him, Amsterdam is certainly the mecca of all things forbidden by God, but then again it's also home to burka-wearing women and mosques with loud calls to prayer. It's just a matter of where you are in the city, Allebéplein or Spuistraat. Whereas other villagers ignored the imam's warning – it didn't suit them, after all a sermon doesn't fill a stomach – and fled to Europe as soon as they had the chance, my grandparents remained steadfast, their loyalty to Allah and the village imam unwavering. They wouldn't set foot in the land of the pagans, not even on holiday. In fact, every summer they tried to convince their children to return home permanently. Surely they had made enough money by now, what else did they need to do there? They had more than enough to keep themselves dressed and fed until they died, what more did they want? Their sons all had big houses in Sivas with all the bells and whistles, and they even earned a passive income by renting out their other houses. My uncles on my mother's side had done well for themselves; they'd all become successful contractors, and all without much education and speaking only broken Dutch.

Mother had grown up with five brothers, all of whom went to primary school. She, however, did not; it was a sin to send girls to school because they would inevitably distract the boys in class. Moreover, they didn't belong there; educated women lose their character when they try to become equal to men, and no one wanted that. Mother was in charge of preparing her brothers' lunchboxes, washing their clothes, holding a lamp over their shoulders so they'd have enough light to read and write in the evenings, and occasionally providing them with a foot massage when they were tired from walking the many miles to and from school.

Despite the fact that Grandma threw the topic of reimmigration in her children's faces every summer and begged them to come home, mainly because she was lonely in her old age now that everyone was gone, her children had already sold their souls to the devil of fortune and enjoyed a good life in the Netherlands. All except Mother. She was always making hawkish attempts to broach the subject and convince Father to return to Turkey. She argued that we should stay in our homeland, where we could be more ourselves, where we could speak our own language, be around people who shared our morals, manners and religion. People like us. Back in Holland, things were going downhill: the children of immigrants all spoke Dutch and were losing their mother tongue; the younger generations weren't even practising Muslims and had fallen captive to those pernicious Western ideas taught in schools; they believed that freedom and individuality were the most important things on earth, and that you should be able to choose and criticise everything in your life with no respect for authority or the community, without any obligation to conform to the whole. In fact, they were learning the opposite: to question every possible authority, to doubt everything, to assume nothing is true. A person could only be happy when they felt secure, and there was no security in the Netherlands. Security is the one thing that every organism longs for, an unsurpassable feeling only found through membership of a substantial community, and such communities only existed because the people in them shared a sense of belonging and an emotional bond: the same ethnicity, language, religion, morals and customs. These things were the source of feelings of solidarity, loyalty, shared destiny and the obligation to help one another. Anyone who thought they could live without them was destined to an icy existence based solely on economic gain. 'A nation is nothing but a big family, and we will never belong to the Dutch, nor will our children or grandchildren; we do not conform to the rules of their community, we look different, we have different ideas. And if we did conform, we would give ourselves away, surrender our own identity and community.'

Didn't Father see that his children were becoming increasingly obstinate and less malleable, that they were straying from their true selves? In the Netherlands, children were raised to believe in the big 'I', to see individuality as the most important thing. 'That's why they have no security, no community, no sense of mutual trust or commitment, that's why they're all so unhappy, so spiritually lonely, so full of internal doubt; they're defenceless, fragile and possess a total lack of drive and ecstasy. You learn to reject authority, to figure out your own path using trial and error. As a result, people make all kinds of unnecessary mistakes and become incredibly selfish. Adjusting to others, occasionally sacrificing your time for the greater good, taking other people into account, all that is out the window. You're only true to yourself, no one else. How many Dutch people would die for their country, for their beliefs? *Very* few. That is a fundamental difference in our mentality!'

Mother didn't want to lose another child to that decadent culture: Defne was still young, only eight, and with her she intended to do things differently, enough was enough. Defne could go to school in Turkey and easily adapt to the Turkish education system and culture. 'If the tree is still wet, you can bend it in all directions.' On top of that, she'd heard that there were special Quranic boarding schools here where children could spend their days learning about all the facets of Islam and go on to become religious teachers themselves. Wouldn't that be wonderful? Wouldn't God be delighted, to see them commit their child to His service, away from worldly influences? Away from the Netherlands, away from the devil's influence? Surely, Father could find a job here with God's help. As long as your intentions were pure and you took a step in the right direction, Allah the Almighty would assist you in your time of need.

'No way. I'm not going anywhere, and neither is Defne, not even if you drag us across the ground,' I declared the last time she brought it up. 'No one asked you for your opinion,' she retorted. Every time the topic came up, I had a slight panic attack, not because I worried for myself – because either way I wasn't going – but for Defne, who was unfortunately the product of their sperm and egg and still underage.

I devised a plan to kidnap Defne if things ever got to that point. I could lie to Youth Services that she was being abused by the begetters and get her taken out of the house. It wouldn't even be a lie – although they weren't abusing her physically, Mother's plan seemed worse to me than that. But what if Defne told them I was lying? She could speak for herself, of course. Plus, the Youth Services were terrible, I'd heard that from Lucas, who didn't come from the sort of strict family I did. Shit. I didn't know. I was better off trying to talk Mother out of it and enlisting as many people to help me as I could.

But before this became necessary, Father informed her that returning to Turkey was too risky financially and would put us in a precarious position. He had a steady income in the Netherlands, while in Turkey unemployment and inflation were high and wages were low. He would have to save up a lot of money before making such a big step. At that, I was ready to drop down on my knees and thank God for income inequality.

Until Mother heard that those Quranic boarding schools also existed in the Netherlands. My heart skipped a beat when she mentioned it. I hadn't thought of that, of Turkey's long arm, or I guess you could call it a voluntary prosthesis. Mother was already working out a plan. Besides, it wouldn't hurt to have Defne out of the house, they'd have more space at home, and Halil could have his own room. I did everything I could to get Halil on my side. At first he was indifferent, but eventually he realised that this could have a huge impact on our little sister's future and those schools were nothing like the weekend schools we went to, that they were way more radical and could seal her fate for ever. We approached the begetters together and talked them out of the idea, but it was mostly Halil who convinced them; obviously, they didn't listen to me.

Hell, Continued

Father thanks the taxi driver and pays him. Defne puts the stray kitten back on the ground: 'I hope we meet again, sweet kitty. Unfortunately, you can't come inside with us, but take care of yourself!' She seems confident the Kümbetan kitten can understand Dutch. Halil is already climbing the stairs to Grandma and Grandpa's house. Mother whistles at him.

'Excuse me? Where do you think you're going? Who's going to carry up these suitcases, the porter?'

Halil walks back to the taxi van, opens the luggage compartment and hoists a heavy suitcase on his back.

'Jeez, what's in here, a dead body?'

'Stop whining, you're not a woman. Come on, I didn't breastfeed you all those years for nothing.'

Mother has a theory that if a man is flabby or 'effeminate', it's because he was weaned on artificial milk. Or because women were having children far too late and were no longer able to produce tigers, and thus gave birth to these half-boiled boys who couldn't put a dent in a pack of butter. 'You can't make good oil with old olives,' as our entirely uneducated yet all-knowing house philosopher says.

Halil huffs and puffs his way up the stairs with the massive suitcase, risking his life as there are no handrails in the village and the staircase is entirely self-supporting. Just a single row of steps, completely exposed. One wrong move and you'd fall eight metres down. There's a barn under the house, but they don't keep cattle any more. Grandpa got rid of all his cows a long time ago, once his children's money started rolling in.

As a toddler, I fell down these stairs multiple times. At the bottom is a square stone basin, about three metres deep, filled with water. It used to be for the cows. One time, I don't remember exactly what happened, but Mother said I slipped on the stairs, fell into the water and hit my head. I was bleeding, and naturally I couldn't swim, so I almost drowned. She rescued me just in time.

Come to think of it, that wasn't the only time I had a near-death experience in the village. I once fell off the balcony when I was a baby. One of Mother's dim-witted second cousins was holding me and somehow managed to drop me. I must've been one lucky kid, because there was a pile of hay under the balcony to break my fall. Of course, if you ask Mother, it was Allah who protected me. Fortunately, I'm a very open-minded person and don't rule anything out, even the existence and special protection of Allah, although it does make me wonder why other people don't receive this same protection, for example an innocent girl in Somalia who's about to be circumcised with a blunt razor blade. The sun and moon shine upon us, as does the Father, praise be to God. Those are the types of questions that Mother doesn't have an answer for, I suspect. Most of the time, she knows so much. Perhaps it's easier to close your eyes to reality than to your own beliefs. A comfortable conservative will stop building dams because he feels safe on dry land. But he still has to make sure that other people keep the water out.

Just as the devout remain firm in their faith despite all setbacks, despite all the children dying of cancer and all the injustice and misery in the world, so I remained firm in my disbelief despite all blessings.

Father takes a suitcase and heads up the stairs as well. Mother and I don't have to carry anything heavy, we're women. We pick up a couple of light bags and head up to the house. Grandma opens the door beaming, even her pupils are smiling. She wipes away her tears of joy with her head-scarf. She hugs me so tightly that I gasp for air. She's a strong woman. 'Oh, how I've missed you, my dear children,' she says in an elderly voice. She plops four wet kisses on either side of my face and then proceeds to suffocate Defne. 'Ouch, Grandma, not so tight,' my sister squeals in Dutch. Defne often forgets that she has to speak Turkish. Mother says that starting today she doesn't want to hear another word of Dutch until we get home. Defne repeats the sentence in Turkish.

'Sorry, my dear, the apple of my eye, I missed you so much that I lost myself for a moment, I'm so sorry if I hurt you,' Grandma says exaggeratedly. I see Defne pinch her nose with her fingers. I wave at her to cut it out, but inside I have to laugh. I pretend to look angry, so she'll understand that it was rude. She pinches her nose again anyway. Grandma reeks of cow manure, just like everybody around here. She may no longer have cows of her own, but she still stays busy helping the women in the neighbourhood with theirs.

Mother swats Defne's hand away from her nose and commands her to walk inside. Then she embraces her mother with tears in her eyes. 'Oh, how big they have grown, *mashallah*!' Grandma says. 'Come, come, let's go inside, and welcome to you too, my son-in-law, welcome!' she says to Father, motioning us in. I walk wearily into the living room. There

212

are no couches, only colourful, hand-woven pouffes on the floor. Both the floors and the walls are covered with carpets, each one different. The pouffes have the same patterns as the carpets, with all kinds of random figures and bright colours, with fringes on the sides.

The first thing I notice are all the mosquitoes in the room. Oh, I forgot to mention how horrible they are here. For some reason, they never bother me in the city. In the Netherlands, you'll get one or two of them at night, but in Kümbet they are fucking everywhere. They buzz constantly, during the day, the night, inside, outside, it's enough to drive you mad. If there's a plate of food in front of you, there'll be at least twenty mosquitoes on it. The mosquito strips hanging from the ceiling are completely covered with the little black devils. I almost vomit. I count seven strips, all completely full; they obviously haven't been changed in a long time. Grandma and Grandpa don't seem to mind the mosquitoes, so who knows, maybe these are the same strips we hung last summer. I'm already dreading the night.

We chat with Grandma about the trip. She asks why we didn't bring our other Grandma from the Netherlands like we usually did. 'She prefers Holland,' Mother says. That is true, Oma hates Kümbet as much as I do, if not more, even though she was born and raised here. I think it brings back too many awful memories. Besides, Oma likes her comfort. She doesn't want to use a squat toilet or sit on a pouffe on the floor or deal with power outages and mosquitoes everywhere; she wants hot water from the tap.

Grandma is disappointed to hear it, she would've liked to spend time with her old friend. Grandpa was still outside, he'd been to the mosque to pray and had just got home. Mother waves angrily at me to sit up; I'm sprawled out with nausea.

213

You can't lie down in such a shameless position in a man's presence, even if he is your Grandpa or someone else in the family. The same goes for your father in a lot of Turkish families, but luckily ours isn't strict about it, and I'm allowed to lie on the couch or put my feet on the table when he's around. I remember how the begetters used to argue about this. Mother accused Father of not caring enough to teach me the traditional rules of female etiquette that I would one day need with my future husband. She often irritably accused Father of allowing me too much freedom – he even let me sit with my legs crossed. How utterly scandalous. Women were supposed to sit with their knees together, without leaning back on the couch or stretching their legs out in front of them, and most importantly they should never sit with their knees pointing outwards, which is known as manspreading nowadays. Only men could sit like that. Men could sit however they wanted; they didn't have to assume any special position in a woman's presence.

After Mother's prodding gaze, I jump to my feet to greet Grandpa. Mother beckons me again and points to her hand, signifying that I should kiss Grandpa's hand. I hate kissing hands, even at the end of Ramadan. Halil goes first. I greet Grandpa and say that I'm happy to see him, then I bend forwards and plant a soft kiss on his hand. It feels more like a gesture of servitude than of respect. I'm really not a fan of hierarchical family relationships.

We spend a little while catching up, and then the real misery begins: an entire week here. A week of sleepless nights because, other than the calls to prayer, it's way too quiet and way too dark, not like Amsterdam, where I'm lulled to sleep by the sound of passing trains, cars, subways, the television, Netflix, a podcast, and where there are so many street lights it never really gets dark.

The days drag by. I can't go out for a walk even though the natural landscape is the most impressive thing to see here, if not the only thing. Women aren't supposed to wander around outside, and if you do you'll almost certainly be harassed by young men who've probably never seen a chick in their lives, let alone a nicely dressed one. The women here stay home and go out only when absolutely necessary, and only fully covered. In other words, the men here have only ever seen beautiful women on TV, and the only way they can release their sexual frustration is by watching porn. I've never seen them doing this myself, but Halil told me that he'd heard from local guys that they spend most of the day jacking off to audiovisual erotica. Understandable, I guess, it's not like there's anything else to do in Kümbet. Nothing ever happens, there's nothing to look forward to. There's no form of entertainment to speak of, and every day is just like the last. There are no shops, no cafés, no community centres, no cinemas, no swimming pools. Just houses, cows and shit. That's why all the local teens dream of nothing more than owning a car so that they can drive to the city or, even better, move. But you can't just buy a car, you need money, and nobody has any money. There is, however, a brand-new mosque. You can't miss it; it towers over everything in the village. It wasn't there last summer. Grandma told me that Sultan Erdoğan, as they affectionately call him here, had it built for them. It's a massive, bulky structure, painted in eye-catching colours, an ultra-modern building among all the crumbling houses. The minarets jut into the sky, unabashed and uncompromising. I decide to go and see it for myself with Halil. When I'm with him, I'm not harassed by men on the street, only ogled. I ignore their gaze, though their eyes burn into my flesh. I can't help but notice one unfortunate-looking guy of about thirty wink at me like an imbecile with a chilli flake in his eyes.

215

It isn't time for prayer yet, so the mosque is empty. We are the only people there, which is convenient because it means I can see the men's hall and Halil the women's. The men's hall is absolutely breathtaking. In the centre is a massive chandelier just begging for attention. The carpets are soft, colourful and intricate. The windows are decorated with images of red tulips and the ceiling with Ottoman motifs. The colours in the wall ornamentation are overwhelmingly beautiful. The hall is so large that our voices echo. Say whatever you want about mosques, they have a way of stirring the soul. Defne notices the echo too, and she amuses herself by shouting random phrases like 'Amsterdam-West is the best' and singing 'Head, shoulders, knees and toes'. Then she starts running around and playing a game where you can't touch certain spots on the carpet.

In the courtyard outside, which is reserved for the men (and women can enter only if there are no men present), there are comfortable benches, vine-covered fences and walls, flowers, lemon and plum trees, and a fountain. Colourful little birds chirp about. It's quite picturesque, so different from the busy streets of Amsterdam; it's quiet and peaceful, no one is in a hurry, nobody cares about punctuality. But I'd take Amsterdam any day. All the silence around here drives me crazy, especially at night.

The grass in the garden looks so soft and inviting that I want to strip off and lie in it naked – it is certainly hot enough – I might have actually done it too, but then I think of the headlines in the Turkish newspapers tomorrow: 'Woman lies nude in mosque garden'.

After we've seen everything else there is to see, I want to have a look at the women's hall. I need to get out of the men's area anyway as it is almost prayer time. Not to mention the fact that I am on my period, which makes me unclean, but fortunately no one can see that. Halil doesn't want to come; he's afraid that a woman would walk in, and he'd be mortified. I tell him to stop whining, that it's just a quick peek, but he refuses adamantly, so I go in with Defne.

I push open the door and am immediately perplexed. Not by the beauty but by the lack thereof. The women's hall is much smaller and has no decoration to speak of. It is utterly drab, with no microphone, no *minbar.* Women obviously can't preach themselves or have their own imam, all they can do is listen in on what the men's imam is saying in the hall next door. There are no bookshelves laden with heavy volumes, because what are women supposed to do with books? Surely they wouldn't even understand them, it's all much too complicated. Let them focus on taking care of the children and baking bread. As the Turkish proverb goes: women have long hair but short brains. Thus, there is no reason for them to wipe the dough off their hands and have an opinion about matters that are none of their concern.

We walk outside. Halil is chatting with a man who looks about forty-five. The guy had probably asked him who he was, where he came from, like everybody does around here. The locals always want to know our begetters' names – usually they've never heard of them – and who our grandparents are. Then we're enthusiastically invited to drink tea with them at their house, which I never accept because the last time I did Halil wasn't with me and the couple asked me if I would marry their son. They wouldn't take no for an answer. These people would do anything to save their children from their fate by sending them to the Netherlands, so if things had gone south, I might have found myself trapped. In an extreme case, I could have been raped or kidnapped while they tried to claim consent and force my family to rescue me from my own sin by marrying me off to the man in question and taking him with me back to Holland. Mother had warned me about this, apparently it had happened to a girl from France. So, I guess I was lucky; I didn't get raped. Maybe because the son wasn't home.

The next question the locals usually ask is: 'Which do you like better, *Hollanda* or Turkey?' Naturally, they're curious about Europe, a place they've never been to but have heard about all their lives. They are, after all, the ones who stayed behind. Some, like Grandpa and Grandma, preferred to live in poverty than perform manual labour in a non-Islamic country. Others were denied permits because there were already enough migrant workers. Either way, their fate was sealed. Apparently, this man had asked Halil this question as well, because I heard my brother saying, 'Both have their advantages.'

'Of course, you like it better there. Here's there's nothing, just cow dung,' the man says with a smile, exposing his crooked yellow teeth. 'Remember, young man, your homeland isn't where you were born or where your parents were born, your homeland is where you fill your stomach. And from what I hear, the Netherlands keeps you very well fed. You get government benefits if you can't work and all kinds of assistance if you have a low income. The state will pay your rent, make sure you're first in line for a nice house and give you money for your children. Your kids go to school for free until they're ready to work, healthcare and medicine are affordable, inflation is low and groceries are cheap. You should thank Allah that you live there and not here. We're just barely scraping by. We don't dare to shit for fear of going hungry.'

How you should answer the question depends on who's

asking. If you say you prefer the Netherlands, another person might accuse your of denying your identity and tell you that you should love your homeland despite all its disadvantages and lack of facilities. But if you say you think Turkey is better, they might insist that you're wrong and start going on and on about all the problems here. In this case the man continues: 'No doubt the Netherlands is economically better off, but that doesn't mean you should give up your language and religion. You have to know where you come from, where your roots are. You have to find a balance.'

So yeah.

'*Inshallah*, you and your children can also come to Europe one day,' Halil says.

'One shouldn't say amen to a prayer for the impossible,' the man replies, his eyes to the ground.

As we walk back, Defne complains about the pebbles in her sandals. The roads are all unpaved and used by cows, cars and pedestrians alike. Every time a tractor goes by, you're left in a cloud of dust that sticks to every inch of clothing and leaves your mouth full of sand. Most of the cars around here are pimped with illegal exhausts so they can go faster, leaving behind a trail of black smoke. It smells terrible.

We pause for a moment so Defne can empty her sandals. I forgot to tell her to wear sneakers instead. A swarm of children passes by. They're different ages and a variety of heights but all equally skinny. They stare at us in awe. Their clothes are dirty and ragged, their shoes worn, with toes sticking out. Some shirts are too small, others way too big. One boy is wearing flip-flops twice as long as his feet. I feel awkward as I take in the pitiful scene. These children, living in a deep state of poverty, are standing there, gazing at our little sister, a girl their own age, dressed in the latest collection from

H&M, clothes that I bought for her myself. Mother had made sure to alter the sleeves so that Defne would get used to covering her arms.

The contrast with these children was so stark that I found it unsettling.

I hear the girls talking about how cool Defne looks, going on about her hair clips, something they'd never had. 'She looks like one of those girls on TV,' says one little girl in a stain-covered shirt. I feel a lump in my throat. Any one of us could just as easily have been one of them. It's pure coincidence that we were born in Amsterdam-West and not in Kümbet. If Father's father hadn't been a young, healthy man who was selected to go to the Netherlands, we would've grown up the same way. I want these children to have what we have; I see myself in them. They look like us.

One of the girls can't stop staring at Defne's sandals. Finally, she walks up to Defne and points to her feet. 'They're *really* pretty,' she stammers. I can't stand it. The Little Prince was right: what kind of world is this? Everywhere you went you saw hard edges, sharp edges, drought. But how often can you be the *gutmensch*? Even if I were to take every single person in this village back to Holland with me, what good would it do? What about all the other villages? And all those other countries where things were even worse? The Netherlands can't take them all, nor can Europe.

Moreover, I'm not so sure it would be a good thing if everyone had access to our way of life; our planet couldn't take it. What if every soul on earth had a car and a refrigerator? There are just too many of us, and economic migrants get the short end of the stick. They can't blame war, and the lack of economic opportunity in their middle-of-nowhere town isn't a valid reason for requesting asylum. We, the Euroturks, are the products of a deal. Europe needed us to help rebuild after the Second World War, and we're still there.

These kinds of questions gnawed at my mind and conscience. Not death itself, but rather the need to kill in order to survive and evolve, and how it was God's cruellest joke on humankind. You could be either hunter or prey, and often you don't get to choose yourself. Fate decided for you. We're all living under the same sun but not in the same light. If it's true that everyone gets what they deserve, then why do the good and innocent suffer?

Last week, Mother and I went into Amsterdam together to buy clothes for Defne. Dam Square was full of activists wearing face masks and carrying around laptops so they could show people videos depicting the horrors of the meat industry. They were trying to get people to go vegan, claiming it was unethical to torment a living being with a consciousness, feelings and the ability to feel pain, purely for human consumption. Mother was confused when a young woman marched up to us and made her smooth, unsettling pitch. She handed us a flyer full of pictures of bloated pigs, chickens piled on top of one another, and cows that, the girl claimed, were raped over and over again so that they would continue to produce milk. If they birthed a calf, it was immediately taken from them, leaving both mother and child in distress. It was time for the objectification of animals to stop. Now. She asked what we thought of this and whether we might be willing to switch to meatless alternatives and stop buying dairy products. I translated for Mother. She replied that she thought it was a noble cause and was glad to see this young woman standing up for animal rights. She agreed that the way these animals were being treated was appalling and strictly forbidden by God. I translated for the woman and told her that I respected what they were doing as well. She thanked us and asked if we might consider going vegan. Not only would it save animal lives, it would also benefit the environment and our own health, because meat was full of antibiotics and hormones.

Mother thought that was nonsense. 'Tell this woman that she doesn't need to worry about that, that God created the animals for our service and that she is free to enjoy a piece of meat without feeling guilty about it. Besides, if you buy organic halal meat, you don't have to worry about additives, and you can trust that the animals have been treated well.' I hesitated to translate this accurately but in the end I did. The woman was at a loss for words, but the look on her face said enough. It was a look that could be understood in any language. If she told Mother she was wrong, she would be saying that Mother's entire worldview was wrong. 'I'm sorry, madam, but animals do not exist to serve us, they have their own lives and their own pleasures, just like we do. This is a very wrong way of thinking, and I'm sorry to hear that you're not open to another point of view. There is nothing ethical about tormenting and killing an animal for your own enjoyment when there are plenty of equally delicious and nutritious alternatives available. Muslims can be vegans too, you know!'

I translated this, and Mother said: 'Let's keep shopping, Büsra. This girl isn't going to shut up.' So we did.

At H&M there were all kinds of light summery clothes in pretty colours. I picked out a few things for Defne, shorts and a couple of sleeveless tops. But Mother told me to put them back. Defne was eight and it was time for her to start getting used to more modest clothing, she wasn't a toddler any more. 'We don't need to buy very much. After summer vacation, she'll have to start wearing a headscarf and long dress to

222

school, so we won't need these clothes any more anyway. And no animals or other creatures on them, either. You can't pray with an image of a living being on your clothes.'

Damn it. For a second, I forgot that, at an Islamic school, little girls aren't allowed to show skin. Not even in gym class, which was separate from the boys, as were swimming lessons. And there were no showers; it was inappropriate for your classmates to see your genitals, even if they had the same ones. According to the Islamic doctrine, you have to cover your *awrah* from everyone except your spouse, so that includes other women. It also means that you can't get a bikini wax. In cases of life and death you can be seen by a male doctor, but only if you've done everything you can to find a female one. That's what I learned.

I wondered how a woman could ever get an IUD under these laws. If you ask me, the religious leaders should give that a little more thought. Maybe it would lead to new schools of Islam. The more schools, the more joy.

I can't help but notice how many pregnant women and people with disabilities there are in Kümbet. There are also people suffering from all kinds of mental illnesses. The place is pretty much an open-air psych ward. The other day a girl about my age knocked on our door. I opened it, said hello and asked her who she was. She stared at me intently for a long time and suddenly proclaimed that I was her long-lost sister. She pulled me into a tight hug and drooled all over my blouse. I didn't know what had hit me.

'Oh my sister! I love you! I missed you! You were in my dream!' Just then, Grandma showed up, handed her a packet of biscuits and told her to go home, that there were a lot of men in the house so they couldn't invite her in. In Kümbet, the men and women visit separately, so if there are men over, it's normal for a female visitor to be rejected at the door. The girl was delighted with the biscuits and trotted down the stairs, repeating over and over again that I was her sister. When she reached the bottom, she turned around and shot me a look that was at first serious, then elated. Her clothes were dirty and ragged, and I could see her unkempt feet sticking out of her broken sandals.

'What was that all about?' I asked Grandma.

'That's Nuray. She's not well. She keeps coming by because I'm the only person around here who gives her any attention. I feel sorry for her, may Allah heal her.'

'What exactly does she have?'

'Nobody knows, a disease of the mind, but the doctor is too expensive, and her parents don't even have enough to eat. Sometimes she can get really wild. If she sees a cucumber, she'll start trembling and running around like a chicken with its head cut off, she'll scream and shake, sometimes she even faints, which is why I always make sure there are no cucumbers in sight when she comes by, otherwise there's no calming her down.'

'Cucumbers?' I wonder if she's joking, if I've landed in some kind of tragic comedy. But Nuray wasn't the only one. There were more people in the village with strange conditions, some physical, some not. At first, I didn't understand why, but then Halil explained that it's because so many people married within their own families. Marrying your cousin was more of a rule than an exception around here. Even the imams approved of it. Of course, I'd completely forgotten.

It reminded me of a friend I had in high school, Esra. She was a smart girl, in the pre-university track like me, but she had three severely disabled sisters. They couldn't do anything by themselves. They needed help going to the toilet, eating and walking. I went over to her house one time, and I was utterly bewildered. It was a huge house, with long, wide halls and huge rooms. It looked kind of like a hospital. They'd received it from the government so they could care for the three sick children. There were all kinds of special devices lying around. I got a nasty feeling in my stomach when I met her sisters. Their bodies were all out of proportion, and they just stared at you with an angry look in their eyes. They were clearly in pain and would start screaming at any random moment.

Every time Esra invited me back, I lied and said that I had plans. She was used to that and didn't seem surprised, but I couldn't shake the feeling that I was secretly afraid to see them again, which weighed heavily on my conscience.

One day, we were talking with a group of classmates about our begetters' last names, a topic that came up a lot during breaks. Some were annoyed that they'd been given their father's surname when their mother had a much prettier one. Then Esra said that it didn't matter in her case, because her parents had the same last name. They were cousins. Suddenly, I realised that was why her sisters were the way they were. Eventually, I dared to ask her about it.

'Hey, Esra, honestly, do you think that your sisters might be handicapped because your parents married within the same family?'

'No, not all,' she said. 'I'm normal, aren't I? Besides, the Prophet, peace be upon him, said that you are permitted to marry your cousin. If that were such a bad thing, the Prophet, peace be upon him, would never have said that. There are lots of people who marry their cousins and have perfectly healthy children.'

I nodded, but deep down I wasn't convinced.

A few kilometres after our encounter with the children

who had admired Defne's sandals, we took a break. We still hadn't reached the green field between the mountains where we wanted to lie in the grass. I drank a big gulp of lukewarm water and passed the bottle to Halil, then I saw Defne poking at something with her stick a little further up. She'd been walking with the stick the whole way, like the shepherds who all used them to keep their flocks in line. The sheep wear bells around here, so you can hear them ringing from afar.

'What's that, Defne?' I asked. I saw something white, about the size of a football, in front of her shoes, and walked over to get a closer look. It looked like some kind of pottery. I bent down and turned it around, and found myself face to face with a skull. A human skull.

Hope

We're back in the Netherlands, and the new school year has started. My laptop is broken – it won't charge. If I want to finish my assignments for tomorrow, I'll have to work on a computer on campus. As I'm getting ready to go, Defne walks in and proclaims that she's 'bored to death'. School is cancelled due to a teacher workday, which they've been having more and more of lately due to labour shortages.

'That's a pretty dress, where did you get it?' I ask, as if I don't already know the answer.

'Mum made it for me,' she says proudly. 'Look, it flies up when I spin around!' She does a little twirl.

Mother used to make clothes for me too. It saved a lot of money. Women in the neighbourhood often came by to ask if she could shorten a hem, alter a dress or fix a tear. She always did. She couldn't say no, even when she didn't feel like it. Soon, more and more people started asking her for help, even the neighbours' acquaintances and relatives. Word spread that there was an excellent seamstress in Kolenkit who would alter their clothes for free. Things got a little out of hand, and eventually Mother was fed up. She complained to Father that if you gave these women a finger they'd take your whole hand.

'I don't mind taking up a hem here and there, but now they're asking if I can whip up a couple of dresses for them if they bring me the fabric. They have no shame. I have a life too you know, and it takes hours to make a dress, especially one that would cost hundreds of euros in a shop, like those party dresses they want.' Father was always saying that she should open a shop and charge people for her services.

'Surely you're not suggesting that I ask my neighbours, friends and family for money, Ismail?' she replied irritably.

'Well, you could. What would be so wrong with that?' Father was much more entrepreneurial and down to earth than Mother.

'No, it wouldn't be right. You just can't do that. Not everything revolves around money.'

Then stop complaining, I thought.

'Okay, then don't come whining to me about it,' Father said. Apparently, he and I were in agreement.

Mother does that a lot. She'll complain the whole damn day about something, but as soon as you offer a potential solution she'll adamantly refuse it and keep right on whining. She expects you to listen and only to offer magic solutions that she can agree with, even though they don't exist. It really gets under my skin, and it seems I'm not the only one.

I'm in the loo adjusting my headscarf with a few pins when Defne walks in wearing sunglasses and licking an ice cream.

'It's really hot,' she says. 'Why aren't you wearing short sleeves like me?'

'Why do you think? You know Mother would never allow it.'

'Why don't you just pack another pair of clothes and change in the toilets at school? And when you get home you can put the long clothes back on, dummy.'

She licks her ice cream and skips off. I'm amazed. Did I

hear that right? Suddenly, I can't stop laughing. This little girl has spunk; she is already preparing to lead a double life. On the one hand, I'm glad she's a rebel like me, but I already feel sorry for her. Get ready, sister, there will be times when you feel like a total schizophrenic.

Asure

I'm in the kitchen making lentil soup. Mother is in the living room watching this show where single people come on television to talk about what they're looking for in a partner and what they have to offer, and interested viewers can call in. Later, they select a few potential candidates to come on the show. They sit on one side of a screen and the contestant sits on the other. They can't see each other, but they can talk. While the audience, the country and the entire European diaspora watches.

They talk for five to ten minutes, usually about what they expect from a marriage and what their life goals are. Their responses are all suspiciously similar, and they always sound so nice. You can't help but wonder how it's possible that they're still single or have had multiple failed marriages. Whatever happened, it was always the ex's fault.

Then there comes a moment when the screen is taken away and the contestant gets to decide whether he or she wants to have dinner with one of the candidates. It goes on like that for hours. Every. Single. Day. All the housewives tune in. I've always been surprised by how Western these Turkish TV shows are. You rarely see a headscarf. And you never see them in series and films. The female characters dress provocatively and have sex before marriage. Men drink alcohol, go out and even celebrate Christmas. But when I'm in Turkey or when I look around, I see a very different reality.

Turkish comedy is also very different from Dutch comedy. It's never about politics or religion, and social issues rarely come up. It's mostly jokes based on stereotypes. Stories about stupid types of people doing stupid types of things and other types of people with sarcastic things to say about it. Kind of SpongeBob–Squidward style. They aren't familiar with more advanced forms of comedy, apparently.

When the show is over, Mother will FaceTime with relatives from Turkey for hours. They always ask about me, and that's when I retreat to my room at Oma's or say I have to study. I hate FaceTiming with family. I feel no connection to them whatsoever; all they want to do is judge me. The last time I talked to my grandma in Turkey, she asked if I wore the shirt I was wearing outside the house. She thought it was too tight: 'you can see everything,' she said. She also asked why I was wearing mascara and reminded me that this life is temporary and that I sin too much, that this makes her very sad, that she had heard this from Mother. Of course. She probably gossiped about me for hours, day in and day out, with people who could then use my sins to make themselves feel more righteous. Just as silence is nothing without the noise before and after it, so is righteousness nothing without sinners to scoff at.

I absolutely hate being reminded of my sins, constantly having to live with the prospect of eternal damnation. So now, I run away. I don't need to hear it; I don't want to hear it. I wonder what they'll say if I take off my headscarf.

I'm sure it will be nothing but guilt and doom.

*

231

Today is also the day of *Asure*, the tenth day of the Islamic month of *muharram*. In Sunni Islam, it's a celebration of Moses leading his people out of Egypt and into Canaan, freeing them from the pharaoh's oppression. In Shia Islam, it's a day of mourning and self-flagellation, but I don't know all the details of that. We're Sunni. Mother is fasting because of the holiness of the day, which she hopes will bring her God's good graces. On top of that, she's also making a dessert known as Asure. It's a custom that's not shared by Moroccans or other non-Turkish Muslims. I've done quite a bit of research, and I haven't found any mention of it in scripture, but the same goes for the celebration of the Prophet's birthday (peace be upon him), Ascension, and other typical Turkish-Muslim holidays except for Eid al-Fitr and Eid al-Adha, but whatever, I'm not complaining, because this delicacy is absolutely divine. When I was a kid, Mother said that the Prophet, peace be upon him, had improvised this concoction after a war when food was scarce. He commanded his followers to bring him everything they had to eat, and he used the ingredients to make this dessert, which consisted of almonds, hazelnuts, dried peaches, pomegranate seeds, sultanas, white beans, milk, rice, chickpeas, coconut flakes, water and sugar. It looks like a soup and is generally eaten warm, but it's sweet. I look forward to it every year. The idea is to make a massive amount, at least four large saucepans, and to distribute it to your neighbours; they do the same. So at the end of the day, we get a bowl of Asure from them and they get one from us; it's an exchange of virtually the same thing, with a couple of minor personal variations.

Originally, you were supposed to offer it to the poor, but since we're all equally rich (or equally poor) on our street, we just give it to each other. After all, we don't know anyone poorer than ourselves. The same goes for Eid al-Adha: you're supposed to give meat to the poor, but we give it to our neighbours because truly poor people are hard to come by in the Netherlands.

I look at my screen. It's 4.30 p.m. I finish my make-up, put on my Heineken polo shirt and jeans and leave. The street is full of men in orange vests armed with leaf blowers. If you ask me, the leaf blower is one of the most superfluous machines ever made. It's autumn, what difference does it make if there are leaves on the ground? Removing them is downright nit-picky. As if anyone in this neighbourhood cares that there are leaves on the pavement. If the council wants to blow its money, it'd be better off just giving it to the people.

When I cycle past one of the men, he turns the blower in my direction, sending leaves and grit in my direction. I squeeze my eyes shut as the dust fills my mouth and nose. I spit. I hit the brakes and glare at the man with a look that demands an explanation. 'Sorry,' he says. 'It was an accident. Good thing you had that rag on your head, otherwise it'd be in your hair. I guess it's good for something!' I say nothing and climb back on my bike.

That afternoon, I found myself in a heated debate at work. A group of Israeli tourists asked me if our meat is kosher.

'Yes,' I said, thinking halal and kosher are the same thing, or at least that's what I'd learned at the Quranic school. I had assumed that the tolerance was mutual. While eating, they asked another waitress just to be sure, and she said that it was halal, not kosher.

They were furious. Because of me. They were all wearing those same little hats that devout Muslims wear, only theirs were smaller and only covered the crown of their head.

Accusing me of lying, they demanded to speak to the manager and refused to pay.

'This meat was slaughtered in the name of Allah, the One and Only God, you call him Yahweh, we call him Allah, but it's the same entity, you see? Just another name,' I explained in English, but they weren't having it. Then my boss showed up. After twenty minutes of arguing, the boss demanded that they either pay or he would call the police. Then, he asked me to apologise. An apology doesn't have to mean that you think the other person was right. It just means that you value your relationship with that person more than your own ego.

They all left a bad review. I expected the boss to lash out at me. My nose, forehead and armpits were dripping with sweat, but to my surprise he gave me a compliment instead.

'Well done, it's okay to play Jewish tricks on Jews, that's the language they speak.'

After the incident, I decided to go on my break. I ordered my plate from the cook – salmon this time – and went to the loo, where I ran into Karima. She had only been working there for three weeks, but I felt like I'd known her a lot longer. We clicked immediately. She was always upbeat, liked to joke around and made it easier to get through a long workday.

'Hey girl. How's it going, tiger?' I asked. She didn't answer and just stared at her phone. When she finally looked up, I saw that her eyes were red, with dark circles under them. She looked tired and overwhelmed and wasn't wearing any make-up, which was unusual for her. All of a sudden, she threw her arms around me and started to cry. I could feel her shaking and inhaled the sweet smell of her perfume. If she weren't so emotional, I would've asked her what she was wearing.

'I've got a huge problem, Büsra,' she said, sobbing.

'Hey, take it easy! What's going on?' I asked, as I detached myself from her grip and stroked her back like a primary school teacher does when a child starts to cry.

'Nick and I broke up,' she said.

'Oh ... is that it? Why?' I asked, and she cried even harder.

'My parents won't accept him because he's not a Muslim. They want me to marry Hamza.'

'Didn't you see that coming?' I heard myself say.

'No, I knew they wouldn't accept him, but I don't know ... I guess I always hoped, but they really ripped me apart; they were way angrier than I'd expected. And if they find out what I've done, I'm dead,' she sobbed.

I felt it coming.

'I lost my virginity. They'll kill me if they find out. I thought I could have a hymen operation, but apparently that shit's been banned in the Netherlands! Fuck! Just when I needed it!' she wailed, banging on the sink.

'Who cares what your parents think?' I said, a little too quickly, realising that I was in the same boat.

'No, I don't want to be cut off from my family for the rest of my life, I can't do it, it's too much. I'll marry Hamza if I have too. But they're still going to find out that I'm not a virgin any more.'

'It'll be okay, we'll see if we can work this out together. Come on. You're not the only one, you know. If necessary, you can just lie and say that you used tampons,' I said.

'Do you think he'll believe that?' she asked.

I noticed I was struggling with my own advice. As long as all women kept doing that, things would never change, this nonsense would never stop. Deep down, I even blamed her. Blamed her for not standing up for her own happiness. But then it occurred to me that I was doing exactly the same thing. Why was it so much easier to tell other people what they should do? Why was I so quick to blame her for not standing up for herself, yet I didn't blame myself? Why couldn't I give her the same benefit of the doubt that I constantly gave myself?

It's always easier to give other people advice.

After my long day at work, I had to walk home because my bike had been stolen for the fifth time that year, an unpleasant side effect of living in Amsterdam-West. Walking felt a lot less safe, so I kept my keys in my hand and gripped the small can of deodorant in my coat pocket, thinking it could be used like pepper spray if necessary. On the way home, there were always groups of Moroccan guys hanging out on the street who, at any moment, could decide to taunt me in that slimy, intimidating tone. Sometimes they chased you all the way to your front door. It wasn't nearly as bad if you were wearing a headscarf, which became clear to me in my post-headscarf days.

I would love to be able to walk the streets at night without having to fear for my safety, but that just isn't a privilege that women enjoy. If only Lucas were with me.

The Mustafa Incident

Today I went bowling with Mustafa, Halil and my little sister. Defne had been saying she wanted to go bowling for a while, and today worked out for everybody. It's also her birthday. Mother emphatically said: 'You're not going because it's her birthday. You could do this on any other day. Right?'

'I guess so,' Halil said with a sigh.

Mother didn't want us to adopting the customs of infidels, so birthday celebrations were strictly forbidden, as were all other modern celebrations like Mother's Day, New Year's, Valentine's Day, Christmas and Easter. At Quranic school, I learned that the Prophet (peace be upon him) had said that whoever imitates a people becomes one of them, thus by celebrating the infidels' holidays you became an infidel. Last year, when Halil brought home a cake on his birthday, Mother wouldn't eat it until the next day, otherwise God might have thought we were celebrating. She does the same thing on New Year's Eve whenever a neighbour or relative invites us to see in the New Year together.

'We're just coming over for fun, same as we would any other day, not to celebrate,' she'd repeat over and over again. When she saw that the neighbour had gone to a lot of trouble getting things ready and cleaning up the house, Mother still felt guilty. The extra effort made it feel like a special day after all, which she had specifically wanted to avoid.

After the bowling, we went out to dinner at a good restaurant, Mustafa's treat. He had also bought a present for Defne. A Monopoly set. While we were there, I decided to take a picture. 'Smile for the camera, guys.'

Halil said he had to bounce and couldn't wait for me to snap a picture. 'I'll take a picture of just the three of us then,' I said in disbelief.

Later that day, I set the photo as my profile picture on WhatsApp. There I was, smiling next to Mustafa, him with his arm around me, and Defne on our laps. Moments later I got a message from an aunt.

'Is that your cousin in your profile picture?'

'Yes,' I replied.

'You two sure look good together. Maybe you should get married. Do you get along well with him?'

I looked at my screen confused. Was I reading this right?

I typed: 'Ummm ... Auntie, are you crazy? He's my first cousin.' Most of the time the only way to answer an impertinent question is with another question.

'So? It's perfectly normal to marry your cousin. I was just trying to give you a compliment. You're a pretty girl, and he's a nice-looking guy, both eligible. And you get along so well with each other! Why not? Aren't there lots of people who do it that way around here?'

I blocked her. She would probably get all indignant about that too, but I didn't care. Half an hour later, just as I was going through my notes for class, I got a call from Mother.

'Why do you have a picture with Mustafa?! Are you completely out of your mind? He's not your husband or your fiancé, and there you are sitting side by side, smiling, practically sitting in each other's laps. And why wasn't Halil in the picture? Did you three go off without him? Did you secretly meet up with Mustafa? Shame on you! What will people say now that they've seen this photo?! No one is going to ask for your hand now, everyone is going to think that you're already betrothed! Take it down right now and come home!'

She'd hung up before I could even get a word out. I popped a piece of gum in my mouth and started chewing so hard that I bit my tongue. Damn it, why the hell did I teach her to use WhatsApp? This time last year she was still walking around with an old Nokia and panicking every time a text message came in. Now I'd really shot myself in the foot. I deleted the picture and went home to my begetters' house. To be honest, I didn't want to delete it – I hadn't done anything wrong, and I was tired of making concessions. And yet, time and again, they had me by the throat. I still let them scare me with their threats.

I prepared to make my case.

As I walked into the living room, a hard object struck my head. It hurt. Tears welled up in my left eye. It was Mother's house slipper. Not the soft, fluffy kind but a hard Turkish one with a wedge heel. I held my hand over my eye and asked her if she was completely out of her mind, which was essentially a rhetorical question.

'Me? No, you're the one who is out of her mind! You don't know your limits, young lady. I've had it with you and your behaviour! Why are you, as a young, adult, single woman posting a picture with a man to whom you are not engaged or married? Do you want people to gossip about you? Do you want people to speculate that you're in a relationship? Or do you think Mustafa might secretly like you, and you actually

239

do want to marry him? If that's the case, just say so and we'll arrange it, instead of sneaking around with him behind our backs!'

I looked at her, stunned. Somehow Mother managed to exceed herself every time.

'You're getting crazier by the day, you know that? You're losing it! What's wrong with a picture with my cousin? Why do you have to make such a big deal out of everything? Why does everything have to be sexual? What have I done to deserve this? I'm twenty fucking years old, and I'm getting whacked in the eye with a slipper! You know what, fuck you!'

Mother stood up furiously. 'Who do you think you're talking to? You think now that you're twenty you don't have to show respect any more? Where are your manners? Where is your honour for the woman who brought you into this world, who nurtured and raised you?! When man tried to cut down the tree with an axe, the tree reminded him that the handle was made of his wood. I gave birth to you, young lady, not the other way around. Know your place!'

This was how Mother operated. She never engaged in substantive debate, never responded directly to criticism. If she was the one dissenting, she saw dissent as a sign of self-confidence and exhortation, but coming from me it was pure insolence. I had been born to two people with three hundred idiotic, unjustifiable auto-pilot restrictions that over the years I had been forced to accept. If you asked questions, they had a gift for responding with very long sentences that had no relevance whatsoever to the question that had been asked. As for pride, Mother had practically invented the word. This was the reason why, after a while, I just couldn't push back any more. I was so tired. I had already wasted so much energy on these kinds of altercations over the years. I preferred to maintain a positive attitude, or at least a somewhat stable mental state, over convincing them that I was right, because there was no way I would ever convince them. The fact is, one simply cannot win over an obsession, because the obsessed person actually cares and you don't. In general, ambitious people are more dangerous and vulnerable than ordinary people. If someone has already made an irrational decision to stick to their guns, you cannot rationally convince them otherwise, and pointing out that an irrational person is being irrational is an inefficient use of your time. You're better off ignoring nonsense than trying to refute it. Forcing people, against their capabilities, into a straitjacket of reasonable thinking is asking for trouble. Reasonableness shouldn't try too hard to be itself in the presence of unreasonableness.

But apart from being a cause, is stupidity also an excuse?

If a person cannot hear, then sound doesn't exist to them. But that doesn't change the fact that sound does exist. If a person is colour-blind, they can't see colour, but they know from other people that there is something out there that they can't see. The fact that there are billions of believers in the world doesn't change the absence of a god in our lives. It's the same with stupid people: they don't have any problem with their own stupidity; it's mostly the people around them who suffer from it.

Usually, numbers are used as evidence that God exists. If you ask me, the opposite is true. When it comes to making decisions, about anything really, I have made a habit of ignoring the tastes of the collective. This has generally proven to be an infallible compass given that things bought too eagerly are usually of inferior quality. Never resign yourself to the decision of the majority.

The begetters can pull out all the stops: they can swear, pinch, hit, throw things, make denigrating, degrading comments, use psychological warfare, get aggressive and shout nonsense. They can say the most abject, belittling, hurtful things, but woe is me if I do the same; then they're outraged and play the victim. They're extraordinarily deft at lighting fuses on powder kegs and then innocently washing their hands of the matter when things ignite. Then they act as if I'm the one who is freaking out and being disrespectful. They turn it all upside down. And that's how it's always been. They want me to say yes and amen, especially because I'm a woman, and to come crawling back with my tail between my legs. Actually, it's only because I'm a woman; if I were a man, they wouldn't react that way at all and wouldn't have a problem with anything I do. I'm not supposed to answer back or respond critically, I'm supposed to be submissive; really, I shouldn't even respond at all, I should simply let myself be enslaved. I should kneel before Her Highness. She was as arrogant as they come, but I was the brat for having the audacity to go against her, I was the one breaking the code, especially the code for women. I was the slippery eel. Mother wanted to shape me into someone who would bow her head in shame and swallow her tongue along with all her emotions and frustrations. Someone who would back down and blame herself for fear that otherwise it would all blow up in her face, who would finally say, 'Yes, Mother, I'm sorry, you're right, I hope you can forgive me one day.'

But that was never going to happen. At the same time, I was overcome by the feeling that she had already won, and with flying colours. I took down the photo; I chose to keep my relationship a secret; I wore the clothes they approve of in their presence; I didn't tell them about my job at the restaurant; I didn't go out; I was usually home early in the evenings; I didn't go on holiday with friends; I went to the beach in secret; I'd

242

been thinking more and more about dating someone they might accept; and I never stayed the night anywhere. In other words, I wasn't living my life the way I wanted to live it. I occasionally rebelled, but in the end she always won. Was I really such a rebel? Or was I someone who thought she was rebelling but still remained within *their* boundaries? Was I not the very embodiment of defeatism, seeing as she still defined the playing field?

When I stood my ground and insisted that there was nothing wrong with that photo and that she was a twisted, backwards idiot who wanted nothing more than to impose her medieval rules on me, I touched a nerve, which really wasn't that hard considering that Mother has a lot of nerves; she's basically a walking clitoris. She came charging at me and grabbed my forearm. I pushed her away; she almost fell. I saw the sweat pearling on her forehead, and she spewed unadulterated verbal slurs, the blue vein on the left side of her head bulging as if she were going to drink my blood.

Then Father intervened. Not because he was suddenly struck with compassion but out of sheer calculation.

'Don't, Fatma, there's no need for that. Surely you can talk this out?' He sensed that things were about to escalate again, for the umpteenth time, and that I wasn't going to put up with it any more. A side effect of getting older is that you become less and less inclined to do things you don't want to do. The haphazard physical attacks were a sign that Mother was weak, that she was at her wits' end, that she wasn't even going to try to use her words. Maybe she wasn't going to win this time?

'A person who won't listen has to feel it! You're lucky to have such a decent father; some fathers would have knocked your teeth out, which you absolutely deserve. It's too bad your uncle is not your father, then you'd see!' Mother shouted.

I turned towards Father and asked, 'Why don't you say

243

anything? Listen to what she's accusing me of! For a picture with Mustafa! Do you think this is normal? Why don't you ever stand up for me, why do you just stand there? You know damn well she's in the wrong here! A psychiatrist could write a whole dissertation on her!'

I saw Father hesitate, and that did me good. Father was more of a hesitator than Mother, and those who hesitate possess an ethical consciousness, an internal set of norms and values that either accepts or rejects certain actions and ideas. After all, you should never deny your certainties the right to err. Mother was the type of person who saw doubt as the ultimate enemy that you shouldn't give in to, even when it crept up on you in a moment of weakness. She thought doubt stemmed from a lack of knowledge, whereas doubt actually tends to increase as you gain knowledge. Everywhere was foggy except where she stood.

But Father's hesitation didn't last long. 'Büsra, stop it! Now! You have to respect your mother, no matter what she says or does. She raised you! Learn some manners! And your mother does have a point, even if she tends to exaggerate. Knocking your teeth out is not a solution, but she is right. You know how our people are, how they gossip and speculate. If you want to take a picture with Mustafa, go right ahead, but you don't need to make it public. Why do you feel the need to share a picture like that? Last time, you posted a picture of your own face on WhatsApp and Facebook, you can't do that! Just pick a nice quote or something, or a pretty flower; stop with all the attention-seeking slut behaviour. What's so hard about that? Why is it so much to ask? Are you really so unhappy if you don't post any pictures?'

I didn't even blame Father any more. By now, I know better than to be disappointed in others.

Mother starts getting all riled up again, like a mouse running in a barrel of flour.

'You wicked girl! Smiling in a picture with a young man, how dare you? Fear God! You are playing with fire! Men his age have a lot of hormones. You may not have any wrong intentions, but they do! If you give a man that kind of attention, he can develop feelings for you. Because you are a woman and he is a man, and that's that! Family or not, that's the nature of the beast, if a woman and a man are alone together, the devil is there with them. The Prophet, peace be upon him, said so himself. Do I really have to tell you that? Why did we send you to classes for all those years if you didn't learn anything? Lesson number one: a woman and a man, it's like putting wood and fire next to each other, no good can come of it!'

'Fatma, exaggeration is also an art, and you're going a little overboard. We know Mustafa. You're getting all worked up for nothing. If she takes down the photo, problem solved.' Father said.

'Listen to yourselves! Mustafa has a girlfriend! And he's my cousin! I'm surrounded by guys at school and at work, aren't I, and it's not like I have feelings for all of them. Where is this coming from?' I tried.

'I don't know what you do with your fellow students and co-workers; unfortunately, I have no insight into that, but I hope for your sake that you don't portray yourself like you did in that picture! You can certainly engage in normal interactions with men as long as you keep your distance and maintain a businesslike composure. You don't have to laugh and giggle and squeal, you don't have to touch them, be stuck to them like tape, act all casual and smile with them in a photo. Know your limits! Gender differences exist for a reason. It's not for nothing that Allah commands us as women to cover our beauty, and the Prophet, peace be upon him, instructed us to lower our voices when we talk to a man, it's so we don't arouse their lust. When are you going to accept this and apply it to your life? By your age, most girls in Turkey are on their second child, and here you are, still so childish and naive, fluttering around as if you know everything. Or you're pretending, I'm almost sure of that. You're going to let your own honour, and this entire family's honour, be damaged by gossip! A woman's honour is more important than her life, don't you understand?! Get that into your head instead of always being so damn stubborn! I'm not in favour of all this mingling between men and women, but that's just the way things are nowadays, it's inevitable, but you still have to lay a firm boundary as a woman. The ball is in your court!'

For the thousandth time, I stood there and took it. I looked at Mother. The face of insanity. Then I shoved the earbuds I'd been holding into my ears, to protect myself from her eternal drivel. I saw Mother rattling on, like the buzz of an annoying fly on an unbearably hot summer night. I closed my eyes until I felt an unconscionable slap on my right cheek. My ear was ringing. I had no intention of escalating things further, so I walked back to my room. I felt that familiar salty taste on my tongue. I lifted my eyes to heaven and spoke to Allah.

'Why didn't You give her the kind of daughter she wanted? Day in and day out, I am being punished for being myself! Why?'

No answer came.

Education

When I was seven years old, I used to go over to Eva's house to play. She lived on our street at the time, but eventually her family moved to the suburbs. Her mother bought books and magazines and read aloud from them every night. Sometimes I was allowed to stay and listen. I remember feeling jealous. Mother never did that. While Eva's mother helped her with her homework and read to her every day, I was teaching mine the alphabet and how to pay for things. The roles were reversed at our house. Eva had activity books full of word searches and puzzles that I wanted to solve, but she wouldn't let me; she wanted to do them herself. Mother would never buy me books like that; they were too expensive. I saw them when we were waiting in a queue at the supermarket; they cost four to five euros. 'For that money, you could buy eight loaves of bread,' Mother would say.

One day, I said to Mother, 'Isn't it nice that other kids have a mother who can read to them? Too bad you can't, but that's okay.' The next day, a book suddenly appeared on the table, and she asked me if I wanted her to read it to me. I immediately sat down beside her, ready to listen. Using the pictures, she made up a story, and that's how the reading fiasco began. Sometimes she needed a moment to figure out how to connect one illustration to the next, but it didn't matter. I appreciated the effort. I gave her a kiss on the cheek and patted her on the headscarf.

The strongest hate is the hate that was once love. The strongest hate is disillusioned love.

I cycle past the supermarket. Memories flash like a panorama before my eyes. There was a time when Mother couldn't read prices, so I had to go shopping with her and help her pay. I had to check the receipt twice, just to be sure, and even then she didn't trust my arithmetic skills. She always thought we were paying too much or too little for things, even when it really was correct.

I bike past the library in Bos en Lommer. How I loved the library as a child; it was my home away from home. After a while, I'd read through all the books on the shelves. The first time I ever set foot in a library was on a field trip in primary school, before that I didn't even know that such a place existed. It was love at first sight. A whole world opened up to me, a treasure trove of exciting stories, *Donald Duck* comics, computers with internet, DVDs, a chocolate milk machine, and all of it free. Except the chocolate milk, that was 50 cents. After the tour with my class, I wanted to go all the time. Since I was still too young to walk there by myself, I was dependent on Mother. I had to beg her every time. Father was always at work. Sometimes she said yes, even though she couldn't read or clearly wasn't in the mood. I always borrowed the maximum number of books allowed, eight, because I knew it would be a while before I could convince Mother to take me again. She only wanted to go every five or six weeks, otherwise she thought it would be too much of a good thing. I always read magazines in the library and saved the longer books for home. I wanted to borrow movies too; we'd recently got a computer, albeit without internet, but it did have a DVD player. A neighbour had given it to us when he got a new one. I took out a library card for Halil too; that way I could borrow eight more books under his name – it's not like he was going to use it anyway. That meant I could borrow sixteen books at a time, but Mother refused to carry them all, so I used his card for magazines and movies, which were significantly lighter.

When I turned twelve, I was finally allowed to go to the library by myself, and I could hang out there alone for hours. I'd buy chocolate milk with the money I occasionally got from Father for helping him deliver the mail and brochures. We always had to be careful not to run into any other PostNL workers, otherwise Father could lose his job because of me. Sometimes I did the entire route for him; he got the afternoon off and I got ten euros. In retrospect, that was peanuts compared to what I was earning for him, but I was more than satisfied with it at the time. Every now and then, I would borrow a couple of books for Halil; he never came to the library, he was always out playing football. But he was happy I thought of him and usually read them too, as long as I brought them home and took them back. My favourite author was Carry Slee. Her books opened my eyes to worlds I knew nothing about. I read about kissing, boyfriends, getting drunk, going out, smoking and drugs. Whenever it was about kissing or sex, I'd get butterflies in my stomach and this tingly feeling between my legs. I had no idea why my body was acting so weird, but I was glued to those stories and would spend the entire weekend after I got home from Quranic school and the entire Christmas break in my room reading. After finishing a good book, I could be on cloud nine for a whole week or upset or angry or sad, or I'd just keep rolling it around in my mind, wondering what I'd actually read. I wrote down the words I didn't know in a notebook so I could ask my teacher about them later and note their meaning.

We didn't have Wi-Fi, which made reading the only fun activity at home, especially since the only alternative was studying Quranic texts. Mother came storming into my room all the time to complain that I never did my Quranic school homework. When was I going to memorise a new *surah*? I'd been working on the same one for two weeks, and the teacher at the mosque was starting to lose patience. If I ignored her demands and turned back to my book, she would take all my books away and lock them in a drawer, the same one where she kept the gold coins from her wedding. She still has them, by the way. Turkish women keep those things until death as a kind of alimony in case their husband leaves them, or a war breaks out, or a genocide begins and they have to flee. Or that's what she told me when I asked her about it.

I hated it when she took away my books. I didn't want to learn verses from the Quran. It was hard, boring and complicated, and I didn't understand a word of it. Why did I have to memorise bits of text written in a language I didn't even understand? It all seemed so useless to me, but Mother said that it would make God love me more and bring me more prosperity in life, and I believed every word of it and was willing to suffer. I picked up my little pink Quran and got to work. I had a trick for memorising things: if you started reading it in a certain rhythm it was easier to remember, like a song in a foreign language.

The teacher would quiz me every Sunday; I didn't want to experience the shame of not knowing it. She had very high expectations of me and insisted that I could learn faster than the other kids. Therefore, if I failed, even once, she was extra disappointed. And annoyed.

'It's important that you work hard to learn about the things that please God, Büsra, or do you want Him to be disappointed in you? Surely, you don't want bad things to befall you, like your parents getting sick or you growing up to be unsuccessful and unhappy, or going to hell? Do you want to spend eternity in the magnificent paradise? Do you want to be protected from all evil and adversity? Then you have to show that you are willing to give everything for God, even your free time – especially your free time – and do your best to know His Book. That is what God expects of you. You are clever. He has given you this gift for a purpose; you should use it to worship Him.'

It's generally true that whoever lies knows the truth. Though I doubt that's the case with the pious.

It didn't take me long to notice that I was quicker than the other kids. At the beginning of the Quranic school year, we all knew the same number of verses, but by the end of the first semester I had already memorised significantly more than everybody else. I wondered why that was. At school, I was also the first to finish my maths, Dutch language and spelling, while the other kids were easily distracted or didn't understand the assignment. When they didn't want to have to stay after school, they would ask me for the answers. At one point, I told them I didn't want to share my notebook any more, but they threatened to exclude me at breaktime. Other kids offered me sweets, and sometimes fifty cents or a euro. Then I was happy to hand over my work because it meant I could buy chocolate milk at the library. I just assumed they were lazy, but I later learned that they genuinely found the work difficult, especially the language exercises, which I had no trouble with at all. It must have been all the books, because we didn't speak Dutch at home and hardly ever watched Dutch television.

When I was about five, Ms Eline had suggested putting me in special education because I hardly spoke a word of Dutch and never said a word. In the years that followed, I'd managed to catch up by reading.

The library also reminded me of all the hours I spent there with Mother, helping her study for her exams. She had to take the national Civic Integration Exam, which requires basic knowledge of the Dutch language and culture. She needed the internet to study, but you could only use the library computers for half an hour per day. First, we used my half hour, then Halil's. She didn't have a library card herself because adults had to pay a membership fee. Mother passed the exam on the first try while almost everyone in her class had to take it multiple times. That's pretty impressive for someone who first had to learn to read; everybody else in her class had at least gone to primary school. She was incredibly proud of herself, and rightfully so. That night we ate cake, but since all the cakes at the supermarket contained pork gelatine she had to make it herself.

She had already received praise from the teacher on several occasions. He encouraged her to persevere, which she had no problem doing. After six months, she passed level one. Her teacher had already lined up a couple of work opportunities for her.

'I can help you get a job at a pharmacy or in a nursery. Or in a nursing home cafeteria. Would you like that?' Initially, Mother said yes, but she soon backed out when she found out that she was pregnant with Defne. It was a total surprise – apparently she had been on the pill and never forgot to take it – that's what I heard her tell my aunt on the phone. She wasn't the least bit happy about it, she didn't want another child, and besides our flat was too small, but abortion is

252

forbidden in Islam (the pill is allowed, at least in the school that Mother adheres to).

I was eleven at the time and didn't know which pill she was talking about, but after a little googling I figured it out. Moreover, the imam had made it clear that a woman had no business working if the man of the house already earned enough for the family to live on. She should focus on raising her children, maintaining the household and worshipping God. So that was the end of that.

As I bike past the bus stop, I see an Andrélon shampoo ad depicting a woman wearing a headscarf. Someone has defaced it, linking her eyebrows together with a black marker. Some of her teeth are coloured in black. Male genitalia have been drawn beside her head. 'Camel fucker,' they've written, and 'No more migrants!'

Favours

It's Saturday afternoon and I'm working a full shift at the restaurant. At 3 p.m., I go on my first break. I had already ordered my meal from the cook, and it's ready. I take my plate and look for a place to sit. Mohammed, the dishwasher, is eating too. I pause to consider whether I should join him or whether we should sit separately. You never know with those untrimmed beards. If he weren't Arab but white, I wouldn't think twice about it. It would be downright rude to sit at a different table and not exchange a word with your co-worker. But devout Muslims have no appreciation for that. I've seen him praying in the broom cupboard, he doesn't shave his beard, he doesn't touch alcohol, and I heard him ask the boss if the meat was halal and if he could leave work early on Friday to go to the mosque. He only speaks English at work, and I haven't actually talked to him myself. The fact that he speaks English means that he has recently arrived in the country, like most of the Yemeni and Palestinians who work here. I'm curious about him, why he came here and why he doesn't speak Dutch. I decide to sit with him, and if he has a problem with that he'll just have to tell me. I do as the Dutch do, and Mohammed will just have to get used to it. It won't be the last time that a woman talks to him.

I ask if I can sit across from him. 'Yes, of course, sister! Sit, please,' he says in English. Those Arabs with all their 'sisters' and 'brothers' at the end of every sentence whenever they're speaking to a fellow Muslim. Kind of endearing, really. But, whatever, I'm allowed to sit. 'How are you, Mohammed?' I ask.

'Fine, fine, *alhamdulillah*, and you? What was your name again?'

'Büsra,' I say.

'Aaah, *Booshra*, sorry, I forget.'

Arabs and Moroccans always call me Booshra. It's Büsra, not Booshra, get it right. But I don't bother to correct him, I'll just be Booshra.

'No problem, I forgive you,' I say. 'Do you like the food here?'

'Yes, yes, I do, really good food, *alhamdulillah*, sister.'

Of course he likes Turkish food, who doesn't? Turkish–Greek cuisine is truly the most refined. Dutch cuisine, to the extent that such a thing even exists, is totally unsophisticated. I remember the first time I stayed for dinner at Lucas's house. We ate boiled potatoes with green beans and a piece of meat in a puddle of gravy. There were no spices in it to speak of, only salt. At the table, everyone started mashing the potatoes and green beans into a homogeneous mess. It didn't look the least bit appetising to me, and I was really confused. Lucas started it, and at first I thought it was because he had been to the dentist that day, but then I saw his sister doing it too. I thought, maybe they're mashing some food for the cat – after all, there are people who feed their cat from their own plate. But soon I realised that all that smashing was part of the meal. So, I did it too. The Dutch way of making rice is equally primitive and should be outlawed. They boil it and drain the water. You can't call that rice.

I ask Mohammed where he's from and why he doesn't speak Dutch. From Yemen, he says, and explains that he's enrolled in a Dutch course but finds it a very difficult language. After work – he works all day everyday – he goes home and studies his vocabulary, but it's not going very well. I ask him why he's here. There's a war in his country, and unfortunately his family is still there, and there's pretty much no chance that they will ever be able to join him here. He got lucky. I ask him a few questions about the war, but it soon becomes clear that it's still an open wound and he'd rather not talk about it, so I let it drop. I ask him what he thinks of the Netherlands. He says he hasn't seen very much of it, none of it really, all he's done since he's been here is work, but he's impressed by the infrastructure.

'But the language is very very difficult,' he says, shaking his head with a sigh. He asks me what I'm studying. When I say Dutch, he looks pleasantly surprised and asks if I can please help him learn the language. Maybe I could tutor him and explain the things he doesn't understand. He has an exam coming up.

If only I hadn't sat down at this table.

That evening, when I got home to Oma's, I was exhausted. I heard the doorbell ring. It was Ensar, Halil's best friend.

'Hey, Büsra, where are your parents, do you know?' he said panting. His forehead was dripping with sweat.

'Aren't they home? I don't know, I just got home from work,' I said, feeling the pain in my feet from the busy workday. I could barely stand.

'I really need to borrow a car, and fast. I rang their doorbell, but they aren't there. You have their house key, don't you? Can you loan me your dad's car keys? I'll bring them back tonight!'

'Why don't you ask Halil?'

'He's not answering.'

'What do you need the car for?'

'It's a long story, I'll tell you later, there's no time now,' he said, almost stuttering he was so stressed.

'Okay, one second, I'll get the keys, but please bring them right back, otherwise Father will be really mad at me.' I gave him the keys from Father's jacket pocket. The apartment was indeed empty. He dashed off. 'Thanks! I'll bring them right back!' he hollered over his shoulder as he raced down the stairs.

Half an hour later Father came over with Oma and asked where his car keys were. He had been out with Mother and Defne visiting a friend and now he needed the car.

'Ensar came by and asked for the keys, he said it was an emergency, so I gave them to him,' I said nervously.

'You did what? You loaned my car to that numbskull without asking me? Do you hear yourself? Are you out of your mind?!' He was seething.

Shit. I knew Father wouldn't like it, he's one of those people who cherishes his things like a hen cherishes her eggs, but even more possessive, especially when it came to his car. Once his own brother had asked to borrow it because his was at the garage, and Father refused. He even lied and said that he needed it himself. Father is of the opinion that people shouldn't expect him to take on all their problems. People make their own beds and then they have to lie in them. He wouldn't ask anyone for anything, even if he were on his deathbed. I don't know why he's this way, maybe some kind of childhood trauma. He has to do everything in his life himself, without any kind of love or support from anybody. He left home at fifteen to work in a textile factory in the Netherlands. His family had him registered as older than he was, which is what they do when they want to marry off underage girls too. Even when I was little he was always telling me and Halil not to expect anyone in the world to help us, that the only person you can truly depend on is yourself, that even your shadow will leave you in the dark, that everything in life revolves around money and power, that all you need to do is sweep your own doorstep. Father talked about his childhood a lot. How hard he had to work, how he had nobody, how much he had wanted to study, that his primary school teacher had told his father that he was highly intelligent, that they should keep him in school, but no one cared about him. School was something he only ever dreamed of. As Carl Jung said, the greatest tragedy of the family is the unlived lives of the parents. Father taught us that it was silly to care about others; after all, they didn't care about you. He was the type of person who saw being smart as being unscrupulous. To this day, he still lives in the past, just like Oma.

'Yeah, sorry, I maybe should have asked you first, but he was in a big hurry and said he'd bring it right back,' I muttered, still trying to save the situation.

'What makes you think that you can loan out my damn stuff?! I've never let anyone borrow my car, and you hand over the keys to some stupid kid? Unbelievable. You really are an incorrigible idiot!'

And then came a slap. That one stung for a while. Oh well, at least Ensar was able to do whatever he needed to do.

258

Lunacy

It's Ramadan, but I'm secretly not fasting. I can't be thirsty all day in this weather. I wonder if Allah minds, given that in his supposed omnipotence he doesn't really need my suffering. If you ask me, I've already suffered enough for Him by covering my entire body and sacrificing dozens of other essential freedoms and pleasures. It's give and take.

Mother is in the living room watching Ramadan programmes where imams answer questions all day from viewers who call in. Yesterday, someone asked if your fast still counted if you got a drop of water in your anus while washing your bum. It still counts. Another person wanted to know if you were allowed to break your fast during the *iftar* if it was being held in the home of relatives who earn money selling drugs or through other illegal activities. That wasn't allowed. But what if they had both a haram (illegal) income and a halal (legal) income? The imam said that either way it was forbidden and would nullify your fasting that day. Then a caller wanted to know whether your fasting was valid if, as a man, you had seen a woman's naked body. The imam replied that if it aroused no reaction in you, your fasting was still valid, otherwise you would have to make up for it the day after Ramadan was over. Another asked whether it was sinful to download movies illegally. The imam replied that most movies were forbidden anyway due to all the immorality in them. But if it was an Islamic film that contained no sinful activity whatsoever, then it's okay to watch it, as long as it's downloaded legally.

While working at Albert Heijn, I witnessed an altercation between the branch manager and a couple of stockists of Moroccan origin. '*Wollah mèh* I'm going to work on Eid, are you crazy, it's not even allowed,' Hussein complained to the manager, Peter.

'Yeah, sorry man, Peter, there's no way, I need the day off,' Ali said.

'Me too,' said Hamza.

'That can certainly be arranged, guys, but you can't even tell me what day the holiday is on. You know I make the schedule three weeks in advance, so I need to know now which day you want off,' Peter says.

'How can we tell you if we don't even know yet? What are we supposed to do? We don't know until the night before when they look at the moon, then we know if the next day is feast or the last day of fast,' Ayoub explained franticly.

'Okay, guys, that may be the case, but I can't have all of you suddenly refusing to come in because it's a holiday, then there won't be anybody to work in the store. Holiday or no holiday, we're open.'

'I can already put in my absence. The date for our holiday is set,' said Hakan, who is Turkish.

'How is it that you already know the date and they don't?' Peter asked, confused.

'Yeah, those Turks, they don't follow the moon. They have their own Islam,' Hamza said dismissively.

'It's true,' the other Moroccans nod.

'Hey, shut up, you guys are driving the man crazy with all your moon this and moon that, who cares about the moon? It's thirty days of fasting and then feast, done, you people always have to make shit so complicated. Peter, don't listen to them, Arabs can pick a fight with their own shadow.'

I never understood how Turks are able to harbour such an aversion to Arabs and yet such a love for Islam.

Every year, it's a topic of debate. All the Muslims in the world determine the end of Ramadan by looking at the moon, except the Turks. We just fast for thirty days each year and then, moon or no moon, we celebrate.

Auntie Kadriye

I was in a lecture when I looked down at my phone and saw that I had eight missed calls. And a ton of messages. Well, this happens to me a lot, as you know by now if you haven't skipped the previous chapters; they say impatience is a reader's greatest vice. Anyway, it was the middle of the afternoon and I hadn't come home late yet, so this was unusual. Mother was demanding that I come to Aunt Kadriye's house immediately. Aunt Kadriye was her younger cousin with whom she shared a sisterly bond. The alarming messages could only mean one thing: Kadriye had been suffering from cancer for two years and things had been going downhill lately. Mother had been over there a lot. The doctors had given up; at least, they'd told us to prepare, which means pretty much the same thing in politically correct doctor-speak. The time had come to say our goodbyes.

I packed my things and prepared to leave the classroom. Since there are only six students in my entire course, including me (Dutch has become so unpopular that the university is cutting the programme at the end of this year – a highly regrettable state of affairs, if you ask me), we are usually in a small classroom and not a large lecture hall, like everybody else. Unless we take courses like history or philosophy, then we're in a large hall. Because of this, there was no way that I could leave the room without everyone noticing. I raised my hand.

'Excuse me, Mr Koppenol, I'm really sorry to interrupt, but I just got a message from my mother, and I need to go, it's urgent. I'll explain later.'

'Urgent? Nothing serious, I hope?'

What was I supposed to say? That it wasn't exactly urgent, that my aunt was on her deathbed, but we'd been preparing for this for months, so it wasn't entirely unexpected? Or that it was serious because she was dying. I have no idea whether this can be classified as serious or not. If I tell him it's not serious, won't he think it's strange that I'm suddenly leaving? So I guess I should tell him that it is serious, but then he might ask more questions, which I'd rather avoid.

'It's not very serious, but I really need to go because it's very important,' I said.

'Okay ... that's fine, off you go then, good luck!'

When I got to Aunt Kadriye's house, it was already full of people. I had to push my way through the crowd to reach the deathbed. I saw her lying there. Lying and suffering. I could only see part of her face because she was surrounded by relatives, acquaintances and neighbours, all snivelling and wailing, and I'm only five foot three. But I saw enough to know that life is merciless, I hardly recognised her. She was incredibly thin; her once full, rosy cheeks had been replaced by pale, wilted skin that sunk in like a deflated balloon. A face of death. No hair, no eyebrows, no eyelashes. Like a store mannequin with anorexia. On the verge of death. She was hooked up to all kinds of cords and cables. You could see that she was struggling with her soul, as Turks like to say. Disease is anything but modest.

I saw that Mother's eyes were bright red. I went over to her. 'We're waiting for Allah to take her, there's no saving her now,' she said between sobs. I didn't know what to make of this emotional version of Mother – I only knew her as a tyrant, never as a victim. I took off my coat and sat down on the sofa next to the family doctor. I got strange looks from many of the visitors, I wasn't distressed enough; everyone around me was wailing their eyes out and I just sat down on the sofa as if none of it affected me. I wasn't overcome with emotion or seized by the sight I had just witnessed. I was supposed to participate, but I was unable to produce tears. I did my best to look sad. I buried my face in my hands and waited for Aunt Kadriye to die, but it took hours. I saw her children, my cousins, weeping too. It was a miserable sight. Her son Ibrahim was only six years old. His mother had spent the last two weeks of her life hooked up to machines to keep her alive.

The doctor explained that cancer produces a fiery pain in the body. It might've looked like she was lying there peacefully, but that was only because she was no longer able to move due to the weakening of her brain. Really, she was suffering tremendously. The doctor suggested that the family consider putting her into a coma and letting her quietly slip away on a morphine pump, otherwise the agony could continue for days and there was no saying when she would actually die. That was out of the question, the family was appalled that the doctor would even suggest such a thing. In our religion, assisting death in any way is an unpardonable sin, as is suicide; you have to suffer until the bitter end, life must be extinguished naturally, when God decides, He could always work a miracle, so we had to wait. We had no idea whether that long, steady beep was coming that afternoon. What if we all had to go home because the machine just didn't feel like it today?

Just as this thought occurred to me, it happened. A soft, almost inaudible beep, and it was done. She was gone. Where to exactly was a good question. Her mother started weeping, wailing at the top of her lungs, crying as she drummed her balled fists against her chest. The others gathered around her and told her to calm herself, to temper her emotions, but she would not be subdued. The imam with the scraggly beard called for attention with his booming voice, silencing the women's cries. I hadn't seen the imam when I walked into the room; naturally, he'd been sitting in one of the other rooms with the men.

'Brothers, sisters, we are gathered here today to witness the irreversible departure of our esteemed sister Kadriye. She was an extraordinarily devout woman, who has had a meaningful impact in our mosques, may Allah accept her deeds, *amin*. Believers of the straight path, she has just passed away, her book of deeds is forever closed, there is no need to worry about her any more, she is with her Creator, while we are the ones who still have to prove ourselves in this world full of infernal temptations, every day. *Wallah*, this life is of an untold and insignificant duration. Every so often, Allah the Merciful and Gracious takes a loved one from us because He the Almighty wants to remind us of the impermanence of this insignificant life. We, in our mortal weakness, often forget this, we are so fixated on our fleeting, worldly, material existence here on earth that we rarely realise that we must prepare for the eternal. Kadriye has done just that, she is most likely, with God's will, on her way to paradise thanks to her great service, all of this is based on what we know about her, that she was a righteous woman who carried out many noble deeds and did not overtly sin. And whatever she may have concealed from us is between her and her Creator. She has fulfilled her task on this earth with verve; we should therefore rejoice for our sister! As for us, dear brothers and sisters, we must continue to fight the devil every day. Do not despair! Allah calls His most beloved servants home early! We all share this final destination. We knew this already, that one day each and every one of us will give his soul back to God, we know this the moment a person is born. Death spares no dear children, even the loved ones of the Prophet, peace be upon him, all perished one after the other, at a time when he needed them most in his struggle against the polytheists and oppressors. But this grief did not stop him for a moment from constantly remembering and worshipping Allah the Exalted. He was not guided by foolish emotions, nay, on the contrary! Of course, he mourned, that is human nature, but in moderation. He knew better than anyone that this life means nothing, and he never lost himself in agonising emotions and suffering. Dear brothers and sisters, do not give in to those doubts that creep up on us from time to time. Pray regularly, visit our mosques frequently, monitor your children's faith, for every pious child you have raised will be a testament to you before Allah after your death. Donate as much possible, for every penny you give is also your testament, and help your fellow Muslims, for I tell you, the *kefen* has no pockets! Do not sin any longer, reject the evil, the sinful, and exhort one another to do good! Draw each other towards virtue, for you will be grateful to each other for it! Change with your hand that which is sinful; and if you cannot, with your tongue; and if you cannot do that either, abhor it with all your heart! And that is the weakest faith. And let there emerge from you a group that calls for goodness and forbids the reprehensible (the sinful), for it is they who will attain success.*

---

* From a verse in the Quran (3:104).

This is also our final station, in a few years or perhaps even tomorrow!'

The people in the living room were overcome with collective ecstasy. I applauded with clenched fists. The insidiousness of illusion is its power of persuasion.

Eid

I heaved a deep sigh when I saw the first wave of visitors in the living room. It was going to be a long day. Today is Eid al-Adha, which means serving around the clock, endless washing-up, making small talk about other people's lives and pretending to be fascinated by their stories, most of which are purely gossip, and bursting into laughter like canned laughter in American sitcoms. The sense of conviviality that people share on such occasions is truly a mystery to me.

I sit at the table staring into space, daydreaming, as my gaze falls on the plates and bowls of lavish food that I've spent the last few days helping prepare. It is all greedily consumed by our already corpulent guests.

I look, but I don't see. I'm surrounded by people making sounds, but I've stopped listening. Just as in the first wave of guests, I'm again ambushed by stories about couples getting divorced after just six weeks of marriage.

'She'll never find another husband, she's second-hand goods now. She would've been better off staying with him. These girls today, they're like china dolls, they break at the first little spat, then they just get divorced and destroy their own nest, as if it's nothing.'

'Yes, but he was beating her, so it is understandable, that's a step too far nowadays.'

'Come now, nobody ever died from a few slaps, for all we know it was nothing, and she just screamed bloody murder so she'd have an excuse to get out, look at what our mothers had to endure from their husbands, and it's not as if the woman is always innocent, who knows what she did or said to push him over the edge, Mehmet isn't someone who would hit a woman for no reason; in most cases, it's the woman's fault, not the man's, believe me.'

I get up and walk into the kitchen, I can't take it any more. As I enter, someone makes a comment that my dress is too tight, that I should go and put on something else. It's so nice how people project their own shame and prudishness onto others. And always with that whole whore–virgin dichotomy. Nevertheless, I go and put on a different dress. I could kick myself. Why do I always give in? Why can't I be furious, insolent, immodest, dangerous, bad? Why can't I take up space, why do I stay sweet and cute, why can't I just be myself in all my glory, the role model we so desperately need? Is it because I sometimes can't find the strength, is that it?

I look out of the window and see the new neighbours in the apartment across from ours making out. They're students, and they don't have any curtains on the windows yet. It's the only apartment without curtains. Mother can't get over the fact that anyone could be so shameless and care so little about their own privacy. 'Only the Dutch!' she declared. When we bought new curtains a little while back, we briefly took the old ones down so we could hang the new ones. Even for those few hours, Mother couldn't stand it.

'I feel so open and exposed,' she kept saying. 'Everyone can see straight into our apartment.' Eventually she taped news-paper over the windows.

From the balcony, I see people walking on the pavement below, some with a phone in their hand, others with ear-buds in, yet another trying to calm a screaming child. I see a woman on a cargo bike and boys on scooters. I see another woman with her mobile phone tucked into her headscarf, chatting away hands-free.

One day all these people will be dead, I think suddenly, just like all the people who walked here before us, who crossed the street, who tried to calm a screaming child. Future gen-erations will only ever see these people in photos and videos. There may be a couple of works written by a handful of people that stand the test of time, but these people won't, because the vast majority of the world's population is doomed to be forgotten, never mentioned again, their existence here on earth entirely inconsequential. Each generation takes itself so seriously, but eventually every era will be pushed through the hourglass of history, pulled by the relentless gravity of evolution. Who wouldn't feel melancholic and nihilistic about that? I do. Perhaps I dwell too much on the fact that human existence is utterly absurd. All I see is the will to survive, but I also see a lack of science to make us want to survive, which is why people seek gods. These people will all be erased from the earth; it's a fate we all share. We are playing the role history has assigned us. And if the climate crisis wipes out the human race, God can just start all over again with a new Adam and Eve, only this time He shouldn't make the same mistakes in the design, and the woman will keep her hands off that damn apple. Though, let's be honest, that apple was more God's problem, He's the one who made such a drama out of it, not Eve. Moreover, there have been so many other design flaws that I just assume we'll leave Human 2.0 to the tech nerds. Maybe we should give some other God a chance, this one has had more than enough time to prove Himself. Besides, I'd rather have an Adriana and Eve. It would save us all a lot of trouble.

'Büsra, pour Canan some more tea,' I hear Mother yell. I don't mind pouring tea for Canan, I like her. She's a neighbour of ours who divorced her aggressive husband and now earns her own living cleaning toilets at Amsterdam Central Station without speaking a word of Dutch. At night, she makes stuffed pastries, egg rolls and mini pizzas that can be frozen and sold to bakeries and restaurants in the neighbourhood. I have nothing but respect for a woman like that. She was done whoring herself out for that man. All those Turkish housewives who constantly complain about their oppressive husbands would never dream of getting divorced and actually having to work themselves; they could really learn from her example. I'm more than happy to defend any woman who dares to go against the grain.

I grab the heavy teapot from the stove and take it into the living room, where they are talking about the daughter-in-law of one of Mother's aunts who doesn't want to have any more children. Even though she already has two and is already forty-two, her mother-in-law thinks she should have a third. Two is not enough.

Then, my aunt asks me if I might be interested in some suitor she knows. He's a painter, well off, has his own place, and his family comes from the same region as my parents. He doesn't even mind that I'm still in school, she already checked. What a sweet and patient man he must be, he is willing to wait for me. She had taken the liberty of showing him my photo, I was approved under the unyielding condition that, once we were engaged, I would wear only long robes that sufficiently covered my legs and curves. No jeans or leggings or anything like that. That would attract attention, and he was a jealous type. And once we were married, I should only work part-time. Motherhood was so much more important. He was too good to pass up, my aunt had known his family for years and they were very decent people.

'No, thank you,' I say. 'I'm not interested. I'm not even thinking about getting married yet,' I say, for the umpteenth time that day.

'But, why not? He has no problem with you being in school. Why wait any longer? He's a perfect candidate, don't let him slip away!'

I did my best to swallow my irritation. I didn't feel like getting into another heated argument about all this, but you know what, fuck it, I was going to do it anyway. I knew exactly what to say to get them riled up.

'I'd prefer a highly educated person. To me, education is the most important quality in a man.'

And yep, they let me have it. Who did I think I was discriminating on the basis of education? My own begetters weren't educated, did that make a person inferior or less capable of being an upstanding husband or father? What on earth did education have to do with marriage? How absurd to want such a thing! All that mattered was that a person was good and pious and blah blah blah, that his heart was in the right place blah blah, that he takes responsibility and fulfils the role of a real man and blah blah blah blah blah.

'And where are we supposed to find this highly educated man for Madam the Queen way up on her cloud?' Aunt Durdane sneered, suggesting that I was the one who was being haughty and making 'unreasonably high demands'. She used broad strokes to make her argument: 'Let me just say that I know more good low-educated people than high-educated people. High-educated people are cunning and crafty, low-educated people are sincere.'

I was so sick of their pathetic rhetorical fallacies.

'This is my criterion, and I'm sticking to it, sorry, it's my choice, I'm the one who has to marry him, not you,' I said. I wasn't going to accept any kind of arranged marriage, but I couldn't say that. Otherwise, they would catch on to the fact that I didn't respect their customs and beliefs, so I just played the academic card. I knew it would be virtually impossible for them to find someone who would fit the bill. No intellectual would rely on his begetters to arrange a wife for him. This was something for pathetic little men who lacked the charm to find a nice wife for themselves or who were otherwise too pious to engage in any kind of dating or flirting.

'Don't be so pig-headed. Just give him a chance, no one is saying that you have to get married right away or that you have to agree, but give people the chance to come by, that's what decent women do,' Mother says.

'Tell you what, I'll just give him your number. Talk to him and see what comes of it,' my aunt insists.

I feel the rage boiling up inside me.

'No. No means no. Don't push me, I don't like that.'

'But, why not?!' Mother demanded, throwing her hands into her hair. Or onto her headscarf, actually.

'You can just try, can't you? He really is an excellent young man, I know him from our neighbourhood, he goes to the mosque every Friday, whenever I have a heavy bag of groceries he comes out to help me with it, he greets everyone, has no bad habits, helps his parents out financially, his mother told me,' my aunt says.

'A man like that is hard to come by nowadays; most of them are junkies. He must be very well raised, may Allah bless his parents,' Mother says.

'I'm sure he's perfect, but I would prefer someone who is educated. I've been very clear about that.'

'There she goes again with her bloody education!' says Mother, who looks as if she could snap at any moment and keeps casting knowing glances at Father. At the time, I didn't know that this discussion was going to start coming up more and more often, and they would only become more adamant.

I decided to change tactics.

'I would prefer to work, save up some money and buy my own house before I get married.'

Mother: 'Why on earth would you want to work when you could find a man to do it for you?'

Me: 'Because I don't need a man.'

Mother: 'You really are a stupid girl. You know what, you do that, buy a house so that whatever man you marry can take advantage of you. He won't have to life a finger to buy a house because he'll already have yours. He can have you for free. And if you're so easy, he'll eventually leave you for another, because you were hardly an investment. Why would he stay with you? Things that cost nothing are of no value!'

I bit my tongue and left the room. Then I grabbed a paper and pen, for as the Little Prince so beautifully said, 'It is a little lonely in the desert. It is also lonely among men.'

Fishing Age

I am drowning
in the fish around me
the fish, who present themselves

as sympathisers and kin
So misleading
not from the heart
inauthentic
I miss the contact
I fucking crave it
I yearn for contact
but the aorta has grown shut
Their hearts
are still beating
but they are dead
Not brain dead
But heart dead
Eyes that smile but don't shine
without sparkle
the pupils ... rarely rigid
Though I flee,
I am snowed in
and wrapped up
Go with the flow
is the motto of the fish
They take every possible hand
and call it friendship,
love
While I
turn my back on
everything that is not possible in love
I leave them
to time
and I hide myself in myself
They call it asocial, inappropriate
I call it humanity

I call it loneliness
And I like loneliness
Because it's the only thing
that protects me,
that keeps me from
becoming part
of this terrarium
I see humans, but no humanity
I see fish
Eyes that don't shine, without sparkle
the pupils ... rarely rigid

Betrayal

My phone buzzes. Lucas.

'Hey baby,' I say.

'Guess where I am,' he says.

'You're at your internship, right?'

'I'm right behind you.'

I turn around, and there he is. I get a hug and a kiss.

'Surprise! Hi!'

We're standing in front of the university. Today was the first day of his internship with an Amsterdam company; he's studying architecture and this internship fits in perfectly with his course. He deliberately picked Amsterdam over The Hague so he could visit me more often. He was still of the opinion that we didn't see enough of each other. We'd been bickering about it a lot lately.

'You just have to confront your family, you don't have to do what they want, you can follow your own path, you don't deserve this, we don't deserve this,' he said. He didn't understand the half of it.

Of course, he was absolutely right. Of course, it was only natural that two people in a relationship sleep together, visit each other's homes and are free to go out whenever they want, but I couldn't turn my back on my family and leave home. No, I wasn't ready to do that. Yes, I hated the begetters, but I loved Oma and Defne more than anyone in the world, and I couldn't go on without them. On top of that, I was afraid of the loneliness that I knew would follow such a radical decision. It would be a definitive choice. I loved Lucas, but I didn't know if he was worth such a sacrifice. Wouldn't I be making life incredibly difficult for myself, and for what, a guy? Wouldn't I be better off coming home with someone my begetters could at least somewhat approve of, someone who was a better fit, a Turkish Muslim like me? He had to be out there, right? But wasn't it terrible of me to be fantasising about relationships with other people when I had a boyfriend? Surely a charming young man like Lucas didn't deserve that?

I didn't know, I just didn't know any more, my mind was running in all different directions, I felt emaciated. I was sick and tired of myself. And, more than anything, I was fed up with that little voice in my head. That little voice that droned on in the background and the realisation that pretty soon everything would be different. No matter which of these two hardly cheerful options I chose, I knew that I would have to make a choice. Uncertainty had nestled itself into my brain and was looking down on me smugly: how was I going to solve this one? If I chose Lucas, they would never respect my decision, so that was out of the question. I had already tried to bring up the topic with Mother, Father and Halil, and it was made abundantly clear to me that I would be cast out of the family, even if Lucas were to convert to Islam. Even if the Pope were to convert to Islam. Not that I expected otherwise: prejudice is the modus operandi of the incompetent. I had mistakenly lost myself in the hopeful thought that doggedness can usually be conquered by love. But no. To understand the world, they have to keep things simple for themselves, which means pigeonholing things, slapping labels onto them and living by the rules. I was longing for the impossible. The only person who might be open to it was Oma, but she didn't have a say.

So, I had to choose. And quickly, because the longer the relationship went on, the harder it would be to end it and the more unfair it would be to him. I was better off doing it now. It would also be better for my own well-being; I knew that sooner or later I'd get caught, it would all come out, so there was no point in keeping up the worthless charade.

'How nice to see you here,' I said. 'I missed you.'

I kissed him passionately, running my hands down his back, as if preparing him for the dagger that was about to come.

'Let's catch the tram around the corner and go to the movies. Then we can grab a bite to eat and I'll let you go, which I won't want to do, but unfortunately I'll have to, gorgeous.'

He kissed me again; this could go on all day, again and again, we just couldn't keep our hands off each other. Wandering around Amsterdam with Lucas was a bad idea; it would be tempting fate, provoking the gods. At any moment, I could be seen. By someone from my neighbourhood, my family, Halil's friends, you never know, they were everywhere. But I also knew that if I said all this now, he would be disappointed. But ... this was going to keep happening now that he was doing an internship here. Perhaps I could survive today, and maybe the second or third time as well, but what about all the other times?

I supressed my reservations and surrendered to the moment. I grabbed his hand and we headed for the tram.

After the movie and dinner, we walked outside. It was

freezing cold; my hands had a blueish tint. I gave him one last hug and was overcome by a feeling of safety.

I had missed him, I realised. I missed him every day. Lucas is special, I was just as in love with him then as I had been three years ago, if not more. He's one of those people you'd want to be stuck with on *Survivor*, trying to spear a fish together. I had always been attracted to his ability to cheer people up, even without intending to; he was just like that, always cheerful. He radiated loyalty and reliability; he had a kind aura about him. He was funny, animated and knew how to flatter you with compliments all day long. He's the kind of gentleman I like: he's there for me, he's caring and committed, always available, calls me every day and showers me with unexpected gifts. A lot of the girls I know who are in relationships can't say the same. Flowers, chocolates, books, perfume, an album of my most embarrassing photos – I got it all. Or he'd make reservations at a private sauna or for a massage. Or we'd suddenly go swimming or to the theatre or a cabaret performance, or take a walk in a national park or the dunes. Life was never boring with Lucas; he always had a plan and all I had to do was surrender to it. He made me feel like an unrivalled vision.

Lucas sometimes joked that my begetters cared so much about me that he was jealous. It would seem that way, with all their calls, their constant surveillance and their strict rules for my own good. Lucas saw these rules as signs of love, care, compassion and concern, while I saw them as forms of suffocation, oppression, distrust and curtailment of my individual freedom and fulfilment, so that I would ultimately become nothing more than an extension of them. When one feels useful and has the urge to give others that same feeling of usefulness, there is a good chance that people will be harmed.

I was not an individual, I was an extension of Mother and of all other women, destined to preserve my family's honour with my vagina, and that was the reason why my parents were doing everything in their power to make me who they wanted me to be: a polite, chaste woman who met all the requirements of the community. Someone who stays in the background, a gentle servant, a maid, a pedestal for her husband, for the entire world of men. Not someone with her own opinions, her own goals, her own convictions and commitments. I was a womb and nothing more, a hot meal, a future mother; my role was to facilitate, everything else was secondary. I was supposed to walk arm in arm with Mother to the market, help her select the most excellent head of cauliflower and spend the rest of the day planning what we would make for the hard-working men of the house, so that one day I could do the same in my own home. I was supposed to enjoy meeting up with other female relatives at HEMA or IKEA or in Turkish cafés around the market. I was supposed to drink coffee and make small talk with all the women in the neighbourhood, with aunts and cousins and other girls, and beforehand I was supposed to make sandwiches and biscuits, which would inevitably be praised, and when they asked for the recipe, I'd say it was a secret and, with the tiniest bit of self-confidence, I'd add that although the first batch was a total flop, I had managed to work out the kinks, at which they'd all conclude that whatever man catches me is a lucky one indeed. One of my many aunts would then predict everyone's future based on the grains at the bottom of their coffee cups (which, by the way, is technically considered idolatry in pure Islam, but once again the doctrine is out the window). Then I'd be obliged to nibble on sunflower seeds and talk about things like where butter is on sale or the problems of people who were dumber than pigeons and thus found themselves in all kinds of predicaments that I had no desire to get involved with, nor did I care to know about their lives or misfortunes. This was Mother's wet dream; these were the poles around which a woman's life should revolve.

Lucas often said that I must be exaggerating, that they were just looking out for me, and if they ever got to know him, they would most certainly accept him. All I could do was sigh. Clearly, even after all these years, he hadn't understood a damn thing. It was so bloody hard to explain these things to someone who saw too much freedom as a disadvantage and knew nothing about collective cultures; someone who was fascinated by conservatism and religion, and its tremendous power to bring structure to people's lives. We had many disagreements about this, and he always had to make comments on my criticism. I believed that life was about searching for yourself, finding yourself, being yourself, developing yourself in total freedom. I was a fundamentalist individualist; I wanted to turn inwards and listen to my own feelings, nothing else.

'Babe, I get where you're coming from, but freedom isn't everything, believe me, sometimes you can lose yourself in it, there are so many dead ends, and if, in a moment of weakness, you're pulled down the wrong path and unable to resist, you're in for a hard time in life. Freedom is elitist, you have to be able to handle it, otherwise you can fall into a void, whereas a lack of freedom can sometimes shield you from those paths in advance. Besides, the good life is about community, security, goodness, wisdom and peace. We've lost those things, you haven't. I observed this first-hand with the Muslims I grew up with. We've lost that in our culture, and the worst thing is that most of us don't even know it. Freedom leads to loneliness. In that sense, we're not that different from apes.

Three-quarters of them live in groups. Although they're highly intelligent, they haven't transcended the concept of the troop. They're not individualistic, and really neither are we, and that makes us unhappy; humans are the only animals who don't accept what they truly are. We're creatures of a pack, monkeys, just a little balder and a little smaller, but we want to be loved and affirmed; we want hugs, we want conversation, we want to look other people in the eye. The demise of religious communities is pushing people into other subcultures – where they hope to be welcomed with open arms by the group and find a sense of purpose – which may end up being worse than those found in religion. It's the way we're programmed, there's no escaping it. You complain about your culture and all the things it imposes on you, I get that, but atheism can be pretty ruthless as well. You've got people who spend decades of their lives rotting away in care homes, young people with no sense of purpose, broken families and no sense of community, tons of divorces and all the consequences that come with them; let's just say it keeps the psychiatrists and psychologists busy. Over the last sixty years, we've lost all our values, put unborn lives at stake, degraded our elderly and undermined the family. We've found ourselves in a postmodern landscape of our own making, devoid of tradition, folklore and church. Cohesion has been lost. Islam is the last collectivist ideology that has managed to stay afloat, and that's commendable. The idea that you can fully develop yourself as a woman, which feminists are always advocating for, doesn't correspond with the need to care for your children. You have to pay someone else to do it, and that's where things go wrong. Well, actually it all starts with having children in the first place. Highly educated women usually get around to that just before or even after the age of forty, when physically it's barely still possible. It's a fine line, and there are many scientifically proven disadvantages. Make no mistake, our way of doing things might seem better to you, from a distance you might see us as a bright full moon in a sea of darkness, but look closer and you'll see the craters. People experience peace and security when they belong to a larger group that strives for cohesion. And, of course, there are rough edges to be avoided; of course, individualism is important for the development of things like science; and, of course, too much community spirit can undermine diversity. But don't fall into the same trap we have – nowadays we're even giving paedophiles the benefit of the doubt because how can you blame someone for something they can't help? Sure, let them live in family neighbourhoods, why not? Unbelievable. If there's one thing that could even make me think of murder, it's that. Pure degeneration and nihilism.'

He kept going: 'Rationality, as a radical rejection of feeling, tradition, faith, intuition and the human will, is irrational. Bonds used to be richer, deeper. All that's been eroded, we have become a soulless people, there's no harmony, we live for profit and want what we can't have. We're culturally depleted. We have a massive ageing population and low birth rates. Who is going to pay for the welfare state? And you know, babe, every human on this earth needs like-minded people around them, we find ourselves in one another, we're social animals and can't escape that. That's why half the Netherlands is on antidepressants. All our relationships are transactional and calculated, and in the end our society will go bankrupt. A healthy population is able to have both. We downplay everything, we don't even know why we should get married or bother having children any more. Your people have a clear culture, honour, respect; you should value it, cherish it. The only god we have is money, that's it.'

284

He sounded like Mother. If I didn't know better I would've thought she'd put him up to it. If you were to put him behind a curtain and give him a voice transformer, I would've sworn it was Mother rattling on; his tone may have been slightly more academic and his language more culturally Christian, but it was Mother all the way. Only, unlike Mother, he had no problem with multi-ethnic extramarital relationships. With friends like that, who needs enemies? But just because Mother and Lucas believed the same lie didn't make it truth. I was angry that he sounded so much like her. Angry and confused. I felt stung. I'm sure he meant well, but time and again, he refused to take my side in this fight. His speech was like a gust of wind into wildfire within me.

Maybe there were no facts, maybe there were only experiences, observations and interpretations that will inevitably contradict someone else's. Maybe reality is not independent of these discussions, but rather bound by how each person sees it. Lucas and his view of freedom and individualism reminded me of a David Foster Wallace joke: a young fish is swimming along and encounters an older fish; the older fish asks, 'How's the water?' The younger fish doesn't know what water is.

Belonging

It was a weekday in November. Lucas had run out to pick up a package at the post office, and I stayed behind at the house with Koos. He at his desk behind his laptop, me on the couch with a book in my lap. The TV was on. I was eating nuts for lunch. I was on a health kick. I hadn't been feeling well and had been battling a constant cough for days, and it seemed to be getting worse. It felt like the phlegm was coming out of my ears. Coughing was painful.

I don't know how it happened, but I was chewing and talking at the same time and all of a sudden a nut became lodged in my windpipe. I couldn't breathe. I did everything I could to cough it up, I flapped my arms around like a pigeon trying to take flight, but to no avail. I couldn't make a sound, I couldn't breathe, couldn't cough. I was stuck, completely paralysed, this was it. I could feel my head getting lighter and my skin turning different shades of purple. I was going to pass out or die. Or both. Suddenly, I felt Koos's strong arms around me and two hard upward thrusts in my stomach. The nut flew out.

Out of gratitude to Koos for saving my life, I was exceptionally nice to him. Every time I came over, I made sure to bring him some kind of food or drink that he liked. If he asked me to do something, I immediately did it, and if he didn't ask, I did it anyway. If his wife wanted him to run an errand or do a household chore, I did it for him, even when he told me not to. I always stopped for a chat with him, asked him how things were going and if everything was okay, and if I could do anything to help him. Last year, for Christmas, he gave me a gift card for a high-end department store.

'I put fifty euros more on yours than on Valentino's, shhh!' he whispered. Tessa's boyfriend had only been given one hundred and fifty euros, and I had to lie and say that I got the same. All I got him was a DNA test kit, the man already had everything anyway, and when I'd done one, he'd been intrigued by my results. According to my test, I was 40 per cent Greek, 33 per cent Mizrachi Jewish, 15.8 per cent West Asian, 9.2 per cent Scandinavian and 2 per cent Inuit. I was especially surprised by the Jewish part. I also wondered how I could possibly be part Scandinavian, until Koos explained it to me.

'We were Vikings, we pillaged and raped. You probably have an ancestor who got raped.' Right. I had no idea what I was supposed to do with this information.

When I told my family about my results, the begetters were angry and indignant. 'We're just Turkish, that's nonsense. Those companies lie to you so you don't feel like a Turk,' Father said.

'Jewish? *Astagfirullah*, are you crazy? We're Muslim!' declared Mother, who apparently didn't know that Jewish is also an ethnicity.

At Christmas dinner, Lucas's Catholic grandmother told everyone that she had donated to charity. My begetters did that on religious holidays too. She also gave out money to her grandchildren and their loved ones, me included. My grandma did that on our holidays too. The only difference was that Lucas couldn't be there.

Six weeks after Christmas dinner, Koos got his results. They were about as diverse as the top of the banking industry: 100 per cent Scandinavian.

The End

Now that Lucas was on his internship in Amsterdam I was out and about with him in my own city twice a week. I was constantly on my guard, and my heart pounded every time I saw someone in the distance who looked like an acquaintance. At home, the arguments continued when I came home in the evening, only now even fierier. Mother had recently discovered that I was on the pill; she recognised the packaging immediately because she took it too. I lied and said that I only took it to regulate my cycle, but she wasn't convinced. She said that she was going to ask our GP why I had asked for it. We had the same doctor: Mrs Kaya, a Turkish woman who wore a headscarf and whose father had apparently known Mother's father. She also went to our mosque and was good friends with Mother. I knew that as a doctor she wasn't allowed to tell anyone why I was on the pill, so I wasn't that worried, but still, when Turks get together, you never know what kind of gossip will go around. Let's just say if I needed an STD test, I wouldn't go to her.

Mother's suspicions only increased. She immediately told Father about the pill and that I'd been hiding it in my socks. Father was shocked and didn't believe for a second that it was for my period. Halil told me that he'd heard overheard them talking and that Father was going to secretly follow me the next time I went out early.

'They really don't trust you any more,' Halil said, who still believed my excuses. It was clear that my bubble was about to burst. I found myself standing at the edge of a ravine.

I had to make a choice; I couldn't live in both worlds. I'd tried to for a long time, and I was tired of putting out fires. I couldn't do this for ever, the truth had to come out. My heaviness in recent weeks had been caused by a desire for deliverance; after all, the greatest suffering is the fear of suffering itself, so I tried to rid myself of all the doubts in my heart and mind. I was better off preparing for the inevitable. It was time to start letting go.

I left. I would break up with Lucas that afternoon.

Sometimes you have to let somebody else be right, especially when that's clearly what they've wanted for a long time. So, I let Mother be right. Of course, she took it as a compliment, and not with false modesty, mind you, but with a dramatic display of victimhood and threats to kill herself. She had plenty of instruments at her disposal to get what she wanted. But make no mistake. Sometimes a choice is written off as a conclusion, but this was by no means my conclusion. Mother is mentally ill, and illness deprives you of any ability you might have had to withdraw from yourself. And those of us in good health have a duty to help those in need, even if the cause of their distress is their own stupid, sick, reckless or malicious behaviour.

I walked to the tram knowing that it was the last time I would walk down this street, on these paving stones, that I would never walk through that front door again, and that I would probably never see Lucas again. Some solutions are an invitation to learn to live with the problem. If you wait too long to say goodbye, you'll be left behind alone.

Now it's the morning after. I was up all night typing long emails that will never be sent. Lucas is no longer a part of my life. I chose sanity over open-mindedness, which meant that there was no good-morning message when I woke up. Not that there's anything good about this morning, I'd hardly slept a wink.

I have class in one hour, I should get going. I step into some pants. Right leg, then left leg, up and button. I grab the first blouse I see. A blue one. More buttons. Fucking buttons that always come undone. Socks. And then the headscarf. Always the headscarf. Which colour goes with my outfit today? The one I was wearing yesterday when I said goodbye to my lover, the one that got soaked with my tears on the train? Or the red one I wore on his birthday? Or the cream-coloured one that I took off at the beach to go swimming with him? Maybe the black one I wore to his grandfather's funeral. Or none at all. No headscarf. I don't want to wear it any more; I can't wear it any more.

I drape the black scarf over my head and let the ends hang down on either side. Just grab a pin and fasten it. It's not that hard. I've been doing it for years, but today it feels impossible. Why do I still wear this thing anyway? Because that's what they want from me? The same reason I sacrificed the person I love? How much longer was I willing to torment myself to please my oppressors? How much longer would it take for me to break the chain?

I let the headscarf fall to the floor. It's not me. I am this, the person looking back at me in the mirror right now, without a scarf, with swollen red eyes and a runny red nose.

291

I decide to head out just like this. Jacket, boots. Oma asks where I'm going in this state.

'School,' I say.

I shut the front door behind me and head down the stairs. I'm outside. I feel the wind in my hair. Unprotected. Exposed. I see a neighbour staring at me. Halil is on the balcony.

'Huh? Where's your headscarf?' he asks.

I don't look up; it takes too much energy. I walk to the metro station. 'Büsra! Where are you going? Your hair!' I keep right on walking, undisturbed. I push my earbuds into my ears.

When I arrive at the final station, I see Maartje. She doesn't recognise me. I don't say anything. We walk in the same direction, I'm right behind her. When we reach the classroom, she notices. So do other people. So does the teacher. They don't really know what to say. Nor do I. I'd rather nobody said anything.

When I get home, Mother is waiting at the front door. She's already called me twenty times. She shouts and yells and bombards me with questions. She's completely distraught, but I don't let it bother me. 'I've decided not to wear a headscarf any more. It's my choice. That's all I have to say about it,' I say. I didn't want to have to explain anything. I didn't have an explanation. I didn't want to wear it any more, full stop, that was the only reason and that was enough. I didn't need to evangelise my decision, I wasn't one of those people who was against all dogma and couldn't keep her opinions to herself, as long as they spared me theirs everything was fine. But, of course, that didn't happen. I don't call Mother the devil incarnate for nothing. Indifference is the desire of anyone with evil intentions, it is something that she is not capable of.

My argument was met with fierce opposition. Father joins in. Then Halil. Defne. Oma.

Halil tries to calm things down by taking a more intellectual approach: 'Büsra, explain it to us.'

'There's nothing to explain,' I say. 'As you can see, I have decided to go outside with my hair exposed, nothing to get all worked up about, it's my choice.'

I go to my room and lock the door. I hear Mother ranting and raving while the rest fall silent, or they are privy to something I can't see. Father asks where they went so wrong with me. They pound on the door, shout all kinds of things, but I don't open it. I just put in my earbuds and turn the music up loud.

An hour later, Uncle comes by and knocks on my door. Mother must have called him in – he's her right-hand man in these matters. I decide not to put on a headscarf just because he's here, I'm done with it, for good. Uncle is angry. Furious. He asks me with a penetrating look in his eyes if I have no shame, no fear of God, if my family sent me to the Quranic school for all those years for nothing, if I have no respect for my begetters, for my own mother, why I'm so ungrateful, why I'm dishonouring the family, and why I'm out to ruin Mother's life and give her paralysis. He points at her.

'Look!' he commands.

'Look what you've done to her! Are you proud?' he demands with fire in his eyes. I stare at him, and for the thousandth time in my life I'm able to confirm that, yes, there have been too many cutbacks in mental health services.

I find it interesting how passionate people can be about a fucking piece of cloth.

'And why do you have haram chicken from the supermarket in the fridge? Do you eat like the infidels now too? You already dress, speak and act like them.' The questions become louder and more demanding. My knees start to shake, and I can feel the goosebumps all over my body. I don't want them to see it, I'm actually not scared, there's nothing they can do to me, the reaction in my body isn't in line with my feelings. I refuse to look at Mother and refuse to respond, I say nothing and just kind of look past them. At first I look at the floor, then around the room, and then, finally, at him, cold and indifferent, waiting. I had no idea what would happen next and was kind of curious myself. After all, you are only truly alive when you feel the full force of the storm and stubbornly refuse to take shelter.

He grabbed me by the chin and turned my head towards Mother; I was startled.

'Look what you've done to your mother, you're ruining her life! Is this how you thank her?!' I see Mother weeping, looking as pitiful as she possibly can. Defeatism had a face. Her dream that I might still grow up to become a respectable young woman in her eyes is now completely shattered. How merciless the vulnerable can be, how vulnerable the merciless.

'I live my own life, and it's none of your business, I haven't done anything wrong, she just needs to learn to respect my choices,' I say. Spit lands in my face. They curse. Fundamental precepts cannot be bent without consequences. Moral principles are only as strong as they are in extreme situations.

'Just you wait, I'm going to cut that hair of yours in your sleep, then we'll see how much you like it,' Mother spits. The urge to maintain power is the downfall of many a tyrant. Or of tyrannical ideas. It's our rejection of them that reinvigorates the creativity of evil.

This is the reason why I decided to burn my family in this work. But one mustn't confuse resistance with revenge.

Mother can't complain. She chose to have a child, and

children can turn out to be merciless reflections of one's own behaviour. Blaming genetics is a scientifically responsible way of skirting your own responsibilities, and one that I am happy to exploit. Just as my conviction that I could change her over the years remained fairly unshaken, so too is hers now.

I had opened a bottle of Coke and dropped in a Mentos. This is war, because now that I have seen the light, I refuse to be forced back into the darkness. Is reconciliation still possible? And if so, do I even want it? Isn't reconciliation nothing more than mutually acknowledging that you're too weak to win? Isn't that the paradox of compromise?

Later that day, Mother called up other members of the family. One aunt told her that her imam said I might be possessed, that maybe it wasn't really me doing this but an evil spirit, and that a few healing sessions would do the trick. This would involve me sitting through hours of Quran recitations several times a week for an indefinite period of time, rubbing holy oils on my head and drinking sacred water so that the evil spirit would naturally leave my body.

That night, it took me a long time to fall asleep because I kept having nightmares about Mother cutting my hair. She was crazy enough to do it, though I didn't think she actually would because she probably believed that I was possessed and acting outside of my own will.

On the inside, I wasn't doing that well. I was desperate and searching, but deep down there was a spark of hope for the future that I kept hidden, even from myself. Hope and expectation are the DNA of progress.

The nightmares were followed by another dream. God spoke to me, which is, by the way, one of His well-known methods for proving His existence to mortals.

'Why do you not seek me, my child?' He asked.

'I don't know you any more; I have forsaken you. All I know are the limits of my own disbelief, which I've harboured ever since I first noticed a lightning rod on the roof of the mosque. And I can no longer exceed those limits.'

'But surely you have nothing to lose by believing in me?'

'I think that a life spent as a believer is a wasted life,' I replied.

'You have my permission to live as you wish, as long as you keep believing,' He said.

'Your followers on earth disagree,' I replied.

'But I'm the boss. Let them talk. The devil is prouder of those who act piously than of those who don't believe at all. My religion is like France – it's great except for all the French people who live there. You do believe, even though you are currently deluding yourself that you do not. Otherwise, we wouldn't be having this conversation. And a soul who denies its true colours will eventually turn black. Keep believing. And be happy. Choose your own morals, live by them and die a respectable citizen, that's true virtue, that's the art of living,' He said.

'But what about the rules?' I asked, surprised.

'The power of true morality lies in the space it provides for personal responsibility, my child,' He replied.

'I will live,' I said.

Disenchantment works wonders. The gaping abyss that separates me from my loved ones is now something that I cherish. I had received God's blessing. Nothing could touch me any more.

Farewell

I tried
To write a poem
But I couldn't find the words
To capture my feelings
And give them language
And then I realised
How much smaller my pain would be
If I had found them.
Something briefly expressed
Can be the fruit of great
And long reflection
That ineffable bundle of feelings
Is the source of this work
It is strange
That you can actually feel it
In your heart
And in your stomach
An infernal stump
An impossible knot
They say time heals
But now I know

That that's a lie
The downside of a good memory is
That one can suffer
From the same things
More than once
My life went on
Day in day out
Month after month
Year after year
The pain grew older
Not less
We are now
Strangers
We talked so much
And then suddenly we didn't
Because I loved the rain
But didn't want to chase the storm
Because a sensible person
Tries to avoid grief
But even now that it's done
Everything's changed
Some things
Remained the same
Despite this mad world
And everyone in it
I love you
I hope for your sake
That the next soul
Who will love you
Will do more than just
Get your hopes up
And that soul will come

Or already has
For in the end, we humans
Love the desire
And not the desired
Sometimes
Breaking up is
The only way
To love someone
The idea
Of what we could have been
Mercilessly taunted me
As I fled
But there was no refuge
For a flame so great
So omnipresent
So captivating
So all-consuming
Therefore
I have buried my feelings
Buried them alive
And never visited them again
Or watered the grave
After all
The more you feel
The more you suffer
Love brings obligations
A burning desire
Is not something
To long for
And a sensible person
Tries to avoid grief
I loved you more

Than the love I had in stock
I write about you
Because this is still the only way
To pin you down
And make you tangible
I will see you
When I see you
Whether it's in the afterlife
Or the one after that
You are a big concession
That I made
And that fills me
To this day
With melancholy
And Weltschmerz
My heartbreak
Has cured me
Of fiery love
Just as the pious
Have cured me
Of piety.
And friends and kin
Have cured me
Of friendship
And kinship
And Oma's death from cancer
And the agony it caused her
That she had to endure
Cured me
Of taking life too seriously
And appreciating every day
All the things

That shouldn't be taken for granted
And going through her possessions
After her funeral
Cured me
Of the urge to possess
Since possession is nothing more
Than resistance to decay
To temporality
To death
Nothing brings us closer to ourselves
Than the deepest sorrow
I have learned
To repress my urges
To love the banal
And have become
A connoisseur
Of life
For wisdom looks down on
Joy and sorrow
The woes of the people
Are more richly varied
Than those of the rest
Of the whole animal kingdom
The fleeting melancholy
Of spirited people arises,
Just like their spirit,
From their inability
To find balance
Resignation
Is all one can buy
With dashed hopes
Away with those

Who only want to see
The glass half full
So they can pretend
That they don't need
To refill it
I refuse
To join
The army of radicals
Of the uncritical
Of staunch believers
The best way
To avenge them
Is to do that
Which they cannot stomach
To set yourself apart
I hereby take
Revenge
Because potentates
Tend to underestimate
Their own kind
Although my act is not wise
Because anyone who seeks comfort and peace
Should not resort to acts of resistance
And a sensible person
Tries to avoid grief
A good sleep
Requires peace
The blessing of God
And of your neighbours
And a sensible person
Tries to avoid grief
But I have chosen

A precious virtue
Called sincerity
While insincerity
Is a proven means
Of gaining trust
After which I will end up
With no family
Because I refuse
Hypocrisy
Mediocrity
A proven remedy
Against loneliness
When I looked back
I saw where I had walked
But actually
I had mostly crawled
And those who crawl
Develop a deep bond
With where they are going
As Victor Hugo said
Every village knows a torch
The teacher
And a priest
Who extinguishes it
But what if there were more teachers
Than priests?
Cowardice is often
A life-preserving
Weakness of character
And is the value
Of a life
Not determined

By the degree
To which it is capable
Of suffering?
Perhaps the grandeur
Of my existence
Lies in the recognition
Of the tragedy
That I have strived
For the impossible
Maybe the optimist is
An up-and-coming
Defeatist
Then again maybe not

One must remain true to the ability to mercilessly betray all that is false.

To be continued (probably).

Glossary

All terms are from Arabic unless otherwise specified

abaya	loose overgarment worn by some Muslim women
Alhamdulillah	praise be to God
astagfirullah	you say this if you think something is ridiculous; literally, 'May Allah forgive us'
awrah	for men, the area from the navel to the knee; for women, the area from the neck to the knee (opinions about this may differ)
azzis	black people (Berber)
baslik parasi	literally head price or bride price (Turkish)
Black Pete	Dutch holiday tradition that traditionally involved blackface
drerries	guys (Berber)
ezan	the call to prayer
ezebi/zebi	penis
haram	forbidden

ibne	faggot (Turkish)
iftar	evening meal during Ramadan when you break your fast
kech	whore
kefen	the white cloth that Muslims are wrapped in after death
kehba	whore (Berber)
mashallah	may God protect you
Millî Görüş	religious-political movement that claims to promote Turkey's 'core values' in the face of Westernisation, particularly active in the European Turkish diaspora
minbar	a raised podium
simit	round sesame bread, similar to a bagel
surah	chapter from the Quran
süt parasi	breast milk price (Turkish; e.g. as in payment for feeding the children)
tattas	white/ethnically Dutch people (Dutch)
tfoe	'that is disgusting' (Berber)
tollie	slang for penis (Dutch)
top	faggot (Turkish)
ummah	all the Muslims in the world combined
wallah	'I swear by Allah'
wela	suffix (Berber)
wesh	prefix (Berber)
wollah mèh	no way
wollah teh	'I swear to Allah', with emphasis
zemmel	faggot (Berber)
zenciler	black people (Turkish)

Some Words of Thanks

Special thanks to my good friend Dennis Honing, because some of the jokes in this book are his, and because he has always inspired me in our conversations.

In addition, I would like to thank Herman Langgraf for his inspirational online musings, some of which have been included in this work.